Limited Edition
Original manuscript
Author's first draft

Anne Connolly joined the Royal Air Force at the age of 17 and enjoyed a career in engineering for many years. She then followed her love of the built environment, working on many varied and complex projects in the UK construction industry. Anne has had the pleasure of working with some of the most wonderful people in some of the toughest circumstances. Through this experience as well as her travels, she has gained an understanding of both how complicated and how simple life can be. She now resides in Essex with her family but remains passionate about many of the places she has lived and makes trips as often as she can to Liverpool, Scotland and Devon, to name a few.

Dedicated to David 'Paddy' McLeod.
Royal Air Force
1967-2018

Anne Connolly

A WING AND A PRAYER

AUSTIN MACAULEY PUBLISHERS™

LONDON * CAMBRIDGE * NEW YORK * SHARJAH

A CIP catalogue record for this title is available from the British Library.

ISBN 9781398415782 (Paperback)
ISBN 9781398426153 (Hardback)
ISBN 9781398426160 (ePub e-book)

www.austinmacauley.com

First Published 2022
Austin Macauley Publishers Ltd®
1 Canada Square
Canary Wharf
London
E14 5AA

My sincere thanks to my publishing team who have worked hard to guide me and bring this book to fruition. A huge thank you to my mum, Susan, my dad, Peter, and my beautiful daughter, Rhian, for their continuous support, encouragement, and belief. To my friends, Gillian, Sarah, Lynne and Deborah, for listening to my ideas and for pushing me forward to write Beatrice's story.

Prologue

I have no idea how I ended up here, it has been such a whirlwind. I am about to make the biggest emotional commitment of my life, to without question love and care for someone forever. We are all told this is the part where your life truly is about to start, that you didn't have a life before this and very soon, you won't remember the past, it will just be you two against the world forever. Does this mean what has happened in my life so far is not living? The weather is hot and dry, the skies are blue, and I can hear the river flowing across the rocks as I cradle a rhubarb and ginger lemonade, one of Mum's concoctions. The reason this place is so special to me is because I have lived a life before today and it hasn't been all hearts and flowers. It has been a hurricane of unexpected gut-wrenching change but, it has also been the most awe-inspiring time. I don't think I want to leave my life behind it is who I am.

I have everything and everyone here I could ask for, well almost everyone, we are blessed. As I start this new life, is it an unbreakable rule that my life so far is to be put aside, not worthy of a mention? Do I hide it now and become someone new? I think that is what is expected of me. Just draw a line under all that has happened and step into a new chapter. Yet, there is no way on earth I can forget. One minute I was just a young woman stuck in a dreary hairdressing and beauty college, the next, I was being shouted at by some angry middle-aged man who hated any signs of femininity. Plus, that was only the gentle start, later came the challenges and complications.

I joined the RAF on a bit of a whim. I was young, bored, lost and wanted more, and the RAF certainly gave me more. More headaches, more stress and more laughter. But it also gave me a purpose.

Chapter 1 –
Shopping Shapes the Future

Things have been going okay with the blue rinse brigade. There is certainly no plan for Exeter College to churn out fashion moguls who will be leading the way in style. No hope. We practice blue rinses and rollers on OAPs known in the trade as 'sets' nearly all day, every day. We have learned that according to the law of the beauty college, that everyone attending or leaving must have matching make up. Which we have all learned diligently. We have received our trainee cards that allow us to enter the wonderful world of the salon supply shop. Our first and only trip to the supplies shop is life changing for us all…

Our new gaggle all head up to the other end of Exeter city on foot. We are wearing our compulsory white heals, with our American tan stockings and dinner lady blue dress uniforms, laden with our heavy college bags. Only Star has had the forethought to bring her clumpy Goth boots in her bag and leave the heavy files back in her locker. Oh, Callum has not been forced into the uniform dress, yet. After what seems like an expedition across the Himalayas, we avoid the pitfalls of the cobbled streets, dodge the shoppers hazardous shopping bags and their 'hippo' sized prams, we finally arrive at Daiseez – the very randomly named and tediously trying too hard to be hip salon supplies shop. The cutting edge of Devonshire dyslexia strikes again. We really are stuck in the eighties.

We all have a good look around the cold warehouse shop only to find Daiseez holds nothing to entertain us or make us feel like we need to save up for any new must have amazing gadgets. What a waste of time, we waited weeks for this card on the promise of how amazing this place would be, like we were entering an exclusive club. We all get grumpy and set off back to the college, tired, sore and annoyed.

Elizabeth yelps with excitement as we leave.

"Marines! Look, this is the place where the Royal Marines sign up."

It's right next door to Daiseez, the HM Forces recruitment office. It's situated on Western Way, so aptly named for a shootout like in the old movies. Star rolls her eyes at this extremely loud statement.

"Oh for god's sake Beth, can you just stop. You are so embarrassing; they are just mindless cannon fodder for god's sake."

"It's Eliz-a-beth, and It's not their minds that I find at all interesting Star, it's their—"

Star abruptly cuts in. "Yes, alright, we get it, do you have to act so cheap every time you spot a uniform?"

Star and Elizabeth start yet another argument, and yet again I must step in to be the peacemaker and keep it from boiling over into a scrappy public brawl. They are so different in personality and because of this they are always coming to blows. We will all laugh about it afterwards as I make them relive the situation in good humour over our white Russian cocktails. In all these months, we haven't seen Star smile or laugh when sober yet, she couldn't be more serious about life if she tried. Maybe she should seek a career as a journalist? She'd be great when doing disaster coverage. As for Elizabeth, I wouldn't be surprised if Elizabeth acts up just to wind Star into a rant for her own entertainment, although she also revels in all the attention she can gain from a drama.

"Hello ladies, and erm, gents."

A tall official looking dark haired man dressed in black trousers and a white shirt with gold markings on his shoulders interrupts the squabble, and looks momentarily at Callum, quizzically for tagging along with what looks like a cleaning company outing. He must think he's the cleaning supervisor.

"Are any of you interested in joining Her Majesties Armed Forces? We have a presentation starting in a few minutes, why don't you come in and have a look?"

"That sounds great mate, anything to escape these girls arguing." Callum is keen to get away to any testosterone rich environment after the many months spent with just women day in and day out. Even a warzone must sound like a holiday in comparison.

We all decide to go in and take a look, more so for a rest. Our feet are throbbing and a free drink and biscuit sound great right now, I would do pretty much anything just to sit down, I ache all over. Heals have never been my thing, even after months of trying they really hurt, and I can't walk like a lady. There has been some progress and I still look slightly physically impaired, but I'm no longer a look alike for a butch man in a dress.

Whilst Sarah starts to fret about being late for class, the rest of us succumb to the extreme politeness from everyone in this professional looking set up. We are surrounded by large colourful action man posters displayed in shinny frames showing men dropping out of helicopters. Some are pictures of big grey battle-ships with people lined up on deck dressed in black and white. Some are green soldiers with guns and helmets with twigs in their hair and some are of soldiers playing with small children. An army nurse with a file, and a cook in white is the only female picture on show. Star will have something to say about this, we are in the nineties now. So, why isn't there a female mechanic at least?

This is a multi-service office, they recruit for the RAF, Royal Navy, Royal Marines, and the Army. We all start to get quite excited, the lights go down and the presentation starts. It feels like going to the cinema, except we have tea in place of coke, and a bourbon biscuit in place of popcorn. What are those biscuits that look like they have dead flies in and sugar on top? They are currants really but anyway, I don't know what they are called but they have those too and I head straight for a couple of those.

After the presentation I am totally blown away. Who knew the nice armed forces people did such wonderful humanitarian work? The UN people all get a pale blue beret, they dig for wells to give poor African villagers water. They build medical centres, like little mini hospitals and they help build schools. They are true heroes. All staff go travelling for team building events called 'enrich-ment time' or something. This means walking up mountains, canoeing and ski-ing. It's just like a family we are told. They even have night clubs, gyms, hair-dressers, and shops. Blimey, it's like party time and scouts all in one. They live together in little village like complexes, how lovely is that? It's like a commune, not scouts. Yes, a commune of people who want to do good things. The lights go up and there is a row of totally mesmerised hair and beauty students, alongside some other rather skinny looking teen lads, who are sitting eagerly near the front. One young lad appears to be with his mum, she looks a bit young. I feel a little embarrassed for him, as she looks a bit too keen to get rid of him, and he looks a bit too scared of her to say no.

We look at each other, Callum has the biggest smile I've seen him wear yet, even bigger than when we all had to undress for our massage class. "Where do I sign?" He asks the open air, then he looks up and mouths a 'thank you' as if he has been rescued from a near death experience.

We all start giggling at this point as if we are doing something naughty, but fun. "Yeah, stuff going back to that drossy college, where do I sign?" I say this jokingly, and in a millisecond, I realise that my one jovial sentence has egged them all on. All the beauty school misfits lead into head bobbing agreement like lemmings and, they all head for the leaflets. They start talking to the friendly staff asking what they need to do next. I follow a second or two behind them out of, well, I have no idea why really, I just did. I started to daydream of helping small children in far off lands.

This is all a bit fast, adrenalin is pumping through our veins as if we are about to go on the roller coaster or on a first date. We all head off to our different rooms for the aptitude tests, right there and then, no appointment necessary. That's right, no hour-long emergency meetings just to decide what poor Callum should wear in beauty class. At least here they are a professional and decisive bunch of people who can organise a proverbial piss up. Well, to be fair they did promise us that at least. The social side of the forces is apparently one of their many core strengths, they are just so friendly and happy.

Sarah is applying to join the Army as a Policewoman; her dream is now re-alised. She has already asked about career progression and forensics. Callum is going to be a Marine, not just any Marine, a Royal Marine, the best in the world they tell him. He wisely keeps a watchful eye over his shoulder to make sure Elizabeth hasn't overheard his choice. Elizabeth is off to the Navy as a Nurse, probably with a dream of tending to those poor Royal Marines, with a very lingering hands-on approach. Star is going to be a Photographer in the Army. She is the creative one after all, I can't imagine her doing anything else.

Star has just said to a rather butch looking lady that she doesn't agree with the Armed Forces in principle, she is simply in it for the training. I'm not sure how that little gem will help her gain entry to the Queen's special soldiers, the nice lady's smile looks almost like a tooth clenched grimace now and I am sure she has noted something on her application file. It's an odd sales type event, a bit like buying a timeshare. Do you think they get sales bonuses for signing us up? If so, Star may still be in with a chance.

Oh me, I have decided to try the RAF. I like Blue. I even suit our college blue uniforms that clash with my mandatory deep burgundy hair and gold, okay, brassy orange highlights. I like the idea of flying into help those poor children who need supplies, and then help build them a school. Topping off the mission by building a well so they have some clean drinking water. Not to mention Top Gun! What a cool soundtrack that has. I have recently watched the film and I distinctly remember how serious it was. Yes, especially when they were playing beach volleyball, that did look very serious and caught my attention too. Anyway, they looked very committed to their job. I have no idea what I will do in the RAF other than humanitarian work and beach volleyball. They ride nice bikes and drive a vintage Porsche in that film so it's looking pretty good. I hope the RAF is like the American Air Force. Let's see what they think I am suitable for after the tests are done. Oh, and volleyball. Hmm, I've never played, but I can swim really well, and I play netball, which is fun, so I am kind of sporty?

Chapter 2 –
Einstein Eclipse

They seemed so nice and now they are telling me I am fat!

The tests went on for a while. They went on and on, seven in total. I have no idea, what on heavens earth most of the questions are related to? There were two papers on engineering principles. I never took Physics at school, and I don't have a car yet so, it was all lost on me. I may be lucky and pass the tests as it was all multiple choice. Four answers to choose from after all, so there may be say, twenty-five percent in the bag by default.

To my amazement they tell me I have over eighty percent in each of the seven tests so, the only hold up to my choices is my age, I am seventeen, and my qualifications. I have just five GCSE's, no A levels and obviously at my age, no degree or anything amazing. Then there is my weight and fitness. What the hell are they saying? I am a size ten and a hundred and thirty-four pounds, how can that be a problem? And granted I told the truth about my exercise regime, maybe I should lie like the others did, but I refuse to lie. At seventeen how bad can it be, surely lying isn't the way forward? Since starting college in Exeter, I don't have any exercise other than dancing in the clubs, oh and walking everywhere. Devon is lacking in the transport department. It's much quicker to walk than wait on a bus that only arrives once or twice a day. I used to do lots of exercise, and I do miss it come to think about it. I used to swim a mile a day at the pool, active all day most days and go for long hikes on Dartmoor. As soon as I left a classroom I refused to go back indoors. Since starting college well, I walk to the bus stop in town which is about a mile. I walk to the shops when needed, which is on the same route. Surely, they get you fit when you join? I've seen army movies, isn't it just the same? According to their health chart at five foot three inches I should be no heavier than seven stone and nine pounds. That's just one hundred and nine pounds. It's impossible. I haven't been seven stone anything since I was seven years old. No one tells me I can't do something. I am livid, flamin' fuming, how dare they?

I have been given a huge list of trades to pick from that match my test results, my age, and my lack of qualifications so, I am sent home to think about it. As I am seventeen, I must have parental consent to join up. So, it's time to tell the folks the good news that I want to fly the nest. The chap kindly marks on the list which trades are open right now if I want to join sooner rather than wait. I already know that I don't want to wait, I can't bare the long bus journey to college any longer. Apparently, it's a good time to start now. No idea why and what the chap meant by that? However, they also point out that unless I address my fitness and weight issues I wouldn't get accepted at the next stage. I really want to do this now due to sheer embarrassment. The others are sailing through without any criticism. I'm not sure how much I am influenced just because they say I can't do it, or because I would do pretty much anything needed to get away from hair and beauty college and the endless blue rinses. It's time to see the world.

Chapter 3 –
Rocky Roads to Nowhere

The folks were fine about it. Well, they laughed, made fun of me, laughed some more and then said that whatever I want to do they are right behind me. I suspect right behind me sniggering but, they are supporting me all the same. It is perfectly clear they are not taking this at all seriously. I agreed to embark on a crash diet with Mum's help and to start running twice a day for about a mile at a time. Then the plan is to go back to the recruitment office in two weeks a changed woman for stage two and a fitness reassessment. Then hopefully I'll get to join up but, I'm starving, and it's only been four days on this fad diet. It's some sort of milkshakes. Mum insists she'll help me do this, and that the plan she has put forward will work. I've been for a couple of runs, which were more of a little jog and a bit of a walk, a bit more of a jog and so on…It's all beyond me. I don't understand why anyone goes for a run. I live in the most beautiful place. If you go out, you should be walking, taking it in and preferably you should have a dog with you. Without a dog you look just weird and if you are running in this peaceful place, you'd look really dodgy. I can't look at anything other than the rugged floor or I'll fall over? I haven't done much else really as I am absolutely shattered, seven hundred calories a day isn't enough, and surely it isn't good for you? So much for coming from a medical family. They are going to kill me before I get back to the career's office.

The pressure is on as the folks have told everyone locally what I am doing. So, I don't feel like I can change my mind. It seems to be a big deal. Some of the neighbours are regularly saying good luck when they see me go out for a run. Apparently, young folks today are generally up to no good, and here I am about to join the forces and make a difference. They are so impressed I have no option but to go through with it now. An old chap George from the next street popped in to see my dad and pass him a book on the history of the RAF, detailing their World War Two missions. He said if I read it, I would impress the RAF at my interview. I flicked through it, it had various black and white photos of planes and people stood next to planes. I might read it a bit more when I get bored.

Chapter 4 –
Pink Pride and Prejudice

I'm back at Western Way in Exeter waiting for my final interview with an RAF recruitment officer, Flight Lieutenant Wells. The medical was first, and I think it went okay considering. They said I should have tried harder. That in the last two weeks I could have achieved more but, they put me forward as a borderline pass. I'm through but I feel like I failed, how is that possible? What happened to the motivational speaking staff and the plates of biscuits?

Officer Wells sits in a serious manner, like a news reader holding his note-paper, his elbows are on the table.

"So, how long have you known you wanted to join the RAF Beatrice?"

Do I lie at this point and say longer than two weeks?

"Erm, I have always wanted to do something special. Something that matters."

He smiles, I have dodged the question well.

"Beatrice, there is something we have to discuss, and I want you to think very carefully before answering my next few questions, so take your time."

"Jesus, is he going to propose or is it more math questions?"

"The Royal Air Force has the highest moral code and must only accept those into the fold who also have the highest moral code. Do you understand?" I nod, but I am completely lost at this point. "Have you ever taken drugs?"

Phew, this is an easy question.

"Yes, I have. I had an operation when I was seven and they gave me some in hospital." I smiled at him, I'm quite pleased I got that one right, I had almost forgotten about that operation.

"I meant recreational drugs Beatrice, not prescribed drugs."

Oh, I feel so stupid now…Algebra for the next question, I hope. Anything is easier than this awkward parental style of questioning.

"Oh, no sorry, I haven't" – it's awkward and silent so I add – "is that a problem?"

Sir Wells ignores this. Oh, did I mention we have to call him sir, I was told this just before I entered the room. He must be some sort of Royalty or something? There is no stopping him, Sir Wells moves onto another earth swallowing embarrassing question…

"Beatrice, have you ever had a boyfriend?"

Dear God, is he hitting on me? This is not on.

"Sir, I do not see how that is remotely relevant right now, it is highly inappropriate to ask that don't you think?"

I am scowling now, and I sit more upright in my chair. What an old slime, he must be like thirty-five years old at least, yuk.

"Ah, Beatrice, I apologise" – another awkward silence – "you misunderstand the reasoning in my question. In Her Majesties Armed Forces, it is against regulations to be homosexual."

What is this plonker going on about now? I need to have a rethink about joining this lot, what next, you cannot join if your favourite colour is purple?

"Okay, Sir Wells, can I ask why you are talking to me about homosexual men?"

I ask while trying to stay calm. This previously stoic recruitment officer then laughs, puts his pen down, looks up at the ceiling and taps the table gently with his hand over and over. After a moment he recovers and looks at me.

"Beatrice, I am sorry. I am not being very clear." He clears his throat and tries again. "My fault entirely, it is a bit awkward, and it's just sir, not Sir Wells." He is stifling a laugh, tears glisten in his eyes. It's not that funny, I don't even know why he is laughing? "Beatrice the question is, are you gay as we are not allowed to put anyone through who is gay?"

As I stare at him, still unimpressed by this scenario, he continues. "I mean are you a lesbian?" He stares seriously at me, and I have no idea what to do. "Sorry Beatrice, I don't personally care about anyone's sexual preferences but, her Majesty does you see."

Oh, I see. I take a deep breath, lean forward.

"Sir, are you trying to tell me the Queen wants you to ask me this question?"

Well, the old plonker can't breathe for laughing now.

"No, no, it's a regulation. It's not allowed. So, we are not allowed to admit anyone who is gay or lesbian."

Admit? Not allowed to admit anyone? What the…it sounds like I am being admitted to an institution for the clinically insane. In a panic I just blurt out. "I like Tom Cruise, Brad Pitt and Johnny Depp and, if Clint Eastwood washed his hair, I'd like him too, probably, and it's Bee, call me Bee." It was like I had uttered the magic password to enter a secret club.

That was the last thing I said to him, I was in. He shook my hand, smiling and chuckling to himself, and he handed me a pack of paperwork. He told me to turn up to a different RAF recruitment office, the address was on the front of the pack, it was in Derry's Cross in Plymouth. I was to be there at 10 am on Wednesday, 18 July for attestation. He told me to make sure I brought all the kit off a list contained in the pack of documents, as I would be leaving from that office on that day as a member of the Royal Air Force. Oh, and he told me to dye my hair. Only a natural colour was allowed, not burgundy. What is it with people telling me what colour hair I must have?

I felt anxious then and I could only nod, I was keen to get out of there. What sort of place only lets you fancy certain people, and how you are to wear your own hair? I feel like I may have had got myself into a bit of a pickle. I hope this feeling is normal, maybe I just need some carbs? After all, it has been weeks since I had a decent meal. Another thing, what the bloody hell is Attestation? I hope it's not a flippin' tattoo. I draw the line at a tattoo. I should probably talk to my folks about this gut feeling I have but, given they laughed at me last time I tried to speak to them, stuff it, not a chance. How bad can it be? I'll just go with it. I'm a really grounded and chilled out person, a laid-back person. Actually, a really easy-going person I am told. I will take this in my stride, and I will cope with this fine all on my own.

Chapter 5 –
Buyer Beware

I feel sick after the long car journey. Home in Okehampton to the Plymouth office is a snake shaped journey across Dartmoor. The weather isn't helping, it's near seventy degrees already and it's just after nine thirty. I had to get up at six to get here on time. I've reassured myself that at least today is just a one off. I'm dressed in a plum winter wool skirt suit, and I look like a prim and proper secretary. Mum insisted that I dressed smart and it's the only outfit I had that passed her test. I think Mum has decided that no matter what the occasion, it is best if I pretend to be someone else. She's has been acting weird these last few days, she's quiet and drinking even more tea than usual, and it worries me.

The kit list has cost my parents a small fortune, which I feel very guilty about. Mum and Dad must sign some papers to hand me over to the Royal Air Force like a pre-owned car. For a split second, I know what a post-Christmas puppy must feel like being handed over to a dog pound, once the responsibility of looking after a dog becomes a reality and the festive novelty wears off.

My nerves have set in, I have an uncertain future. I'm not entirely sure what to expect. It would probably be less uncertain if I had read the documents in the pack that they gave to me. It's just that there were too many of them, and then somehow…I was going to read them on the bus on my way home that day. I get very travel sick on a bus, or on any form of transport really. So, understandably I couldn't look at them on the bus after all or I would need the large envelope they came in to be sick into. So, I thought I'd do it later and then later I forgot. None of this has shocked my parents. They patiently listened to me explaining why I have no idea of what was going to happen and followed my words with a silent nod of the head and a smile, as they looked at each other momentarily, and then back at me with raised eyebrows.

There are eleven other new recruits in the Plymouth office when I arrived. We are all asked to line up. I feel very short by comparison. A polite man explains that in a few moments we will be going into the next room without any accompanying family to undertake attestation. There is that word again, Attestation? It sounds like some horrid initiation prank. It makes me question if I need to start holding hands with the others, do we start chanting? Were the victims of the holocaust told to go in for 'attestation' before being led to a gas chamber? I should have listened more at school. I can't cope with the suspense. I put my hand up nervously like a toddler in playgroup. Still, I manage to stop myself from swinging from left to right as I wait for someone to notice. The kind looking man in his crisp blue uniform comes over to and ask what my question is. He must be quite high up in the pecking order. Firstly, he is old. Secondly, he has a large crown like motif on his shoulders. Anyway, he explains to us all, and I very relieved to find out that attestation is swearing allegiance to the Queen while you put your right hand on a bible. It's the traditional way of joining the armed forces, as well as signing on the contractual dotted line.

It does sound a bit chanty when we finally did the deed. All of us read the same verse from a printed card in unison. That's it. I am now a member of the Queen's Royal Air Force! I tell my parents and they look really pleased for me and Mum looks like she may actually cry with pride.

Previously, The Royal Air Force was known to me as 'the raff' but apparently this is not the way we can speak now. I've already been told off once for this error today. We must either say the whole thing in full or, say the 'R-A-F' nice and clearly, as if speaking to a deaf foreign speaking tourist. In short, I have been a member of this elite social club a whole twenty minutes and they are already telling me what to say and how to say it. All I have in return to show for this is a piece of paper. A small temporary identity card called a F1250. I've figured that the F is for form and the number of the form, well I hope it isn't a sign that there are another 1249 forms for me to fill in at some point? Turning to one of the new recruits next to me I cheerfully try to make conversation. "Crikey, they do love a bit of paperwork, they didn't show that in the nice video, did they?" Awkward, I didn't get a reply, just a serious nod and a grunt.

We stand in a cue for half an hour to fill in even more forms, that's twelve forms so far. We spend around another hour sitting and drinking tea, and then sign even more forms. Total forms now at nineteen. I speak quietly to my parents, Dad looks famished, he needs to eat soon. "There was none of this in the film they showed to us, they dug wells. They can probably dig quite a few in this time we are wasting. How will we get anything done?" Dad calmed me. "Okay Bee, don't worry. It's a lot of forms at the beginning, legality and all that." Then Mum chipped in. "Not in our day there wasn't Peter? One form, a quick handshake and we were in." She didn't realise that she has undone all the comfort Dad has achieved, I look down at the form in my hands and I start to worry.

"Four hours have passed already and all we have is this square piece of paper that looks like a dry-cleaning receipt, tea and cake, and a headache."

Dad puts his arm on my shoulder and squeezes me gently. I can't help but ask him, "Am I doing the right thing here Dad? Is it too late to go home?"

Dad offers me a chewy mint and a smile, I guess we're going nowhere then.

Next, we are told that the bus to take us to the training camp has broken down hours away. We are to wait while the recruitment staff decide what to do. They have hinted that we may have to go home and come back another day. I'm almost lost for words that this once decisive and organised bunch may give up on day one and send us all home.

"Isn't this the same lot that were in the wars that saved us all? Was that after tea and cake, and only after the bus had arrived?" I asked my parents, expecting a chuckle from Dad as an answer.

Chapter 6 –
All Aboard

Sat waiting on a train at Exeter St David's Station, it's Sunday, 18 July. Some awful record from the eighties is on constant play in nearly every place we've been. I was hoping for something more awesome to remember leaving home to, other than a song by Prince telling me to party like it's 1999! What am I doing, this is it, and it's no party so far.

I was sent home with a train ticket last Wednesday after more forms and signatures, just to leave home again today for the training camp, this time on British Rail. We will be met off the train at the other end apparently. "That is if there is a bus that works in the R-A-F!" I moan to my dad. It was embarrassing for me to leave home last week to such as fuss, a big emotional farewell from all my friends only to be back again a few hours later. "So, the RAF deploy international aid to the needy all over the world, they sprang into action in the Falklands war. I remember it on the news, Sue." Dad smiles as he chats with Mum. "So, how come, deploying a bus to Plymouth had them completely stumped?" Dad is laughing now, and I am starting to falter. These jokes are a step too far, I think I might cry. "I can't back out now Dad, yet I already feel this is a big mistake. What if I am surrounded by halfwits for the next nine years?" My parents laugh, not realising how serious this is. "Did I mention I have to do nine years before I can leave and return home?" My tears have passed I just feel annoyed about it all now. "Men, don't they have to do six years, hardly fair is it? They said it was to make sure the training wasn't wasted on women" – annoyed I add – "they want their monies worth." My head is spinning, not with the obvious injustice but with trying to figure out why training women costs more than men. Surely the longer time they serve in return, equates to a lower cost of the training than men?

Thankfully, no one could be bothered to do all the leaving thing again this weekend, so I chilled out at home. I already had a night out the weekend before, with everyone crying and being emotional. You'd think I was being sent to my death. I was feeling positive after a few drinks, I have landed a top job that helps people, and I get to wear blue. Which, I already know really suits me. I didn't understand the upset that night, or realise before then, that they were bothered about me leaving. I think it's quite nice. I didn't realise I would be missed and now that I do, well maybe I shouldn't go? Maybe they will miss my parents more than me? My friends usually stay at my house on the nights we go out. My folks make a fuss and Dad cooks bacon butties after midnight when we come home, he insists that we 'must be peckish after all that dancing girls'. The folks are not so bad really. I usually feel as if I am in the way when I am home alone, but when I have friends over it is different, they spoil us all.

As for the Job, I'm still not exactly sure of the details. I'll figure that out in training. The contract my parents signed said I will be given trade training as a Gen Mech E / 4 S of TT. No one know what it means. If I was stood on the main stage at Glastonbury and asked for a hand in the air from anyone who knew what it is, there still wouldn't be anyone waving back at me I reckon. I really want to be something medical. You know, so I can give the children who need the clean water their inoculations or something. Unfortunately, I was told they wouldn't be taking on any medic type trades for a while, but that this trade is very similar. Apparently, according to my results on the psychometric test, I will like this job. If I was to guess, I'd settle on it meaning a lab technician of sorts, maybe a spe-cialist one. It was the latest topic of humour at home when I told my parents what I was going to enlist to be. Dad was laughing because even after his own career in the army he hasn't a clue what it is. He then asked me what I wanted to be when I grew up in a condescending voice, and then he told me to brace myself as whatever this trade code is, it possibly isn't going to match my answer. Then Mum asked me if I'd prefer a surprise and just laughed lots...Even when I thought they'd calmed down, Dad had to leave the room as he found it hilarious, he was purple form laughing at me. Mum was no better.

They are always laughing. They only have to look at one other and they start. Mum started to recite again my seventh Christmas, how all the excitement had got too much for me that it made me ill. That a surprise wasn't really my thing, that I was identified as a control freak at a very early age.

Anyway, whatever it is, I will find out soon and it will probably match me perfectly. I mean they have carried out psychometric testing to be sure after all.

Everyone is now on the train, one bunch of odd-looking misfits and me. One of the girls, Natalie is clearly a diva. She is desperate for a hundred percent attention. There are two guys around nineteen with dark hair and floppy fringes, they both look like they have been sulking since they were thirteen. One man is about twenty-five or twenty-six, he's wearing a cream shirt, some brown cords and a tweed jacket in a horrid shade of matching brown. He may be listed as a missing geography teacher. Oh, and a girl called Rachael who looks quite nice, a typical English rose and to my relief, she seems quite normal, in a posh shop assistant type of way.

It feels like a weird school trip, but no one is in charge, and instead of misbehaving everyone behaves impeccably all the way to Newark station. As the train approaches it slows to a crawl. The station is old and quaint with yellow stone bricks and ornate ironwork brackets that hold up hanging baskets as well as the roof. It's quite beautiful and the weather is warm, about seventy-five, maybe eighty degrees. There's a huge Victorian style clock on the platform wall, with hands so big it would fit well in a primary school. I wonder whether it's enlarged purposefully as the RAF are used to having train loads of halfwits arrive here for training?

We are all off the train safely, the breeze carries a familiar smell of cut grass, the birds are singing, the train has pulled away just as gently as it arrived, just seconds after a whistle is blown and I can't help but smile. There is a feeling in the air that we have achieved. We made it. One of the young men is sneezing, his eyes instantly puff up as if he has been crying. The rest of the group look happy too, as if we are all thinking the same thing, that this will be a great adventure.

It was only a fleeting thought for us as a terrifying, angry man in a blue uniform and black peaked hat storms up to us screaming and waving a black shinny stick around. I can't understand a word he is bellowing, he's gesturing towards the end of the platform to the left. Everyone has started to grab their bags and run. It feels like time has stood still before I realise that I should follow them. For a moment I was a merely voyeur watching a movie scene.

I'm last to arrive in the safe haven of the car park but, there is nowhere to go other than onto an old bus. The top half of the bus is light blue and bottom a greyish blue, it's 'Air Force' blue. The bus is the replica of a five-year-old child's drawing, square in shape with no refined details. I'm glad to see that the said five-year-old remembered to draw headlights and plain black wheels, or once again we wouldn't make it very far.

I feel quite detached from what is going on around me until the screaming comes closer. I could feel a warm feisty breath on my face, like being wafted with a hairdryer and a strong smell of stale coffee. The angry man is introduced to us as Sergeant Bundock. He is trespassing in my personal space, and I am shocked back to reality. He is scaring the living daylights out of me. I think he's going to get violent, and I'm stuck to the spot by terror, stood rigid. I'm too frightened to move, my stomach churns and I am damn keen to say whatever he wants me to say. I can only nod though. I tried to speak when he asked me if I think I should be here, but my voice is missing. My mouth and throat are so dry nothing comes out. He's shouting at me even lounder now.

"Pick up your purple paisley bag, stop looking like a gormless university drop out, and get your bag onto that bus" – sharply followed by – "move! Get your sorry excuse for an arse on there before I feel the need to throw you under the fifteen thirty hours to Nottingham! You tree-hugging hippy waster!"

Right now, I feel like I have committed a terrible crime for merely being me.

I feel clammy, sick and in need of a toilet when we arrive at the gloomy RAF base where we will be tortured for the next six weeks. It looks like a prison from those old war films. There is a plane on a roundabout at the front entrance gate. I don't remember seeing those in the movies. It looks like a large grey Airfix model of a fighter plane, and someone has meticulously put all the stickers in exactly the right places. I don't think my brother ever managed to do the stickers so well on his toy ones, they were always wrinkly. The life size plane is mounted on stilts at an angle with its nose pointing to the air. It's landlocked by grass and circled by rows of primroses and pansies to seal the outer edge of the roundabout. Other than this happy gate display, it's a baron place with cold looking buildings, most with pale grey steel windows and doors. Some small box buildings have olive green doors with white stencilled statements like 'HAZARDOUS KEEP OUT', I am a little scared by it all, okay, very scared by this place so far.

We are all lined up outside the main entrance building. I tentatively raise my hand as I really don't feel at all well. Sergeant Bundock storms over to squawk at me some more.

"What the hell are you doing you useless chimp? You are not in primary school now, you don't raise your fucking hand whilst I am talking, do you hear me?" I could hardly claim not to hear him, my ears are ringing. I feel like I have a ferocious lion roaring in my face, and this lion wants to eat me. I think I might just cry, what the bloody hell? I don't cry, which is reassuring, as I don't usually cry too easily. I would be embarrassed if I did. I'm not sure when I last cried come to think of it. Never mind, I am in too much shock, I just stand here silently, eyes wide open. Sergeant Bundock then leans in to whisper quietly in my right ear and politely asks me what it is I want, and he adds 'sweet cheeks' to the end of his enquiry. Bloody hell, I think this bloke is bipolar, what the hell is a mentally ill man doing in charge of us all. This is bad, very bad. I have made a terrible mistake and I have no idea how to get out of it. I nervously ask, my voice cracking as if I have tonsillitis,

"Erm, I really need the toilet please?"

He nods over his shoulder and says quietly, "Over there in the guard room, go on. Run there and back, and then get back here and fall in sharpish before I change my mind."

I realise now that Sergeant Bundock is Welsh. When he was shouting, I had no idea as I didn't hear his accent. Now though it's very clear.

I find the entrance door after a scurry around, it's to the right of the building, not at the front as you'd expect. I knock, tentatively enter and I quietly ask for directions to the toilet. A nice fresh-faced man in blue uniform walks towards me with keys jingling on his belt. He tells me it's 'first on the right' as he points his entire arm decisively down a corridor immediately to my right. The walls are shiny, they are painted in gloss paint in pale grey. The floor is shinny and dark grey, it's all bloody grey, grey everywhere. My shoes squeak as I walk down the corridor, it breaks to frightening silence in this cold oppressive building. As I enter the room in search of a moment of solace, I cannot wait to lock the door behind me. I don't think I want to ever come out of this tiny sterile safe room, not least because it is refreshingly cold. My face is still burning from the embarrassment outside, I'll splash my face with water before I go back out there.

As I leave, I turn to say thank you and when I do, the nice fresh-faced man has already walked over to where I am, he takes pity on me and say's calmly "Don't worry, it will be fine. It's all part of the training, just keep your head down and do as you are told, okay?"

I nod and force a small smile of gratitude for his kindness. I notice he is really tall now he is so close, and as I look up at him, I feel like a small, frightened child on their first day at school. I have a tear in my eye and a lump in my throat, but I must push it to the back of my mind and 'fall in' outside.

Chapter 7 –
Left Is Right and Left Again

"Luft, Luft, Luft, Rrrright, Luft." Sergeant Bundock is rolling these words in such a rhythm it's like some sort of repetitive sound torture. I can't focus on that right now though my feet are absolutely killing me, as are the back of my calves. Sometimes I wake in the night, and these are the first thoughts in my head 'Luft, Luft, Luft Rrrright Luft'. Can you get Post Traumatic Stress Disorder just from the training? We are practicing marching. We are always practicing marching. I have no idea when I will be using this skill in the future, but for now it seems very important to Sergeant Bundock that we march everywhere and that we march loudly banging our heels into the road.

Basic training as it turns out, isn't very basic. We learn military skills, the politics of war, bomb basics so we can spot a displaced Improvised Explosive Device (IED). Sounds impressive doesn't it. An IED is just a makeshift DIY style bomb but, they jazz it up a bit to sound professional. We pretend to be soldiers in the woods, learn to use weapons and we practice first aid for every possible occasion. The field survival skills are a bit like scouts, with weapons, and a no neckerchief or tea making badges. We learn the shapes of aircraft in black silhouettes so we can tell one from another in the dark, 'oh how handy I hear you say', yes, it's lost on me too. I have learned to make my bedding into square blocks, like sandwiches with a wool wrapper. They call them bed packs. Again, this is of no use to anyone now or in the future. It won't open a well for fresh water, save a dying child or stop a war. It will however get you a serious telling off, Sergeant Bundock style, if it isn't perfectly square at the corners. It must be the width of the pillows, twenty-six inches, and flat and solid enough to use as a shelf. If it's a very bad example of a scratchy blanket bedding pack, it flies out of the window to a soundtrack of abuse. My shoes are like black glass and my shirts have creases in the sleeves that could give you a papercut.

The funniest bit so far has been nuclear training. So worry not. If I am around when a nuke bomb goes off, I know how to die in style. I will lie face down and count to three, I'll not make it to ten to say coming ready or not. Just one, two, three. I think it's most sensible I guess, if you are going to be fried by a nuke it's probably best to have a little lie down. Obviously, there has been so much more, but overall, I can cope with a war situation of sorts. I can shoot you, I can stab you with a needle if you have been poisoned, and I can patch you up again. I can build a campfire, spot an aircraft in the dark and write it in my little black reporting diary.

Next Wednesday we are passing out. Not literally, not even the RAF plan into the schedule fainting. It's the term used to graduate from basic training. We've all passed bar one. He broke his foot and hopefully he'll complete the course once his foot is healed. He slipped on the floor in the barrack block. The Barrack block floors are also like glass, polished to perfection by hand and dangerous to be on. No shoes are allowed indoors, and socks are a must to make sure we don't scratch the floor. So, you spend your evening tentatively ice skating on lake like glossy floors cleaning or ironing the night away. Anyway, walk too fast and accidents happen.

After we graduate, we will all head off to various RAF camps for our next round of training, specific to our chosen job. I can't wait. I am really excited about finding out what mine is and a little reassured as the staff here don't seem to know what it is either. But first, some marching up and down to a brass band in our number one uniform for our families to watch. Apparently, from just this short marching demonstration, they can see how much we've changed from useless lowlife into the RAFs finest, and it will make them so very proud.

Chapter 8 –
The Three W's...

Wet, Windy Wales. This is it, I've been here a week. It's awful, I'm completely distressed on the inside, and I have no idea how to get out of this mess that I have naively managed to get myself into. How did I manage to do this in just one silly college lunch hour? I'd do anything to go back, hairdressing isn't so bad really and some of the old dears are lovely.

I arrived in Wales on another one of those childlike buses, I was the only girl though. Just a bus full of spotty teenage boys with headphones on. We stood on the parade square where we were dropped off at 10 pm. Sorry, I must talk like I am military now, it was twenty-two hundred hours. The Sergeant who was waiting for us took one look at me and then frantically flipped through pages of paperwork on his clip board, pausing every now and then to look up in my direction, frown a bit and then do it all again. He did this four times, and he didn't move from his spot or say a word. The gaggle of hormonal boys started to make too much noise in their huddle so, he finally broke from his repetitive task to shout at us all to stop talking and fall in line. He then walked over to a corporal and started chatting, and they both started staring at me. Am I in the wrong place? Did I get on the wrong bus? I can't have, they called my name, so I got on.

Two hours later, the guys were all dispatched to their accommodation, and they were told that they would be provided with a briefing in the hall of their block at oh seven hundred tomorrow morning.

I'm still here, cold, tired, and fed up of sitting on my kit bag. Apparently, they didn't expect a 'girl', so they don't have any accommodation. I may have to sleep in the cells at the guardroom. Then, in the nick of time, a slightly tipsy and busty lady wanders over. She's wearing jeans, a rugby top and a pair of black court shoes and is sporting the same crew style haircut as the teen boys. She says she is the 'duty waff' and that she will escort me to the block I will be living in.

I am told to report back to the parade square in uniform at oh seven forty-five hours in the morning.

I got to bed by two, and I was up at six trying to find an ironing board so I could iron my clothes for parade. The parade was easy. Once we lined up, we were marched to a hanger with lots of big green machines in it, like the ones you see at road works, only bigger. I am singled out and called to the office where a kind looking Chief asks me how my stay was. He informs me that the officer in charge, 'the Boss' would like to see me when it is morning tea break. Civilised at last, I feel calmed by this guy and shimmer of hope starts to appear.

I felt sick in the first lessons, no breakfast and I am so tired. It transpires breakfast was before parade, I have no idea where. I didn't get the oh seven hundred brief that told the others about welfare matters and the camp layout. So, I pile lots of sugar in a cup of milky tea, I drink it down quick and head off in search of the Boss's door, where I stand and wait outside.

When I am asked to come inside, I am informed that I am the only girl to come to technical training in over nine years, and the female education officer, Squadron Leader Biggleswade is quite excited. She tells me how important it is that I do well. At least I am not the first, although I am told the first few have all left the RAF shortly after training, so I may as well be. She tells me that I must show the boys what we women can do.

When I leave the Chief calls me over and he asks me why I want to be an Electrician. He is concerned given that in my file it says I was in hair and beauty college before this, that it's a bit of a change of direction. He gets quite annoyed when I tell him I don't want to be an electrician and that I have idea why he would think I would want to do that? He storms into the office and declares, "Bloody hell fire Smithy, we have another one for crying out loud!" When he returns, he calmly asks me what I thought I was doing here. To which I shrug my shoulders. I feel embarrassed again as I remember, I have no idea. He stares at me for an uncomfortable time, and I finally remember and tell him, "I am going to be a Gen Mech E." In the most condescending voice, the Chief informs me that it means I will be training to be an electrician, the 'E' stands for Electrician, I will soon be an Electrical Engineer. I feel so sick, still no food and now I feel very deflated to boot.

You would think that was enough devastating news for one day but that wasn't the worst bit. Lunch finally arrives. My course is marched in a file of two by two to the mess for some food. At least I know where it is now. We are late as we had to wait for someone to shout at us and march us there. The mess is a single storey building with a very empty echoing feel to it, it must be the high ceiling or the sparsity of the interior. It's filled with rows and rows of matching young men in blue eating frantically, each sat on white shinny tables seating four, until I arrive that is. I walk in behind my course who are so far ignoring the fact I exist. I feel very lonely already. I have never felt this way before. I have always loved my own company so, why I feel this way in such a busy place, I don't understand? The queue moves swiftly, but before I reach the servery for some lunch, the hordes of blue clothed men stop eating and put their cutlery down. The cutlery clatters to the tables like dominos and there is a final crash followed by silence. They all stop talking and just stare at me, and it's deathly quiet. They remained motionless until I got my food and sat down on a table at the back on my own. Lunch was unbearable. I've never really stood out and I really have no plan to. I'm not going back there again, not ever.

In the technical training hanger, there is one guy that stands out from the rest, he has a quiff of dark hair in a '40s style, he has gentle bluey green eyes, and he smiles with a warmth, a glow that I can feel in the centre of my chest. It's quite unlike anything I've known before, angelic maybe? I noticed first when I had to squeeze past him by the lockers, and my bag bumped into him. I turned to say sorry. I'm still the clumsy one, my legs behave like an over excited puppy when I am in a rush. I think I spend most of my time here on tender hooks which makes my usual uncoordinated traits more pronounced. Anyway, he was towering above me and he just smiled. That's all. Now I see him about a fair bit and it's always the same smile. He seems to stop time. He breaks the darkness and then he passes as if nothing happened at all. Maybe not everyone is horrid or heartless in cold wet and windy Wales.

I can't tell the staff how awful I feel, I have no way out. I definitely can't speak to the education officer even though she is a friendly and enthusiastic woman. She wants me to do well and show the men that women are better engineers than the average man. There is such a divide and a pressure to be better than the guys, it plays on my mind so much I make mistakes instead of doing well. I'm trying, I'm really trying.

I almost forgot to mention, as if that isn't awful enough, there's the weather. There is a hurricane coming in and at my one hundred and twelve pounds, I'm struggling to stay upright when the wind blows in like the Wizard of Oz. I had to hold on to a lamppost on my way back to the barracks last night. I've lost too much weight in training I have no strength behind me to push into a storm. I don't feel very strong these days, I'm often lightheaded and I dream of a nice takeaway at home and a long lie in. Skipping meals won't help this. There is a shop by the camp gates where I can by something to eat back in my room since I perfected my canteen escape. The course, including me, all march to the mess and then I skip going in and head back to the block where I can hide out on my own. A whole barrack block and only me inside, and still they gave me room 13. Upstairs in the middle. Why not room number one?

Chapter 9 –
The Calling

The nice guy I found out is called Adam. He's been in the RAF for seven years and is here on his promotion course, higher technical training. He always smiles and says hello to me now. He noticed I looked lost and asked me if I wanted to catch up for a coffee and a chat about how life is after training, promising me it will be very different. He's been very friendly and a huge support. We met for coffee on a day when I needed a friend more than ever. I am so pleased that it isn't all dreadful, that this place isn't a reflection of things to come. Adam said that the guys on my course are acting like kids as they are just boys, young and inexperienced. That once they are on their own in a section of all ages, sur-rounded by grown men, that they will remember their manners and act with more dignity. He told me that any time I need a friend, or a chat, that he'd be there. He'll make sure to check in on me in the training hanger.

The worst parts are still lingering though. I dread physical training, which is three times a week. Keeping up with the guys is harder now. I'm last in running but, in circuit training I am holding my own, I'm always in the first four or five. Swimming was a horrendous shock and that's my forte. It turns out that it's their big problem. My course whistled and cheered when I came out of the changing room to the poolside, and although it was probably an attempt at humour of some sort, it felt horrid as they still don't speak to me at any other time. They ignore me if I try to join in. The physical training instructor made us line up and stand to attention. He then asked them to each in turn stare at me and score me out of ten for how I looked in a swimsuit, while I remained stood to attention. I also found out that day that my course mates don't like me doing too well, it makes them very bad tempered. So, I must try not to come first in swimming again. I need to pretend to be average or below average from now on to avoid the cruel remarks and a frosty atmosphere. It didn't help that the instructor gave them fifty press ups each for being beaten by a girl. He then walked the line-up to ridicule each of them individually for it.

I sleep little these days as I am so anxious and homesick, I spend my spare time wondering how to get out of this mess. Adam manages to appear and lift my spirits up just when I need it most.

We met for another coffee after the swimming debacle, I almost cried when I told him what happened. It's okay, I didn't cry, my words just got a little choked. I'm so angry, that's why. It was unnecessary for the instructor to do that. I'd come to accept the guy's poor behaviour, but the instructor is something like thirty. Adam is a fantastic listener. He urged me to report what had happened, he said it was not acceptable in any circumstances. There is no way I'm doing that, telling Adam is hard enough, and I feel that ignoring it is the best way forward.

"Adam, I am so grateful that you take the time to check on me."

"Bee it's my pleasure, I am glad you can talk to me, and I hope it helps you. Not long now and you'll be posted somewhere much nicer." Showing his warm genuine smile.

"I hope so. If you hadn't of taken the time to chat to me, I'd have lost it by now. I'd probably have killed one of the boys on my course."

"In that case, I am very glad I could help save some poor chaps life." Smiling back at me, he knows I'm joking.

"Seriously Adam. You are a great listener, a great support and a great friend. Erm, you don't seem yourself though today. Are you alright?"

"I'm fine Bee" – he pauses for a moment – "I do have some news. It's confidential though. Can I trust you not to tell anyone?" He looks concerned, as if he shouldn't burden anyone.

"Tell who, I have no one to speak to?" – I smile and lean forward – "You can trust me, I promise."

"A year ago, I applied for a Commission, to become an officer."

"Wow, that's fantastic news, and they have said yes?" This is great news, I feel so excited to hear such good news.

"Kind of." Adam is looking at me as if I won't like what he will say next?

"What is it? What is kind of?"

"I have to finish here first, and my course has four months left to go" – he hugs his mug of coffee for comfort – "I'm struggling to see the benefit in doing it, it seems such a waste."

I can see a tiny glimpse of frustration break through his calm nature.

"But, as an engineering officer, the training will be invaluable to you, surely?"

"Bee, I'm not going to be an engineering officer."

"I don't understand?"

"A while back, a few years ago now actually when I was on operations, I had a calling to do something else. So, I started to study towards it when I got back home. Now have the qualifications that I need." He is leaning on the table now, as if there is something awkward to explain.

"Right, okay. That's fantastic news then. But what in?"

"Bee, I'm going to be a Padre, an RAF Chaplain."

In that moment it all made sense. I am so pleased for him and yes, I understand sticking out the course to the end will be tough. I find myself giving him back the same sound advice that he gave me, to just be patient and like a storm it will pass soon enough. Before we part, I have a moment of sadness and doubt. I ask him if this means we are friends or, if it's not appropriate anymore as he'll be an officer soon. Adam bestows me with one of his magical smiles, and he assures me that we'll bump into each other again and that we are indeed good friends, and that Chaplains can be friends with anyone.

Chapter 10 –
Escape to Reality

At last, after months of seclusion, hard work and monotonous training, the day arrived when we were told our final exam results and of our postings. It was time to set off for a new beginning. The postings we are given typically last for three years. I hoped I'd be heading for somewhere nicer than another desolate camp in windy Wales at least. The Chief had on occasion quietly said to me, that it is all better when training is over with and we are settled on a proper unit, just as Adam has. He must have seen me looking sad and beaten at times too.

During my time in Wales, I reported to the Boss once a month, where I lied and told her all was well. She in return told me that I must do better as my scores were averaging under eighty percent, only the fourth highest in a class of twelve, and simply not good enough to make a statement. It was nerves though, I couldn't do any better when I was so nervous all the time. Plus, I needed to be careful not to do too well, and that was a tricky balancing act. The guys were relentless with their verbal attacks and grumpiness if I exceeded. In Wales I remained a cross between a leper and a novelty and in the six months I was there, I had only Adam as a friend. Some of the guys on my course were polite after a while but still standoffish. They'd tease each other heavily if they were seen speaking to me, so it was best that they didn't. I learned not to talk, only answer questions, and the guys only talked to me when no one else was around to hear. I stood out more than a giant mole on the end of a witch's nose. I never want to stand out again. I crave the freedom of being lost amongst the crowd, I miss it. I'm not sure that I will ever feel that free again. In this new RAF life, I'm too much of an oddity. I'm so sad remembering how it was, I need to dig deep and block it out. I have no idea how to get out of my contract, and if I did find a way, I am not sure I could leave. I have a duty now, to be good at this role until the next female engineer arrives and takes the pressure off me. Apparently, the RAF head office was monitoring my results as they would like an excuse to close the trade to women in the future. I'm told the monitoring of my annual assessments will continue for three years. I have no choice but to stick at it and do reasonably well. I thought that when I arrived at my permanent base I could quietly find out about the process of resigning, so when the monitoring stops, I am ready, and I can leave. Although, I seem to remember my parents telling me it costs thousands to buy your freedom back, which I don't have, and neither will Mum and Dad I imagine. Not that I can see me asking the folks, how embarrassing would that be? I feel guilty enough and I haven't told them any of it. When I called home, I would tell them as little as possible and that all was fine, I'd fib. I couldn't bear them worrying when there was nothing they could do. I never used to lie, and now for the RAF and to spare my parents worry, I've lied often.

RAF Lossiemouth, this is my posting. It's situated at the top of Scotland on the Morayshire coast. It's not handy for going home at weekends to Devon at the bottom of England, and it's the only place colder and wetter than the damp and grey place in the valleys of Wales. It's as if they did this on purpose, another tragic joke at my expense. It takes fifteen hours to get back home. I guess if I am not going home that often I can at least save up to buy my way out when the time comes.

After a huge train journey to Inverness with three train changes, a car picked me up and took me to the camp. It was quite a pretty drive to get here from the train station and took about an hour. It's a shame I felt sick for most of it. Feeling tired and nervous, the winding country roads and the hills in the highlands of Scotland is not a great mix, I was exhausted when I landed. The guys at the guard room knew I was coming, they expected a girl, and they were very chatty. In fact, I couldn't get a word in. The driver didn't stop for breath when he was handing me over to the team at the gate. I was in my room in the women's barrack block in record time and I felt, well, almost welcome.

This camp is huge, I need to get a bus to the other side of the airfield in the mornings to find the section where I work. It's a lot better than the training camp in Wales, with better facilities and a nicer warmer feel to the buildings. They are mostly painted green not grey and I am stared at only a fraction as much? Probably as I look a little lost as I'm still finding my way. There are other women on camp, lots in fact, the female accommodation block is full. There are plenty of nights out and functions, a good gym, places to eat and our camp is joined onto a village. There are a few shops inside and a few outside of camp.

I am treated a little different, a step backwards at work. I think that's because some of the men have never directly worked with a woman before, and they have been working for many years. They have preconceived ideas about us crying all the time, being moody, being feeble or being generally clueless. I worked hard and completed everything they have asked of me in the first months, so they soon came around and recently it's starting to feel okay. It's such a relief to be in a place where I don't stand out all the time. Where I am spoken to civilly, like a human being and, I am surprised and pleased to find that most of my job is outdoors.

I had no idea I'd like it, and I had even less of a clue that this type of job existed at all before I joined the RAF. The generators and various green machines we worked on at the training camp, well they live outdoors by the jets. You know they never said, they never explained the context of what we were learning. I've missed the outdoors so much. Growing up in the countryside I was always outdoors, playing, exploring and swimming outdoors. The only job I had ever heard of being outdoors though was a farmer, not an engineer.

Okay, the humour and some of the jokes the engineers recite are pretty cutting, if you didn't know it is all just for fun, it's just banter. It reminds me of home. Probably as both my parents were in the Army before I was born. I have been mocked this way before and it's not threatening, not like it was in training. Maybe this child like humour is a trait that all the armed forces people share? It may be too early to tell if it is the same everywhere but, in my section, no matter how bad the day gets we laugh about it. I am at home with this humour, this camaraderie is reassuring and more than welcome after my time in the awful training camps.

The local accent is soft, and my nickname for a little while was Ken. Slightly embarrassingly, it took quite some time listening to the local accent to realise that Ken means 'you know' and it is said a lot to confirm or close a lot of sentences. I was convinced that Ken was either a pretty common name up here or a very popular chap, I just couldn't understand at first what was being said. When I asked about Ken once at tea break, they all fell about laughing. So, I was called Ken for weeks. Now I am Buzzy Bee or just Bee.

I have recently been told that I'm moving out of the general team and on to a squadron for a few months. It's exciting, a change of scene. I will be in a van, and we will go around the squadron checking on assets with my mechanic teammate. The radio will be on in the van, so this sounds like it has the making of a great spring and summer. It's the same job but on the aircraft line, where the planes park basically. I just wish I had made some friends to hang out with outside of work. I have bumped into a few of the girls from the block in passing, but I haven't had a drink with them or anything. I feel shy now, idea why. The guys don't ask me to join them with what they are doing at weekends, I only get to go out to the section drinks once a fortnight. So, weekends are quite dull. I use them as a time to rest.

My first squadron task is supporting Tornado jets on 617 Squadron. This squadron is famous for The Dam Busters. They flew different planes back then obviously, now they fly these fighter jets.

Anyway, they have strange rituals in the bar on their Squadron nights.

617 Squadron do some sort of routine dance to the Dambusters theme tune. When the beer is flowing, they have their arms stretched out pretending to be planes dropping bombs, which has earnt them a nickname that rhymes with Dambusters, the Dumb Bastards. I haven't seen the routine yet, but I suspect that it is mostly the engineers who look after the jets who take part, not the elitist aircrew. These pilots seem to have no humour. They have all grown up watching aerobatic displays and have got themselves confused with being a celebrity. They all wear their sunglasses and the pride of their Squadron's history on their faces, like a smug badge of honour that sets them head and shoulders above other fighter Squadrons. It's ridiculous given the historic Dambusters mission happened in 1943, generations before they were born. Their Squadron's motto is 'Aspres moi le deluge' meaning 'after the flood'.

We have a healthy disrespect for the aviator wearing Maverick followers of 617 Squadron, someone must keep them grounded after all. Tomorrow I will see all this for myself. I am taking over from a chap called Jock who has got a cancellation appointment for his vasectomy. He has four kids already, and apparently this is the only way forward. Did I mention that most of the chaps here are from Scotland and are nicknamed Jock up here? If you call Jock across the hanger, four or five men will turn around to see which one you are pointing at. You really couldn't make it up.

Chapter 11 –
A New Dawn

It's sunny, really sunny, and I am on the squadron with Paul. Paul isn't too talk-ative, but when he does speak it's worth listening to. He is either being extremely witty or quite profound. He's from Manchester, which right now makes him cool by birth. We have some Manchester tunes on the CD player, and we are on the airfield approach when the comm's radio calls us over to a jet on bay eleven. The jet is due to go out and the generator is not working properly. Jets use generators to start. They can start on their own like a car, but it's not good for them if they do.

Six aircraft technicians are stood around waiting and looking sullen when we get there. They hate having to rely on us to come and save the day, it really bothers them. They sulk like over tired kids and look at the floor. I jump out of the van and head to the generator to see what's wrong, while Paul walks over to the squadron line office to ask for some background.

As I unplug the cable from the jet and run the engine to start the fault finding I hear a voice mocking the guys. It's nothing new, but this time I freeze and just listen.

"What's happening here chaps, how many of you are stood beholden of this fair maiden to bail you out and get us up in the air?"

A broad shouldered cinematically beautiful man is walking towards the jet with a wry smile on his face. He's staring right at me with blue steel eyes. I feel the core of me tighten in an instant as I take a sharp breath in. Is this in my imagination, he even sounded like an American movie star?

The banter continues in the background with his flying partner, who is still chatting to the engineers gathering by our van some thirty-feet away. Christ, he's coming over and I feel trapped, what the hell? I can't move. I'm really clumsy and I know that if I move now, I'll fall or at least trip a little bit and loose face.

"So, are you going to get me up in the air, miss?" What? I swear he meant that innocently. He is smiling playfully at me due to the banter with the boys but, I heard that sentence in a way that has made my body tighten again, electricity has just travelled up my spine like a mild shockwave of instant torture. I pull it together just enough to answer sternly,

"We will, but it may take a while. You should wait inside, we can call you when it's ready to go."

This way I can get rid of him without having to move and expose myself and my clumsiness. He looks quite bemused at me as I turn to look at the instruments on the control panel.

"So, you'll summon me when you are ready for me? I like the sound of that but, maybe I prefer to watch." There is a pause, and I am speechless as he coughs a little. "It's not every day I get to watch an engineer work so seriously and pro-fessionally. It brings a warm feeling to my cold heart."

He says this with that same wry smile he first approached with, and he doesn't take his eyes off me for a second. He may be mocking me, but it feels more intense than the usual RAF banter. What a cocky idiot, he must think he is god's gift to women. I get it, he's a flirt, that's all. I can handle this, even if my insides are telling me, I can't. He's American and he's flying in our jets? When did we start an exchange programmes with the yanks? I'm going to give him this put down in the most professional manner, seeing he likes professional so much.

"Sir, I appreciate the sentiment but, I think you'll find that you will be of no use to me whatsoever. You are simply the driver and this fault, well this requires an engineer's expertise. Now if you don't mind." I gesture over his shoulder to the Squadron office building, my raised eyebrows providing the hint he should leave now. Oh shit, I didn't say any of that in the humorous way I intended. I sounded horrid, cold, and borderline subordinate. He starts laughing at this point. I have lost the points I was expecting to score on this one, and it suddenly makes me quite angry. Yet, I have those same electric feelings running through my veins and the deep tensions within my core that I know is not remotely the re-sponse I want to have to this situation right now. These are feelings that over-power my body without a choice. "Have I said something funny, sir? Or is this an American humour moment that is so weak, it's lost on us Brits?" I am livid now, breathing heavily and standing with my hands on my hips I square up to him. I think I'm going to lose my temper. The other flying suit comes over now and quickly senses an issue. He looks at his partner – "All okay here JJ?" – and then at me – "What seems to be the problem here?"

Before I can say a word, blue eyes adds, "Oh, I was a little grumpy with this engineer called?" He looks at me with a nod to my rank on my shoulder, expecting my name. "McBrien," I inform him without moving and he continues. "SAC McBrien was explaining to me about the complexity of the generator's automatic safety systems and interlocks. How they are designed to ensure the aircraft receives power with a one-percent tolerance so as not to disturb the calibration on the avionics or cause any damage to the navigation and weapon systems." He speaks calmly as he somehow adds with all seriousness. "I didn't understand much of it Bob, I'm only a hopeless Canadian boy really, I missed out on the wonderful British education to support such technical wizardry. So, I think we should wait inside" – annoyed now he adds – "I'm sure the nice engineers wouldn't mind calling us when it's ready." As they turn to walk back to the squadron office, he looks straight at me with an intense anger that leaves me with a burning heat raising up through my body. I think it's anger I am feeling too but, I am not at all confident that I have understood what my body is telling me right now.

My thoughts are broken as Paul arrives. "What was that about? Did you piss them off? It's only been five minutes, if he complains and I get another bollocking from the Chief my promotion is on the line Bee!"

I reassure as best I can. "It's okay Paul, it isn't a problem. He was just asking how long it would be and was being impatient with having to wait." I sigh.

"I said we'd let him know when it's ready. We can call it in on the radio as we leave. They'll get the message."

Paul has a rant for a while about Aircrew and their poor attitudes towards ground crew, but I don't hear most of it. My thoughts are with the man who stopped me functioning for a moment and stole my humour, replacing it with an intense need that I am yet to understand.

Chapter 12 –
Beer Calls

We don't use our own bar in the section at Lossiemouth, ever since someone ran onto the airfield naked, we are banned from drinking so close to the airfield. So, we have booked the rugby club for our fortnightly beer call, it's ours for two hours before it opens up to the station, at eighteen hundred on Friday. It works well, as anyone of any rank on station can arrive after our time and we have more fun without having to move on. Banter grows between sections. Beer is in full swing and it's nearly nineteen hundred hours when Sid, a rather outrageous and alternatively minded Corporal insists we all dance to our section song. We are not allowed to be on the floor when this song plays.

Sid is one of life's eccentrics and to be fair, he makes fun out of any situation, although you can't tell if he is smiling or not due to his pruned handlebar moustache. He's nicknamed Sid the sexist but, he isn't really sexist. He just pretends to mock the nature of it, tongue in cheek to make a point. So, he can say whatever he likes to me to shock the lads but, no one else can. To some, I'm their token girl in the section. It's sweet really in an odd kind of way. When he is joking his cockney accent makes it all the funnier, when he is pulling someone up for being out of order, there is no messing with Sid. I don't know if it's a reminder of the times we had in basic recruit training when Sergeant Bundock scared me, or if it is a generalisation of the men of south Wales, or just a coincidence.

'Yes, sir. I can boogie' by Baccara, is the section song and woe betide anyone who fails to join in. I'm positioned on an up ended whisky barrel, picked by Sid so I can't fall too far as 'I am only a girl' and I shouldn't be drinking beer in his opinion. It's a man's drink. Which is ridiculous as the barrels are higher than all the tables, and he bought the beer. The truth is, he places me there so no one can get too close to me to be a pest. Sid is always in control and quite protective and thoughtful really, he just likes to hide it. We are in the heart of the Scottish whisky country and there are signs everywhere in the bar of the various tours and the heritage of the highlands.

The Boss is doing a toast to Scotty Henderson who has been promoted and posted to Germany. The toast is rudely ended as Sid can't wait any longer, he shouts, "It's all bollocks, sir. You boring old fart, on your head son, and let's get dancing." Cheers go up as everyone raises their glass and the music starts. No average dancing is accepted, if you are seen to be doing the NAAFI two step, stepping left, then right with no interest you are in serious breach of orders and you will be made to do a forfeit. The boss laughs loudly like Santa and does as instructed. The beer in his hand he must pour over his head, and he must also start making a prat of himself dancing. Pure Dad dancing in the Boss's case, he's painfully stiff like a robot and he lacks any sense of rhythm. No one is immune to the world of Sid. The crowd are now flailing about like ducks shaking their tail feathers and doing funky chicken dancing. No idea why this is the most popular dance for our section but, it's very funny.

Chapter 13 –
Bob Never Fails

James was walking ahead of Bob, he really needed a beer. Their training flight had left an hour late due to birds on the airfield, and that was cut short further as they were ordered back to base for a briefing. The day started badly at the outset as he had to cover for his Navigator, Bob. Explaining away a false alibi for the night before when Bob's latest girlfriend called him to find out if Bob was alive or dead. She was worried as he didn't call in to see her after work as he had promised her.

"Hey, JJ, wait for me I'll get the first-round in. I owe you for covering for me this morning. I was done for. She was going to realise I was up to something if you hadn't of given me back up."

James was livid at this flippant remark. "I hardly had a choice, did I? You told Joy you were with me all night, that I was uncontrollably upset as my pet dog, my only true friend, the pretty blonde shiatzu called pixie had died! You're a lowlife Bob." He started to rant at Bob, not that Bob seemed genuinely concerned about James's anger. "I bet you've used that one before, haven't you? Work well, does it? Not only does it close the issue, but it also moves all the attention from you, onto me, your alibi." James pushed Bob away when he tried to put his arm around his shoulder. "Don't do that to me again as I won't cover for you twice."

There was a barely a second of quiet when Bob burst out laughing and slapped James on the back of his shoulders. "C'mon mate, stop being so sensitive, are you gay or something? I mean, that would explain your choice of dog." At this glib comment about the imaginary fluffy pet dog, James can do nothing but laugh at his Romeo friend, while Bob continues to apologise by way of explanation. "To be fair James, I have only been seeing Joy for five weeks. I reckon it's over. She's just not too bright and she doesn't understand my humour. I'll tell her this weekend that I've lost interest. I'll think of something sensitive because I can be sensitive." There was a moment pause. "You know I can be sensitive JJ, I mean I held your bloody hand all night over your beloved Pixie."

James couldn't stay angry at Bob, he has no choice but to accept that not everyone has the true scruples of an English gentleman and an officer. "Okay Casanova, you're buying the first five at least, then I'll think about forgiving you." Bob puts his arm around James again, but this time in a very camp way, as he forces a high-pitched voice that almost breaks and stings in his throat. "Am I on the sofa tonight sweetie, please forgive me and let me back into your bed my gorgeous blue-eyed hero?" James pushes him away again, laughing loudly.

As they approach, James notices that the music sounds louder than usual at the Rugby club tonight. "I wonder what chaos is on the other side of this door?" James can only imagine how his day is going to dip to a new low, with Bob on a mission to misbehave and break loose of Joy. As they enter the room there is a crazy party vibe. Bizarrely everyone is dancing to some crazy seventies' song, but no one is on the floor, they are on the bar, the chairs, the tables. A skinny pale blonde guy is dancing on a shelf on the wall, which looks like it is about to give way. He looks a little like a muppet puppet the way he is dancing and balancing on the ledge.

"There's something unnatural about him JJ, look." Bob starts laughing as he points out the oddball he sees, with warm humour and an air of boyhood respect. James smiles as he scans the room, the mood has picked up and whatever new scandal he is going to witness tonight, he thinks it will be harmless light-hearted fun. Then he sees her, the girl from the line, the one who had a severe sense of humour failure.

James

Christ, she looks hot when she is dancing and laughing. I can't stop staring at her, when Bob thrusts a beer in my hand. Have I really been stood here this long? Christ her ass is perfect in those jeans. The way her top is riding up a little as she puts her hands above her head, showing a glimpse of her lower spine. So toned and her skin looks so smooth, I may have to look away just so I can walk. If she weren't such a clear pain in the ass, I'd have to ask her out right here, right now. Hell, I'd want to know everything about her before I steal her away from this greasy sweaty place.

Bob notices my attentions are somewhat captured by her, SAC McBrien. "Bloody hell JJ look at her, no wonder you haven't moved, you have the best view in the house!" – Bob drinks a little and with no reply from me adds – "I think you need to cover for me again tomorrow, I think I may need a new alibi, she needs me!"

What the hell, no chance. "Back off Bob, she's too clever for you."

Bob senses something about my tone and thankfully backs off. "Alright girl-friend, she is clearly all yours then, I know when my fellow comrades are serious about their prey." Bob walks off to start chatting to some girls he recognises from the Officers mess, just some mess staff that he flirts with harmlessly every day. They are butter in his hands, but he won't go there, not so close to home. He prefers to keep his conquests at a safe distance, never to be seen again once the axe falls.

I find myself walking over to where she is dancing, the music has changed and the room dynamic changes too, she is now dancing on the floor having jumped from the barrel. What the hell am I doing, why did I react so much at the thought of Bob going anywhere near her? I want her, obviously, I just want her. I have no idea who she is, what she is like, yet at the same time I know all I need to know to make up my mind. I am acting like a first-class idiot.

I'm stood still close behind her when 'Love Man' comes on, Otis Reading you never fail me. My stance is authoritative, legs apart and beer in hand. I'll just wait for her to realise someone is behind her. As she does, she freezes a little, then tentatively turns around. As soon as I see her stare back at me, I realise I have the upper hand here, I am in control, and she is mine. She has the look of anger, contempt and scared rabbit all rolled into one. I raise my eyebrow with a smile and ask if she's been waiting here long for me.

"Oh yes Cowboy, all my life!" She is not impressed and downright moody.

I've managed to annoy her by my mere presence and completely misjudged the situation. Then, the words of my dad are suddenly ringing in my ear, *Don't marry the one you can live with James, marry the one you can't live without.*

No one so far has turned me down or given me such attitude. This is a first. Being a pilot is a big turn on for the girls generally and my Canadian accent usually seals the deal. She does it for me, I am going to win her over if it kills me, which it might do. She looks like she could pack a mean left hook.

"James." I say, with a smile.

"James what?" She replies. Yep, she's hot.

"My name is James and your name SAC McBrien is?"

Just as she is about to answer an old guy with a moustache comes over with a beer for her and he brings with him a mean stare. "Bee, come away, step away, stay away from those Aircrew lot, they can't be trusted." As he drags her away, he looks at me. "I've got your number sunshine, she's too good for you, she's ours. Step away from what your life can't afford."

Well, I start laughing and raise my beer to him. He is joking I think, but there is a serious undertone. So, it's Bee, Bee McBrien, I like it. Hmmm, I have no idea how to get close to her. Maybe I should quit while I'm ahead? I really need to take a break. I don't know the girl and I am thinking of plans to get close to her. Get a grip, come on, get a grip.

Chapter 14 –
Take Cover

Bee

What is this guy doing here? That's all I need right now. Thank God Sid came along when he did, I was frozen to the spot and here we go again, that feeling. It's like the invasion of the body snatchers. My body is not my own when he is around. I feel like a new-born lamb even clumsier than I was before, and my legs are bumbling. It could just be that I have drunk too much. I may have to hide away and quit the dancing. I can't dance with him in here I feel nervous. We are at the other side of the club hut now, and I think it's safe to turn around, so my back is against the wall. He can't sneak up on me here. I feel like a hunted animal. Not an elegant gazelle hunted by a lion, more like an ungainly goat. Oh, for crying out loud, he's staring at me. What do I do now, please someone talk to me and break this awkwardness? I look at my watch, the walls, and back again. Why is he still staring at me? Right, I'll go to the bathroom that will help me escape, I can think about how to get past him and home without him noticing when I'm there. He's by the door so maybe a window? Is that going too far? Arghhh, I need to get a grip.

The toilets are cold, damp and there is gloss paint on the walls in insipid baby pink. The tiles on the floor are grey as is the paintwork around the doors. Clearly the guys in the rugby club have no idea on how to decorate this old Nissen hut to make it welcoming. The hand dryer provides no heat, just cold air and the place is freezing. It's not helping me think of a plan. Although, wait, this is all in my head, isn't it? So, I don't actually need a plan. I just need to calmly walk to the door and go home. No one will notice. I'm short, it's an advantage in a packed bar. Yes, that's what I'll do. I check my hair, I look at myself in the mirror 'you got this' pull up my jeans and smooth my top, and then turn to leave. One straight walk across to the opposite corner of the club and I'll be through the door, and then I'm home and dry.

Out I walk and okay, easier said than done. It's gone a little crazy in the club, the tunes are louder, *Don't stop believing* is playing, arms are thrown into the air to the chorus along with a rain of beer. There are hordes of drunk men and a few token women singing along badly. The place is packed, and everyone is dancing, or maybe they are so drunk, they are just struggling to stand? It's hard to tell. I keep my head down and weave through the crowd. The lighting is low and there are timber columns propping up the ceiling here and there. Each have memorabilia hung tentatively, and odd jutting out shelves for beer glasses to perch on, but at least they don't move around with waving arms. I can feel the cold air waft in my direction, so I know I am near the door. Thank God, at last, I'm through the door into the small porch. Just a couple more steps and I'll be out and into the welcome cool air.

There's a small step I always trip on, more of a lip at the bottom of the door frame, so I must watch out for that. As I am looking down negotiating the step, I bump into someone coming in the other way. My automatic response is to apologise, and as I'm saying sorry, I look up and it's him, the bloody cowboy. I am startled and the word 'Shit' slips out. I'm lost as to what to do now and well, I'm frozen. We are both silent and stood perfectly still, so close to each other that we are almost touching. Has time stopped? I must move, well one of us must move. I'll do it, I'll go around him, to the right. As I do, he moves to my right too. So, I dart left and try and dash past him. That bloody step, it got me again. As I trip, he grabs my arm and waist to stop me falling face first. He pulls me near to him. He is hot. I mean temperature hot. I feel his body heat radiate like an oven. He is going to kiss me, isn't he? Oh god no.

"Are you okay Bee? Has something happened?" He asks me so gently, I feel like he knows me. He has a look of concern in his eyes, like he really cares.

"I'm fine, you are in the way that's all, tripping me up!" I bark back. I can be such a prat. Why, oh why did I bark back?

He asks again, "I meant has something happened to upset you, you're rushing out of here like the place is on fire?"

He has a valid point; I was making a run for it. I tried to walk calmly but my heart was pounding, so I ended up racing out of there. "It's nothing, I'm fine thank you. I just want to go home now."

I manage to say that with some grace compared to my last snap at him. He looks at me confused and with his hands perching in his pockets at his hips he looks left, purses his lips together, and then looks back at me.

"Okay, well, I can walk you back, make sure you get back okay. Do you stay on camp? Which way is it?" I don't hesitate to respond with a no thank you, I'm fine. I wouldn't know how to say yes, even if it is creepy walking back to the women's accommodation block on my own.

"It's not an offer. I wouldn't be doing my duty if I let you walk back alone. It's not appropriate."

"What?" – I laugh at this point – "your Duty?" He laughs a little too.

"Okay, not my duty then, but where I am from it's not right to let a young lady walk home alone. It's not polite." I am lost for words at what to say. So, I just shrug, and we walk towards the main road on camp.

"My Block is the other side of the main road by the gym." We don't speak again. We just walk at a quick pace. It's strange, a little tense. When I do speak, I don't look at him, I look straight ahead.

"It's this one, I'm okay now." I take a deep breath and decide to turn around and look at him briefly. "Thank you." I don't want to come across as completely rude.

As I rush for the door. "Bee" – he calls out – "goodnight."

James

Goodnight! Is that all I can think of? What an idiot. She's so different. Kinda interesting, in a vulnerable kind of way, but fierce as well. Or is that just a front? She's just odd, probably bat shit crazy knowing my luck but, I want to know her even more now. I am going to have to pull out all the stops, think of something amazing to impress her just to get her to consider talking to me.

Chapter 15 –
Sparkling Wisdom
Bee

The day after beer call, my head is banging. I kept waking up, my sleep was broken on and off all night. His face looking down at me is the first thing on my mind as soon as I wake. I must find a way to get this man out of my mind before I die of insomnia.

I'll walk on the beach today. It's bright again, a little chilly in the wind but, mostly warm and dry. This is pretty much the start of summer for Scotland. Maybe I'll do some shopping in Elgin. It's Mum's birthday soon and I need ideas for her present. There isn't much to do here on weekends. Most folk go out for lunch, then stay out in local pubs if the mood takes them. Some go on a whiskey tour, or maybe down to Aviemore for the mountains. Some head to Inverness for the Lochs. Some go home to their families if they are only a few hours away. It's too far for me to go home for a weekend. Fifteen hours or more to Devon is a bit much so I'll stay put. I should consider a break to go home, a week's leave would be nice soon. Although I won't go for Mum's birthday. It's a bank holiday and the journey will be unbearable to get to the southwest of England that weekend. Until I can go, I'll chill out as much as I can. A long hot shower is a great way to start the day and firm up my plans.

Okay, I've switched my plans whilst I was in the shower. I'll go shopping first, I hate shopping, especially when I don't know what to get. Then a relaxing walk on the beach to make it better. With no need to rush off to the shops, I can take my time and relax. I'll pick up a sandwich in town and have a makeshift picnic.

Elgin is a pretty town with a scattering of various shops, some trinket shops, jewellers, galleries, and cafes. There is a small shopping centre, St Giles. It houses a random collection of shops from outdoor clothing to a chemist. It doesn't seem to fit in with the town. The main high street is so pretty. In the centre is a big old civic hall building and a fountain, surrounded by historic stone buildings, arches and turrets. Then this ugly glass box shopping centre. When you walk into it there are identical glass front facades to every shop. They are soulless, you could be anywhere in the UK. Anyway, I hope it won't take too long for something to jump out at me for Mum. Jewellery is a good fall-back plan as I can post it easy enough. There is a little independent jeweller on Commerce Street, one of the back streets. Right, I'll start there.

I can see a lovely pair of gold and pearl earrings in the window, but other than that, it all seems to be rings. Then that Hollywood voice appears from nowhere.

"So, are we picking rings already? I'm sure happy if you are?" When I freeze and say nothing he carries on. "I think the one second row down, third in from the right would be perfect, or is it too big? Too ostentatious for you classy Brits?"

What on earth is he doing here? I can't stop smiling as he is quite funny. Without turning I reply, "Well maybe I'm an ostentatious kind of girl? Although, you'll have to save up your flying pay first, it's nearly ten thousand pounds. Maybe I'll have to wait for a few thousand years, or sadly, marry someone else. Awe, such a shame."

We both laugh and for a moment it feels like we are old friends. I've forgotten to be careful and keep my guard up and there is no agonising atmosphere. He smiles warmly and adds in a quiet and soft tone.

"Hey, it's odd seeing you here. What are you looking for? Anything in particular? I'm here to buy a gift for my mum, I kinda thought earrings is always a win? Maybe a necklace?"

I can't help but laugh more.

"I'm actually here for the same reason, my mum's birthday. I thought earrings or a locket."

I'm smiling as I turn fully towards him, and I realise his blue eyes are intense but also kind, they stand out, probably due to the golden tan worn on his face. His eyes are thoughtful and knowing. He has a few lines at the top of his nose and to the outer edges of his eyes that make him look masculine, but playful. He hasn't shaved, and the rugged unshaven look transfixes me completely. As I scan his features, I notice his skin on his cheeks is baby smooth, his lips are pale and full and he has magazine perfect hair, dark blonde swept slightly to one side and ruffled. This guy is like a Disney character. No wonder he can joke with me, he is clearly the type to have a long-legged blonde model for a girlfriend. I think I'm quite safe as a short brunette. Ah, I get it now, I'm in the friend zone.

"So, Bee, Great minds think alike! Shall we pick together? I need all the help I can get. My mum is not too easy to please, she's a Brit!"

"Okay, I'm confused?"

"So, your mum is British? Is that why you are on exchange here, to seek out your heritage?" He laughs loudly at this, what did I say? Don't all Yanks love to think they have British heritage?

"Bee, I'm not on exchange. I have a British passport; I have dual citizenship. So, I am in the Royal Air Force just like you. I'm not on an exchange programme." He stares at the puzzled look on my face. "Didn't you notice my uniform is British?"

Erm, I stand stunned and trying to think of what I have noticed so far, other than how he looks, and how he makes me feel, not a lot obviously. "Hey, you haven't noticed me at all have you?" What have I missed here? I best laugh this off. He's messing with me.

"Sorry cowboy, I was too busy working when we met."

"Bee, you don't remember my name, do you?" I stare at him with guilt written all over my face, God I feel really bad about this, but I don't, I don't remember his name. I was too angry at him the first time, and too keen to escape last night. I remember his eyes, his stare, his body heat radiating like a burning hot sun, but I don't remember his name.

"It's James" – he laughs a little – "Bee McBrien, let me formally introduce myself James Jamieson, or JJ for short." It's a nice name, but I feel so embarrassed about forgetting it I'm speechless, and so I just bite my bottom lip with guilt and think about apologising as he continues. "I prefer James, just James." I find myself smiling and fidgeting. *Say something for goodness's sake?*

"Okay, Just James. I am Beatrice, Bee or the guys at work sometimes call me Bumble." – Looking at the shop door, I add – "shall we do this?" I smile and gesture towards the shop again.

James laughs as he replies, places his hand on his chest. "Well if you insist Bee, I mean I thought I'd have to put much more effort in before you agreed to a ring. Beatrice Jamieson, it sounds nice, doesn't it?"

We both start laughing and with the back of my hand I playfully hit him in the stomach as we walk into the shop. "The presents James, not the ring."

A tall thin older gentleman comes out from a storeroom, his clothes are meticulously worn, albeit a little like an undertaker. Black trousers, white shirt, and black tie. The shop is full of wall-to-wall glass cabinets and a glass counter to the front with watches and bracelets displayed. An old-fashioned pale grey till is perched on top of the counter on the right side. It's like stepping back in time, old show tunes play in the background. A soft Scottish accent welcome us.

"Good afternoon to you both, its lovely to see a lovely young couple looking so happy. Let me guess, you are here to look at rings?"

Before I get to reply, James jumps in. "Not today, I'm still to convince her to marry me. So today we are after presents for our mothers, unless she changes her mind whilst we are here?" He says this and looks at me as if this was a real situation and he is pleading with me for the fiftieth time to marry him, until one day, I finally give in and just pick a ring. It makes me giggle. But I manage to pull myself together, pause and wrinkle my nose and shake my head.

"Not yet honey, I'm just not ready." The soft Scottish accent interrupts knowledgably.

"Well dearie, I don't know why you are waiting, he's clearly the one for you. Trust me, I see them all in here and you two are perfectly right together. Life is short, you have to grab happiness when you see it, before it passes by" – he smiles at us knowingly – "like a happy bus dearie, jump on board dearie, jump on board."

We laughed so much, a happy bus? He is clearly on the happy pills. If only he knew we didn't know each other at all. The nice man was sweet and helped us with our purchases. We bought the same pairs of earrings each for our mum's, yellow gold with pearl drops, then said our goodbyes to the quirky shop owner. James pulled open the door, the shop doorbells rang, and he waved me through first. I like this. It feels so normal and natural.

"Hey Bee, this may sound odd but are you done shopping now? Do you fancy lunch on the beach? I know its Scotland and it's freezing but, there is a pastry shop in town that does the best pasties, a British legend of a pie. I often pick one up and shoot through to the beach at Roseisle. It's really stunning, what do you think?" I reply without a hesitation,

"Sounds perfect but, I have to correct you cowboy, a pasty is not a pie!" James rolls his eyes like a nonchalant teen and speaks to the air.

"Oh, she has forgotten my name again, maybe its early onset dementia?" He looks at me now, with a mischievous smile and we are laughing again.

Chapter 16 –
Sun, Sea, and Sand

I am surprised how easy the afternoon was on the beach with James. I felt relaxed but energised. It was like spending time with family, I almost forgot that he is movie star gorgeous as we walked and talked. Once I figured I was in the friendzone, it was so much easier. The only reminder was from time to time, when I looked up and caught a glimpse of him from the side, or when we accidentally walked too close and I felt him near me, I had goose bumps spread across my arms and a chill down my spine. When we sat and ate our lunch, we stared ahead looking into the sea. Still talking, but in a calm and relaxed way. This place is beautiful. Choppy dark turquoise sea and long white sands, a mature forest edges the beach that is full of fluffy fifty-foot Christmas trees, and inside the woods hide picnic benches to sit and eat. I learnt about some of James's childhood, and how he ended up here. I felt so sad when he told me his father, also called James, had died when he was just eleven years old.

James's father was an engineer for Rolls Royce and had a passion for planes, especially the Red Arrows. James beamed when he spoke of his dad. He said his father was influential in developing a new type of civil aircraft engine in the 1980s that could be used in a variety of aircraft. So, this is where James's interest in flying came from. He held dear the fond memories of the times he spent with his dad watching the Red Arrows or making little red plastic Airfix models. I was sure his eyes were wet from the raw depth of the feelings for his father. Confirmed to me when James stood to instigate a walk and a change of subject. James clearly kept the British stiff upper lip part of his genes. He said he had found it impossible to accept his father's death until much later, as a teen, and he didn't fully appreciate yet how this had impacted him.

In the early years, James daydreamed of him returning home declaring it all a big mistake, that his dad had been away stuck somewhere on business, maybe a top-secret project. His mum remarried when he was thirteen, a nice quiet caring man called Eric who was visiting his family in the UK when they met. After writing often and Sunday telephone calls for about six months, they took the plunge. Eric couldn't bear James and his mum, Margaret struggling alone back in the UK, he wanted to take care of them both. Eric was a natural family man who took no time in preparing. He took a lease on a house in Burnaby on the outskirts of Vancouver. Close to his work but more importantly near the best schools for James and situated well for the lakes and mountains. James's stepfather was a futuristic computer analyst and programmer who landed an innovative job some years earlier in Vancouver. The company was called Electronic Arts and they made home video games. Eric was working on a game called FIFA, leading a team building the game platform, although James did not think it would take off.

James was distraught to leave England at the time, he loved everything about his life. His Grandparents, his cousins, friends. He was completely oblivious to his mother's struggle as a single parent as he had everything he needed. He sobbed the most when leaving his dog Bear knowing he would likely never see her again. She was an eight-year-old golden husky cross who was to be left with his Aunt Anne. James's mum thought the journey and quarantine for Bear would be too much for her, it would be cruel to put her through it.

For James this was his last link to his father. Bear had been brought home unplanned as a pup when a littler was found by the side of the road. She was the littlest one, and the only blonde. With piercing blue eyes, a pure white face and brown button nose. She had bonded instantly with James's father, nuzzling into his neck for protection as soon as she was picked up. After losing his father, Bear and James were inseparable. James's concern for Bear came true as she died within a year of being parted from James. She died in her sleep, premature for her breed and James was sure his departure contributed to Bear fading away. This was the first catalyst to James finally grieving properly for losing his father and his life back in the UK. The losses became real again, and his emotions raw and uncontrollable as soon as he heard the news about Bear, he sobbed for days.

James finally seemed to settle in his third year in Vancouver. The first years being a solitary, sad and lonely time. He did have friends in the first two years, the kids in his school were boisterous and fun but James felt as if he wasn't really in the room, as if he was hearing them from underwater at times. There were a few more years of anger and playing up, finally cumulating in James finally settling down when he was Sixteen. He had been on several outward bound's trips with the Scouts, kayaking, camping and hiking which alongside his light-hearted and grossly boyish friends, helped him truly belly laugh again. He also found a strong male influence in Tom, a big Canadian policeman who led the scout troop in his spare time. Ever since then, he enjoyed the nature and experiences in the outskirts of Vancouver and is pretty much Canadian as far as you could now tell. He isn't a fan of football or 'Soccer' as he calls it now. He prefers ice hockey, and his team are the Vancouver Canucks, the same as Tom. James also mentioned his half-sister, Monica, who arrived into the family screaming the house down in his third year in Canada.

Monica is a wayward handful of a girl, a headstrong, lumbar jack shirt wearing rock chic. She is carefree except for her passions for saving the planet. She also spends her time demonstrating for the rights of the indigenous people of Vancouver who are still suffering oppression, injustice, and racism. James rolled his eyes and shook his head when he spoke of Monica being brought home by Tom when she was eleven. She had skipped school and been arrested for breach of the peace; James was so embarrassed at the time but was laughing about it as he retold the story to me. Clearly, he is very fond of his rebellious sibling. He may not be laughing had the charges not of been dropped. James said with conviction, that Monica would either mature into a woman who would change the world in some amazing way, or end up in jail for a lengthy term, and there would be no middle ground.

When the afternoon air became cooler, and the light was fading James gave me a lift back to base in his old red truck. I insisted he drop me at the gate to save his trouble, and James didn't argue. He was tired after talking about personal things. Then we simply said goodbye. No plans, no promises. I think the day will have been a one off.

Chapter 17 –
Forever Friends

When Bee received the call from Sarah, she was shocked. She had only spoken to her two days earlier, on Tuesday. Bee wasn't on her best form and had admitted to Sarah that she was feeling isolated up in Scotland. She assured her that it wasn't the place. The area was outstanding, it was just that she hadn't got anyone to share it with. She hadn't ever had to try hard to make friends, she used to be a magnet for striking up a conversation with a stranger, now she was hopeless at it. She assumed just as it was in training, that she just didn't fit in. She seemed to get on okay at work, but they weren't keen on having a woman join their social outings and adventures outside of work hours. The women in the block where she lived all seemed very polite, just busy, and she was hardly noticed. Many of them were shift workers in supply squadron or worked in the mess. Sarah hadn't had the same issues in her new world, and so she felt terrible for Bee. Sarah was welcomed with open arms by her red cap colleagues. The army police were not popular outside of their squad, so they stuck together and looked after each other with care. When Bee had joined the RAF, she became a rare breed, the odd one out. A female engineer in a man's world, a lonesome trail-blazer and she had resigned to the fact that it wouldn't be easy.

Each of the other college crew had settled well in their new roles. No awkwardness, and no surprises. It was painful for Sarah to know how badly her friend felt, especially as Bee had been the spiritual leader of the group, the one to always make the others feel secure and happy.

Stood holding the phone she worryingly asks,

"Are you okay Sarah?" Bee felt awkward talking to her in the control office.

"Hi love. Yes, I'm fine." Sarah couldn't contain herself. "I have a surprise for you, and before you say no, it's all arranged."

Bee was dumbstruck and a little worried.

"Erm, surprise? What is it, what have you done?"

"I have called the others and we are all free this weekend."

"Okay, I don't follow Sarah, what do you want me to do?"

"Nothing. We are all coming up to see you, all of us. The visiting accommodation block is booked, and we will all arrive tomorrow night. When we get there, we plan to drink lots and cheer you up."

Bee was touched and shocked. She also felt embarrassed that Sarah had told the others how lonely she felt. "Oh my god, really? You are crazy. How did you do all this? I have no idea of where to visit when you get here."

"No need to figure it out, we will just find a pub or something. It's all about seeing you, we will have such a laugh. Star, Beth and Callum are all set to get off work early to catch the train." Sarah had it all figured out precisely, bombarding Bee with information. "I'm finishing at lunch then driving up, collecting them at Inverness train station on my way. The infamous five will be back together. So, wish me luck that my old escort gets me there. It'll be great!"

"Wait, Callum is coming too? How did you get hold of him, I thought he was away? It'll be fun trying to keep Beth off him, you know how she is with Marines." They both laughed, and already Bee felt better.

"Look, I have to go. Make sure the guardroom has a phone number for you so we can ring you when we get there, then you can come and meet us, and we can take it from there."

"Sarah you're crazy, but I love you. Thank you."

As Bee hung up, the control room was quiet. The Sergeant asked Bee what the call was about, he wanted to give her a fighting chance. The lads would make up a story that could lead to rumours otherwise. As Bee briefly explained that she had friends from college visiting that weekend, it dawned on her that 'this weekend' meant tomorrow. Her excitement grew, and she had a spring in her step as she left to go back to work. Her mind wasn't on the six-month generator service she had to finish before the end of her shift. It was elsewhere, reminiscing about old times with good friends. Bee felt blessed to have such great friends. She couldn't wait to hear what they had all been up to since they last saw each other. So much had happened to each of them since that shopping trip. Bee smiled as she grabbed a screwdriver from the tool board. She was now more careful when she was shopping, she thought, as shopping shapes the future after all.

Chapter 18 –
Away with the Fairies

Bee received the call, they had arrived. She was starting to worry as it was getting late, it was after nine thirty. She grabbed her keys and ran down the corridor of her block, her worries cast aside as she was excited to see them.

Sarah parked in the holding bay, hers was the only vehicle outside the guardroom at that time of night which made it easy for her to spot them. All three of them were outside the car jumping, cheering, waving and making a scene to make sure it was a clear give away.

Bee tried to stay calm and look collected, but she couldn't help but run the last bit of the way. She was greeted with a huge group hug, and Beth telling her to 'get in the car quick' she was freezing. Bee then realised Star was missing. "Is everything okay, where is Star?"

Callum spoke more confidently than he used to. "She's not allowed off camp this weekend, her corporal is being a knob."

"What? What do you mean, not allowed?" Bee was lost to the ways of the Army. They were far more authoritarian than the RAF, quite bullish Bee thought.

"Just that, her Corporal has said she can't travel, no reason that we know of, she must have messed up."

Sarah was quick to explain. "Bee in the Army it's different. I am sure Star is quite a handful, you know what she can be like. If she has given him cheek, she'll get confined to barracks as a punishment." Bee found it hard to take in.

"So, are you telling me basically, she is grounded. She can fight for her country, but she is treated like a child? Did they take her pocket money off her as well?"

The others climb in the back of the car laughing while Bee takes the front passenger seat to direct Sarah to the visitor's block.

"Get you RAF chick 'grounded' like your planes you mean. Last into action, first out and all that." Callum sounded every bit the quick-witted marine now,

Bee hardly recognised him. He seemed taller, assured, tanned, and definitely more muscular than she had remembered.

"I bet you guys don't mind the lift when you need to get somewhere though?" Bee retorted with a smile in her voice.

"So, you admit you lot are just our glorified taxi service then Bee?" They continued to chat in good humour until they parked at the barrack block. The left wing of the redbrick building was for females, the right for males. It was situated right across from the NAAFI bar.

"Okay, shall I go and get the drinks in while you guys drop your bags?" Bee was so excited she didn't want to wait, it was getting late, and the bar would shut soon. "I'll get our college round, for old times' sake." Whoops from Callum and laughter from the others faded in the as Bee entered the NAAFI front door.

It was quiet inside, around a dozen or so scattered around the large hall. The busy night in the NAAFI club was a Saturday when they had a DJ and they opened up the dancefloor. She approached the bored looking lady at the bar, disturbing her from her magazine.

"Hi there. A pint of Snakebite please, two white Russians, and a rum and coke please."

"Thirsty tonight aren't you darlin'?" The barmaid smiled and straightened her top, before repeating the order back to Bee to confirm.

"Actually, you better make those two rounds of the same, we have a lot of catching up to do, and one for yourself too." Bee was rocking onto her heals, her bank card in her hand ready to pay, overjoyed her friends had made such an effort to see her.

Chapter 19 –
Pistols at Dawn

They all pilled back to Bee's block after the bar shut with a takeout of crisps, chocolate bars and cider. Then they drank and laughed until four in the morning. They had to be quiet to go undetected. Sarah kept them in check despite being worse for wear herself. She repeated over and over that she was military police now, she could not get caught in the block with Callum being out of bounds in the female accommodation. She decreed that if someone knocked on the door, Callum would have to jump out of the first floor's window and make a run for it.

Callum would turn the music up a little every now and then, hoping Sarah wouldn't notice. Sarah would reach over without a word and turn it back down, she had the attributes of a great policewoman, nothing went unnoticed. She was quite drunk but still pretending to be the grown up. Meanwhile, Beth, who hadn't taken her eyes off Callum for most of the night, would edge closer to Callum at every opportunity. Callum considered jumping out of the window just to escape Beth, but he managed to elude her by popping to the bathroom even if he didn't need to. Sarah fell asleep, as did Beth eventually.

Callum bid Bee goodnight to the sound of gulls' squawks that let them both know how close they were to sea and that daylight was arriving. Callum bent down and looked into her eyes, wearing a warm smile he gave her a quick hug before creeping out of her room.

Bee later woke to a sound of Sarah being sick into a waste bin. "What the hell Sarah, that's disgusting." There was a knock at the door and an unfamiliar voice shouted, "There's a call for you." Bee stepped over Beth who was still fast asleep snuggled under a blanket, using Bee's rucksack as a pillow. Bee rubbed her forehead as she staggered down the corridor to grab the phone.

"Hello?"

"Is that McBrien?" A sharp impatient man barked.

"Yes, McBrien here."

"It's the guardroom, your visitor has arrived, can you come and get her please?"

"My visitor, who is it?"

"Private Fitzgerald, an angry looking woman called, Star Fitzgerald? Is she yours or not?" The distain in the Sergeant's voice when he was pronouncing Star, made it evident he thought she was a waste of his time.

"Star, wow, yes. I'll be there in a few minutes. Thank you."

Bee hurried back to her room, checked her appearance, and checked she still had her I.D in her back pocket of her jeans. She hadn't had a night like that since she joined the RAF, more than a year earlier. She announced to her drowsy friends that Star had arrived as she left the room to collect her.

By the time she had arrived back at the block with Star, Callum was back in her room. Sarah and Beth had managed to rise, clean up the mess and make hot drinks. The window was wide open in the over ambitious hope that the smell of vomit and alcohol would be wafted away before Bee returned.

"Look, she made it!" Bee proclaimed as she entered the room. Her eyes were drawn to Callum, surprised he was back already and looking fresh faced, ready to start another adventure. As the ladies cheered, Callum calmly stated,

"Your Corporal realised he was being a dick and let you play out then?" He plumped a pillow and relaxed back onto Bee's bed, leaving one foot on the floor.

"No, he didn't. Nazi creep" – Star snorted – "he has serious issues that guy."

Sarah was startled, her police training kicking in instantly. "What do you mean Star? You mean you haven't got permission and you've gone against a direct order?"

Sarah had been out of training nearly six months and it was a joke at work that she had not yet charged anyone, which made her more serious and alert to possibilities. There simply had not been the opportunity, she was a police virgin. They hummed the 'like a virgin' tune to wind her up when she came on shift, and she was affectionately known to her team as Madonna.

"Yes, that is what I mean Sarah. I'll sort it when I get back." Star wasn't phased in the slightest. She had found the army discipline neither consistent nor appropriate, and when it wasn't to her liking she pushed back.

"What the hell Star, you are AWOL! Do you have any idea how serious this is?" Sarah was on her feet, hands on her head. She was panicking, thinking what she should do. She is the police. A red cap, army police. No bending the rules, not ever. She should arrest her, surely? This was her chance but in a turn of fate, she didn't want to take it, and she was torn toward doing her duty and her loyalty to her friend.

"Keep your hair on Sarah, it's not that big a deal." Star really didn't see the seriousness of the issue. This wasn't forgetting to clean up, or not completing a task, or pretending not to hear. She had left camp and gone away when expressly told not to, and it carried a heavy penalty.

Callum spoke, and he didn't reassure anyone. "Star has outdone herself this time." He sat up and looked over at Star. "You are truly fucked! You are a legend my friend."

Sarah lost her humour and started to argue with Star and Beth about what should happen next. Explaining that her career in the army police was hard earned. She feared it could be over if she was found with Star and she hadn't detained her straight away. Bee stepped into her old role and calmed the situation before it turned into a fight. She hadn't seen Sarah this angry or emotional before. This was a new and unexpected situation, yet she felt in familiar territory sorting out the group's disagreements.

It was decided best to stay on camp, no venturing out and getting seen at the guardroom again. They would get some food before heading to the NAAFI bar that night. Sarah wasn't happy, but she agreed they would all pretend that they had no idea Star was absent without leave, if Star was caught. There was no live band booked for the club that night, just a DJ. Regardless, the music would be loud, the drinks cheap and it would be busy. All the ingredients that they needed for another night of laughter together.

Chapter 20 –
Bop 'til You Drop

It was warm in the club, and dark. The reunited group took a round table near the empty stage at the back of the hall. Every other table was taken. Next to them was a rowdy bunch of guys of various ages between twenty and forty. When Callum returned from the bar a tall stocky bald guy walked back with him, helping him carry the drinks. Bee was confused by how familiar they were with each other until Callum introduced his friend.

"This is Paddy, he's the skipper for the Lossie rugby team. We were both at the tri-service championships in Twickenham two weeks ago." As polite greetings were exchanged, Paddy shouted to the table next door, "Guys, listen in. We have guests" – the group eyed the ladies up and down and then looked at Callum – "this is Callum, do you remember? He was the one the Marines called 'Vidal' at Twickenham a few weeks back?" With this news, the rugby team stood up politely, said hello and then shuffled around to bring their tables together joining the two groups.

Callum explained why he was visiting, that he had a friend he was worried about. When Paddy heard it was because Bee doesn't really know anyone yet and hadn't settled in, it was declared by Paddy that the rugby team would keep an eye on Bee. She was crowned with a raise of their glasses as an honouree club member.

What Paddy said went as law to the team. He only spoke the truth or wisdom, and he had often had a brilliant idea for some high jinks. Not to mention a fantastic singing voice to start the group singing their rugby anthems after a victorious match. The match today had been in Inverurie against a civilian team, the employees of a whisky brewery. The RAF bus brought them back to camp by seven in the evening. It was too early to call it a night, so they headed to the NAAFI to keep drinking to celebrate their win. Bee was nervous of this bunch of loud men to start with. They all seemed larger than life and extremely confident, and she had become awkward with people.

Soon enough, with the help of alcohol they were laughing and chatting well. The dance floor was full, when suddenly the lights went on and three RAF police were stood just inside the main door. The music cut and the tallest policeman shouted out that they were looking for an Army private who was AWOL. The whole rugby team stood up, shielding Star as they looked over to the police. Paddy was standing tall at the front, he recognised the policeman who spoke as Sgt Stu Wiseman. It was a good friend of his, a teammate who couldn't swap his duty and be with them that day. Paddy smiled and shouted over, "No Sergeant, we don't have any Army wankers in here tonight" – shaking his head and holding up his pint – "we won by the way, we missed you today, didn't we lads?" The team gestured in agreement and shouted out the score, and that they missed him by each raising their drinks towards him.

"Alright there Paddy, good result." Stu nodded but he didn't move. "If you see or hear of anything you will let me know, won't you Paddy?"

"Of course, mate, absolutely" – Paddy replied cheekily without hesitation – "we always do the right thing, Stu. Always."

The rugby team all nodded and repeated sternly and seriously, almost in unison. "Yes, we'd do the right thing Stu, always."

With this, Sergeant Stu Wiseman told his two guys that he was sure all was clear, and to move on. When his guys turned to leave, Stu nodded, smiled and followed behind them, raising a hand to wave a gesture of goodbye. He calmly turned off the house lights before the swing door closed, it was a knowing signal, and Paddy and his team understood.

As soon as the house lights went off, the whole place erupted with cheers and laughter, the RAF police would undoubtedly have heard it. The music burst abruptly, and everyone stood and danced to celebrate. Swinging their arms and giving the 'V' sign towards the door as they sang the chorus. Sarah laughed nervously and then downed her drink as she declared that she was beyond help. The rugby team insisted Star stood on a table and took a bow to everyone in the club, raising another cheer and lifting the atmosphere to festival level.

Beth was otherwise engaged in a celebratory kiss with a short blonde rugby player which made Bee laugh. Callum smiled contentedly as he saw how happy Bee looked. He was proud of the small part his chance meeting with the rugby boys had played in making the evening a success. He knew that when he left the next day Bee would have some new friends.

Paddy saw Callum deep in thought so put his arm around Bee like a bear, not spilling a drop of his new pint in his other hand. He looked down on her as he squeezed her shoulder and told her she'd be alright now, the team would have her back. He told her that if they didn't see her in the rugby club bar for their home games, they'd come looking for her and want to know why. His good friend Taff agreed, and the two guys headed to prop up the bar and watch over the club, satisfied that their parental team duties were discharged. The rugby team and most of the station looked up to these two guys. They were older, wiser and able to make everyone feel welcome. Whilst they often led the team into some ridiculous memory building mischief, they had so far been able to escape any punishment that was due.

The next day over breakfast Callum checked that everyone remembered and more importantly, understood the plan that Paddy and Taff had worked through with them the night before. A plan to get Star back on to her base without anyone noticing, avoiding capture at the gate of the army barracks. They coached her in what to say when she was finally found in her room, or upon arrival at work on the Monday morning. She was either out running, in the NAAFI, doing her laundry or sleeping with headphones on over the weekend. She was to say that she felt victimised by her Corporal and his heavy-handed actions. She was to also tell him in private that if he didn't back off, she would report him for his continuous harassment, which could ruin his career.

Star wasn't guilty this time. She had turned her Corporal down when he had tried it on, and his pride was hurt, and this fuelled his actions towards her. He needed to let it go now or he'd see she would fight back. She needed to stick to the story to protect herself now, and for the future. She was to say that she hadn't left camp and plant the seed the corporal was a bully. She could do this with ease and loved the plan.

Sarah however was not so keen. She was nervous about her part in getting Star back on camp, but she agreed regardless. She was inspired by the RAF policing and their use of discretion, convinced that the RAF police Sergeant knew exactly what was happening and that Star was on their base.

Bee was quiet over breakfast, not because she was worried for Star. She thought the plan sounded robust and that it would work. She would wait up eagerly to hear confirmation that all went well, more because it was fun than due to concern. Bee was sad her friends were leaving. She would miss them deeply, fond of them all and proud of who they were becoming, especially Callum. He had really grown since becoming a Marine. She would miss who she was when they were around too. She missed her old self, bubbly and confident. Bee was anxious that she would fade away again, she was already nervous about going to the rugby club the following weekend. What if no one recognised her? What if they didn't mean it and they were just being polite? As the friends walked to the car Callum could see Bee's sadness.

"Are you okay Bee? The plan will work fine you know, Star will be okay."

"I know. Thank you so much for all you have done Callum, I really appreciate it."

"Make sure you go next week, to the rugby club, promise me?" Callum stopped Bee and encased her in a gentle hug, resting his head on top of hers, he told her all would be fine. He could see she was about to cry, and he couldn't bear it. He was used to the emotions of women after hair and beauty college but, Bee was not like that. He thought she was the tough one and he found it hard to see her this fragile. He felt bigger and stronger after his training, yet his friend looked a shadow of who she used to be.

"Promise me Bee, you will go and have some fun?"

"I Promise, I will."

Callum let her go so Bee could hug the others and say goodbye. They laughed and joked a little. Each pledged to do it again soon, but sadly they knew it would not happen for quite a while.

Chapter 21 –
Mission Impossible

There was less than twenty miles to go until Sarah reached Star's Army barracks in the north of England. They stopped at services so Sarah could change into her uniform. It was a saving grace that she had left straight form work on the Friday, throwing her uniform in a bag on the back seat. Callum had helped polish and iron her uniform to perfection to give Sarah an advantage at the other end. The detour would add a couple of hours onto her drive home, but it would be worth it she thought, if it went well. Star jumped into the boot with her coat and some bags around her just in case she needed them for comfort or cover.

As they approached the camp Sarah spoke like a ventriloquist smiling through gritted teeth "This is it, wait out." Star stifled her giggles. Sarah felt the nerves reach her spine, she worried she would be caught. Sarah left the radio on as she parked up so no noises could be heard in the car. She marched across to sign in at the guard room. A sleepy twenty something Private opened the sliding hatch to see what the formal visitor wanted.

"Hello there Private, I need to sign in my vehicle, and can you give me directions to the medical centre, I have correspondence to deliver?"

"Yes Corporal, please sign into this book and I will give you a vehicle pass. Hand it in on leaving."

"Thank you Private, I know the drill."

"The medical centre is past the barrack blocks, right at the roundabout and it's on your left."

"Understood, thank you." Sarah nodded.

As Sarah passed him the signing in book, his curiosity become the better of him "Can I ask what the letter is for Corporal?"

"It's medical in confidence, test results. I can't tell you I'm afraid."

"Must be important to be delivering it on a Sunday, and by hand?"

"I can't say but, it's for the Brigadier I believe. It's not looking good, that's all I can say." Sarah managed to deliver the answers exactly as Paddy and Taff had instructed. She leaned in. "Look don't tell anyone but, I think they are test results following an indiscretion on his last tour, and he is very keen that his wife doesn't find out. Very hush hush." Sarah nods and taps her nose.

"Understood corporal, officers pulling in favours, looking out for each other I bet, and we are doing all the leg work."

"They have earnt that privilege Private, and don't you forget it!" Sarah was sharp.

"Sorry Corporal. Yes Corporal."

Sarah took the pass from his hand and marched as quickly as she could back to her car, a nervous wreck. As the private watched her, he thought it must be serious for her to be so quick and efficient. He could not wait to tell the lads at work about the news. Distracted by the gossip, he had not asked for I.D and Sarah hadn't written legibly in the signing in book. All as detailed and directed by the seasoned professionals of such crazy antics, the RAF Lossiemouth rugby guys.

The rest of the plan went well. Sarah escaped the barracks after Star was dropped back at her accommodation without capture. That was until she was pulled up for speeding by civilian police, less than five miles away from camp. The local police we very taken with how beautiful Sarah was and how apologetic she was. A gorgeous slender woman in immaculate uniform stood before them, polite and extremely thankful that they were not going to press charges and ruin her military career. She exchanged phone numbers with Gerry, the taller red head of the pair as he started flirting. He mistook her nerves for attraction. Her mistake was giving him her real phone number, and as she drove away shaking, she wondered if he would call and whether the truth would out.

Chapter 22 –
Match Day Nerves

The first home rugby game was against RAF Leuchars, it's part of the RAF championships. Bee was welcomed with the warmth you would greet distant family. They were pleased to see her, and many asked about Sarah and Star's mission. They had heard it went well yet enjoyed the connection and chance to reminisce about the antics the week before.

They asked Bee to help a little, their usual team helpers were on duty or away on detachment which left them depleted. They were desperate to keep the show running like clockwork, so their match rivals were hosted well. Bee was delighted, she didn't fancy standing on the side lines the entire time. Until she made friends she didn't relish standing alone. Keeping busy would help her nerves.

Bee soon relaxed and started to enjoy her newfound place in the club. She had helped make the post-match snacks. Helped stock the bar and chatted to Stan the bar manager along the way. He was a quiet and gentle man. He used to play on the team years earlier and had long since given up the mantle to the younger players.

In his late forties he had served in the RAF as aircrew for twenty-two years before retiring and settling on a remote farm a few miles from Lossiemouth station. He was single and needed it to be that way. Stan had difficulty talking about his time in service, he could talk all day about his tours with the rugby club but, Bee had sensed not to ask too much more about his old times of duty after he had mentioned he was with a Chinook squadron in the Falklands war. His time evacuating casualties and dropping more Marines or Parachute Regiment around Mount Pleasant had left scars in his soul that he had long resigned would never heal. The farm gave him work to do when he couldn't sleep. The rugby club was his social lifeline. He was accepted there with no questions, and the mischievous nature of the sport meant there was always something to smile about, taking away temporarily, the deep and often debilitating sadness he carried.

Bob had convinced James to watch the match and have a pint or two at the club. James had confided in him that he had met someone that he could not take his mind off, and that it was driving him insane. He told Bob that he was disappointed when he saw this girl by chance in the arms of another man last week. Bob didn't understand, as he was used to acting impulsively and decisively as soon as he spotted his conquests, but James was different. He was happy on his own, he was starting to develop the same tendencies as Stan. Given a few more years or tours in operation he would potentially follow suit.

As they stood on the cold and damp side lines of the pitch, beer in hand the half time whistle blew signalling the players to the front of the clubhouse for lemon squash and freshly cut oranges to perk them up for another forty minutes of intense and determined play.

James was stopped in his tracks when he turned to see Bee bringing out the tray of oranges and he tugged on his friends arm to confess.

"That's her, Bob that's the one."

"Well buddy, I told you it would be good to come here today."

"You said it would help take my mind off her."

"Well, fate has other ideas. How about you sleep with her and get it over with, then get back to normal?"

James was disgusted with Bob's suggestion, and took no time telling him how annoyed he was. Bob had issues with women, no respect and certainly no plans of keeping one long enough to share any true intimacy. James held his beer and just watched her nervously.

Bee brought out a third tray of oranges for the hungry mud-covered players and managed to move unnoticed, or so she thought. The players were all focussed on the game and taking instructions from the coach and each other. After placing the last large silver catering tray of chopped oranges on the rickety outdoor table, she collected the empty jugs of juice onto a tray so she could replenish them. Turning she bumped onto someone and dropped the tray, the glass jugs fell and smashed on the concrete floor. Cheers and jibes from the crowd made her cringe as she bent to pick up the mess.

As Bee felt a warmth of another bend down close next to her a familiar voice asked,

"Are you okay Bee? Here let me help you." James instinctively stepped in to help, and the awkwardness she felt disappeared momentarily while he was focussed on the situation.

"Thank you, I can't believe I just did that."

Bee blushed and kept her eyes to the ground, embarrassed more now by James's presence. The large broken pieces of glass chimed as they gathered them onto the tray and then they headed into the club house to dispose of the damage. James tried to change the subject.

"How are you? How have you been? I erm, I didn't expect to see you here today?"

Bee thought before she replied, she thought James seemed nervous and questioned why would he not expect to see her, was he avoiding her now? She thought it best reply politely but with no questions so he can retreat with grace.

"Yes, a good week thanks. I'm just helping out on home games." Bee gave James information but asked no questions. Just the right amount of information so he could avoid her in future. Bee was disappointed to think he hadn't enjoyed the time together a few weeks earlier. She had and he played on her mind on and off.

"That's good to hear Bee." It was getting awkward, silence had descended, and James knew this wasn't a good sign so after seeing she was okay, made his excuses and head back outside to find Bob. He would keep his distance and convince Bob to leave after they finished their drinks.

Chapter 23 –
617 Squadron Calling

Morning tea break had finished when Paul and I are called to the office and told there has been a complaint from the Squadron. There are engineering assets on 617 squadron that aren't working, and that they couldn't get hold of us. Paul is angry, pleading with our Sergeant that they haven't radioed us, no one has tried? We are told to get over to the line office and get the situation under control, and that if we have delayed flying operations, we are in serious trouble.

Speeding over to the line Paul pulls up sharply right outside the squadron office, our big white workshop van with the light on top still flashing orange in defiance. Paul jumps out and strops across the path to the door. He barks at me to stay put, he will sort this. I sense an overreaction brewing that may well end his hopes of a return to windy Wales for his promotion training. I should maybe go with him? No, it's best I stay put as directed.

As I'm looking over the driver's seat toward the office building, there is a tap on my window which makes me jump. It's James, he's in his flying suit and looking as breath-taking as ever. He laughs at me for jumping and signals for me to wind down the window.

"Hey Bee, I was hoping to see you for the last three days and I am afraid I ran out of patience." What is he talking about? "The crew chief owes me a favour so, he called over to your section to call you out on a false job, I'm sorry."

"You're sorry, you will be if Paul catches up with you, he is fuming. Our Sergeant said we'd let the side down and if we were to delay flying, we might be charged. Are you out of your mind?"

I don't know if I am angry, or happy to see him, it's just a mix of odd feelings. Annoyed, I think.

"Hey, I'm sorry Bee, I wanted to ask you last week and I wanted to call, but I have no number for you. I knew calling your hanger wasn't an option as you are out all day in the van."

I just stare at him, no words come out, I have no idea what to say. James speaks without a break, like he just has to say it,

"Okay, so here's the thing. I really had a nice time when we hung out at the beach the other weekend, can I take you somewhere? Just as friends of course? There is somewhere I'd really like to show you and it's stunning, are you about this weekend?"

Erm, this is a bit odd, unusual, I am raising my shoulders and slowly shaking my head unsure of what to reply. I do need more friends up here.

"Erm, yes, but what is it?"

Behind me Paul is returning from the office and James simply said, "Great, I'll pick you up at nine on Saturday morning." He smiles and walks away towards Bob who is lurking by a jet, around a hundred feet away.

The door to the van opens to disturb me watching him leave, and somehow Paul is now in a much better mood. "The dumb bastard's Chief actually apologised to me and said he'd call our control and tell them we are the best ground support crew they have had in years. Apparently, our lot got their wires crossed. They just wanted to invite us to their summer BBQ, how odd is that?"

Despite Paul having a distaste for the squadron team, he is clearly very proud of being accepted and praised by their crew Chief. His chest is puffed out, head high and he walks with purpose for the rest of the shift, retelling the story at lunchtime and at afternoon break to anyone who would listen.

Meanwhile, I couldn't eat at lunch. I felt nervous, and I couldn't even talk to anyone about my pending day out with the most attractive man on base, as friends. I can't call him and cancel, I have no idea how to contact him that won't arise suspicion. He just needs a friend too and we certainly talked like friends for hours. It isn't a date. I am pretty sure it isn't, I'm in the friend zone but, that doesn't stop me from feeling restless.

The day passes slowly, as does the night, and the next two days.

Chapter 24 –
D Day Landings

Okay, so I haven't slept for more than say two hours on and off. I am sure James is going to realise I find him attractive and then being friends will be spoilt. Who am I kidding, he probably takes it for granted women no matter what age or background, find him attractive and is used to ignoring it? I only have dark blue jeans to wear, so let's hope they'll do. A vest top and black zipped up fleece should do it, and walking boots of course. Everyone in the Highlands wears this attire, even when out for lunch in town. So, I will just ask if I need to change when I see him to be polite but, I am quite confident in this rough and ready part of Scotland I'll do. Maybe we are headed to another beach up along the coast, a lake or maybe one of the castles. There are many beautiful Disney style castles up here. I'll wear my hair down and naturally wavy I think that'll soften the utilitarian look I have now fallen accustomed to. I'll wear mascara and I better put something under my eyes to cover up the sleep deprivation. At least with it being an early start today, I will be back home early and then I can get some sleep once the anticipation and nerves have long since passed.

I'm all done, great, ten minutes to go, double check I have my keys and my bank cards and cash in my back pocket. I don't like bringing a handbag or purse, I'll grab my waterproof black jacket. Five minutes left, and I can't sit down. If I wait downstairs by the door that is going to look too keen but, I am keen to get away without anyone seeing me get into James's truck. The last thing I need is questions or gossip. I need to stay below the radar, unknown and undetected. The staring, the jokes at my expense and unwanted attention has left its mark, a horrid time and I often remember about something cringeworthy. I was either getting too much negative attention or being blanked. I have never felt so unwelcome.

Luckily everyone will be in bed until gone ten today as on a Friday night most of the girls will have gone out in Elgin after the beer calls, dancing to finish off the week. I'll have to wait at the window and keep an eye out. He'll know not to beep his horn and will hopefully wait quietly.

Well, James didn't arrive quietly. I forgot the noise of 'Big Red' his Canadian import RAM truck. It roars around the corner and rumbles into place. I shoot downstairs as fast as I could, when I get to the bottom of the stairs I try to calm my walk out of the barrack block, so I don't look too much like I am running away from a crime scene, my breathing is still too fast, so I slow it down a bit more. James has got out of the truck. What? No, shit, we need a quick getaway, or maybe he is cancelling. No, ignore that, he walking to the other side of the truck. Ah, okay. "Hello lovely lady, your ride awaits." James has opened the passenger door and is holding one of his hands behind his back like a butler, smiling and looking directly at me. Lovely but a bit old fashioned, this feels awkward.

The truck is too high up for me, I look like a tired toddler trying to climb in, I miss my step as I turned but I still landed on the seat. A little hard but sat upright thank God. James has closed the door and has run around to his as I fiddle with the seat belt. I can't get the bloody thing to work. James watches and smiles. "Okay, sit back I will do that for you before you rip the seatbelt off like the hulk." I can't help but laugh at that but only for a second, I am reduced to silence as he reaches over me to grab the belt. He is so close to me now, I am frozen. I take a sharp breath in but, I can't exhale, and an electric pulse shoots up my spine. This is so uncomfortable I just want to go back already. Thankfully, James is completely unaware and breaks the frozen spell.

"Right, all buckled up and here we go. Do you have a bag or anything with you? Did you forget it?"

"No, I erm don't carry much, I have my keys, my bank card and some cash in my pocket." – Deep breath in – "am I dressed okay? I kind of guessed we'd be out and about, I'm not underdressed, am I?"

As I say that it is seems obvious, I am not underdressed, as James is in jeans, a white polo shirt, back of the collar up, and there is a multilayer jacket on the seat in between us.

"No, not at all, you look great and, I think I have brought everything we need."

I look around the cab, behind the seat is a cool box and a black square half leather half canvass bag, like one that would carry a large video camera.

"Okay, where are we going?"

James smiles as we head out of camp and turn left. "Can you wait a little bit longer, it's a surprise?"

I look at him as he smiles his right arm high up on the large steering wheel. "Yes, I can wait but, isn't that the sort of question a serial killer would ask before he lures his victim deep into the woods for her final day trip?"

It's an uncomfortable moment before his laughing. "Damn you foiled my plan. Look I can tell you if you want but, we are only ten minutes away, if you can wait that long?"

As James looks over, I don't speak I just nod and smile. Great, ten minutes and I can get out of the truck, it's making me feel uncomfortable being so close to him, some friendly distance would be nice. I stare out of the window at the countryside as we drive along. After a few minutes I am relaxed again by the views; the awkwardness has passed, and I am looking forward to whatever beach, Loch or pub we land at.

We pull into the right at the gates of RAF Kinloss; another station about fifteen minutes along the Moray coast. Why have we come here? So, no one knows us maybe? It doesn't make sense. James flashes his ID and vehicle pass at the guard and he is waved through, clearly, he is a regular here. Ah, wait, maybe he lives on this camp and commutes to Lossiemouth?

"Okay James, I am lost, why are we here?" He looks over and tells me to wait just one more minute. We drive forward and past a low brick building then a large green hanger and turn right onto the beige tarmac of the aircraft manoeuvring area and park in a bay at the flying club.

"Do you trust me, Bee? I thought we could go on a trip with a view?" He is staring at me hoping for a good response, but I am lost for words.

Thing is, I am in the RAF, but I have never been in a plane. Never. Not even to go on holiday. So, getting into one of those tiny little tin can planes is asking a bit much without some warning. As I confess my lack of flight experience James laughs so much, then tells me to jump out as he holds my door open again. I could get used to this chauffer service. James also tells me that I am going to love this, he promises it even. Oh, dear god I hope so. I am not easy scared, so there is hope. I feel silly though confessing about being in the RAF, around planes all day every day, yet I have never been in one in the sky. I wonder what he thinks of me now. Wait until he knows how I ended up joining the RAF, no long-time childhood dream or fascination of aircraft or aeronautical engineering, just a random lunchtime encounter.

We walk to the small green shed like building, with its pristine white and blue sign announcing it is the station flying club, a small framed grey-haired man in matching grey overalls walks over to us with a sprightly spring to his step. His tanned wrinkled face and sparkling green eyes greet James with a warm welcome. "James my good man, welcome, good to see you." He looks at me and smiles. "So, this is the lady you are taking up today? Nice to meet you miss…"

As he holds out a hand to shake mine as I mumble in return, "Beatrice, or Bee for short, as in bumble bee, erm, nice to meet you." James is beaming back at him, clearly, they have spent a lot of time together and James wastes not a moment more. "David, thank you for preparing this for me. The skies are blue, the charts are good, it couldn't be a nicer day for it."

I must admit, I look up to the blue sky and I am very excited about this now, I bet the views are amazing. David interrupts my gazing. "Okay then Bee, if you follow me, I can give you a safety briefing and there is a form to fill in while your man here, checks over Charlie Alpha Foxtrot and loads your bags."

I walk closely behind David to the club office. He manages to tell me I have a lovely man in James, that he's been an asset to the club since he arrived helping younger pilots with their training notes and logbook data entry. He is old fashioned and has misunderstood, he thinks James and I are dating. I don't know how to interrupt to correct him. "All done now, grab yourself a quick brew lassie while James and I finish off the pre-flight paperwork."

I hold a warm white mug of tea. The mug has a picture of a huge rotund beige plane, it looks like a bottlenose whale with wings and a large jousting lance strapped to its head protruding out of the front. I haven't seen anything like it. As well as the picture of the plane, there is the station emblem and the words 'The mighty hunter Nimrod MR2'.

I overhear talk of fuel volumes and wind speeds, Zulu something or other. I am not really listening. I am transfixed looking out of the misty window at the little plane we are going to fly in. I am nervous but in a good way and if truth be told, I would have been really happy just to have a look up close at one of those Nimrods' instead of going anywhere.

Anyway, we wouldn't be doing this flight if it wasn't safe, so no need to be nervous really. I feel the anticipation though. It's a once in a lifetime event that is about to happen, maybe I do like surprises after all. Mum always said I was terrible with any surprise, always ill with an upset stomach, tantrums and tears too so, they stopped surprising me somewhere around seven years old with the exception of Christmas.

"Wakey, wakey Bee, we are ready, are you okay?" I look back at James so calm "A little nervous maybe?" James has put his hand on my lower back to guide me out, reassuring me all is well. My stomach flips inside out, maybe Mum was right after all. It's like a dream, I know all is well, I am just a bit over-whelmed. I'm smiling so hard my cheeks are sore. I think he knows I am okay with this, although all I can do is nod and smile as I follow orders about getting in and out of the plane. I am to stand on the black sandpaper looking patch bits, not the white part of the wing. Then how to get inside, where to hold on the canopy, what I can and cannot lean on.

Adjusting the belt and braces that clip all together like child reins is fiddly. It is tiny in here, all dials, fuses, and toggle switches. James passes me a pale green headset, and he shows me where to plug it in, although he tells me we don't need it just yet, he will tell me when. The plane has a single joystick to drive it, not one of those two-handed steering wheels like in the movies. In fact, there are two joysticks, one on my side too and peddles that I can't reach. I swear to God if he asks me to get any more involved, I will freak out. The cool box and bag I notice are already in the back strapped in, sitting alongside a small fire extin-guisher.

"Right Bee, we are flying for about fifty minutes, but it will feel a lot shorter, time feels different up there. Calm and peaceful, okay?"

"Okay, got it. Anything else?" As I smile at James again, I can tell he is excited too, maybe it never wears off no matter how much flying you do?

"Yes, lots actually, we will put the headset on, I will call into the tower, taxi to the strip, then we hold still, call in again and then when cleared, we will move to the strip and take off." I'm nodding along, following the plan so far. "The take-off will be smooth, it is great conditions today. We are going across water to the Isle of Skye, we will be at two thousand feet, I will come in lower when we are near so we can see as much as we can, but we have certain paths and rules to follow so not to scare cattle or wildlife." I keep nodding. "It'll be fine though we have a land rover waiting the other side for some sightseeing, all you have to do is relax and enjoy!"

What is happening, have I taken someone else's place, these things don't happen to me. I mean, I guess in the RAF we can do this right? I just never thought of it before or heard of it.

"I'm closing the canopy now Bee, okay. Arms in tight so I don't catch your jacket and you can put the headset on now." As James pull the bubble shaped canopy over the top of us and clamps it into place, he shows me the air vents either side of the long-complicated control panel; they are tilting vents like in an old-fashioned car in case I get too warm up there. Shit, this thing is basic.

The engine is on, and we start to move slowly "Kinloss this is Golf Echo Charlie Alpha Foxtrot requesting access to runway 2 for take-off, two P. O. B." I lose the rest, I am looking around us and then before you know it, we are moving along a runway, and we are up.

"Wow! This is amazing." I start laughing, an odd thing to do but this is just mind-blowing. I see below those huge Nimrod planes all lined up, perfectly in formation on the ground, now they are looking as small as our plane. I see the golden sand of the coast already.

James is pleased "I knew you'd like it Bee, hold on a second while I check course."

I sit peacefully, happy not to say a word as the view goes on forever and the water lapping the sand is meditational. The sea is deep turquoise, I see something in the water, James notices my interest is fixed on something.

"I'll get a little closer, I think it's a pod of dolphin or maybe whales, they have sightings of Orca up here."

Sure enough, when we get a bit closer it is a group of bottle nose dolphin, six of them. We don't linger as there is a little one in the middle and James wants to stay away.

"They probably have no idea we are here at fifteen hundred feet but just in case Bee, I would rather we stayed back, I hope that is okay?"

"Of course it's okay, being kind to nature is more than okay to me. James, where I grew up, we were constantly annoyed by visitors who didn't respect the animals or the rivers. People can be ignorant, can't they?" James looks over and smiles at me, he gets it, he understands.

Before I know it, we are coming into land on a green island with a small airstrip, the sea is on the left, the coastline weaving in and out like a wobbly drawn line and there are dark green mountains in the background. I can feel the wind is blowing us from the left as we sway a little side to side, James is adjusting to stay on course but, I'm more concerned about the three little white croft style houses that are getting bigger, just before the runway starts. In a blink they are gone, and we are on the ground, rolling along the runway and I now notice he had been talking to the tower for the last few minutes. I could never fly, I haven't got the concentration, I could never cope with all those buttons, and I'd stare out of the window and get lost in the view. I would end up on the local news…**Fox**-trot **U**niform **C**harlie **K**ilo-**ed,** she's missing at sea.

My cheeks are aching from smiling. I sit patiently as James brings us into the parking bay. My knees are a little wobbly getting out of the plane, reversing backwards onto the black sandpaper strips again. Luckily James has come around to my side to help me, a guiding hand that is most welcomed.

"Well, what did you think? Did you enjoy it?" James is smiling as much as I am, he seems really pleased he has made me happy, unless this is how you feel every time you fly, and it just doesn't wear off?

"I have no words, it is just surreal, beautiful and you were right, I feel like we have only been up there for, like I have no idea? What is the time, it's like time stopped?"

James is nodding away as we walk indoors to check in, as if he knows exactly what I am trying to say. The airfield staff are great, it takes only a few minutes to book in the plane, and a young chap with short but full curly black hair is waiting on a seat in the small bare lounge, he's holding a folder for James.

"Sir, your vehicle is outside, fuelled with a spare in the back and a torch, and here are your keys. The folder has the map and the house keys. If you need anything, anything at all, call the number on the back and Ken will help you. Return your folder and vehicle here to the desk tomorrow before you leave. I hope you have a lovely stay." The young guy doesn't look at me at all. He seems shy and awkward, maybe only seventeen-ish.

I start to laugh, an actual chap called Ken, priceless. James and the nice young chap shake hands and he is gone. "Why did you laugh?" James looks as if I have been rude, shit. "I am so sorry. When I first came to Moray I though everyone was called Ken as…"

Before I get to explain, James's eyebrows have lifted, and he smiles. I don't need to carry on. "Hold on a minute James, he just said hand back the keys tomorrow? What does he mean, tomorrow?" I am instantly suspicious, so this is it is it? Flashy pants pilot fly boy thinks he can swipe me off my feet and take me away and I don't get a choice? I'll bloody see about that; I don't bloody think so. He will have done this a dozen times eh, works every time does it? What a wanker, quick leg over and then shouts next.

"Whooooah there, no, this is not what it looks like Bee, it's just a hike, no big deal and you can only have the cottage booking overnight, not just for a day, we are heading back tonight, I promise."

I am seething, James has dropped the bags and is holding his hands up like he's been told to freeze by the police.

"Really, you think I am going to believe that, why book a cottage at all? What was the point if we are going back tonight?" I go to turn and leave, then end up doing a full bloody circle clumsily as I realise, I can't leave. I am stuck here, and I hate being stuck. Hands on hips angry, breathing noisily through my nose like an angry dragon, I could bloody swing for him. "Well?"

James lowers his arms stares at me and patiently smiles.

"I have brought food with us to cook, a cold picnic first for our first stop at the fairy pools and then salmon and new potatoes to warm us up after while we sit by a fire and thaw out with a hot drink. It may be summer, but it gets cold up here. I was worried we'd be cold. Plus, we haven't seen the sea view from the cottage yet. Sam at work raves on about it, so I was keen to go, I'm sorry if you thought…"

Oh god, that is quite nice and more refined than creepy, now I think about it, and now he thinks that I think he was intending to seduce me which; clearly isn't on his mind at all, I mean why would he? I'm definitely not his type, I'm short, dark unruly hair, not remotely glamorous or sleek, and I am a junior rank. Shit! Shit! Shit! I feel like a right idiot. I feel my face start to burn, and I couldn't be more embarrassed, I raise my hands up to cover my face, slowly close my eyes and take a deep breath to think. James comes closer.

"Hey, I am so sorry I didn't mean to worry you or embarrass you Bee, I honestly thought this would be great, I thought after our chats on the beach about nature, that that you'd love it as much as me?" James cups my upper arms gently and I lower my hands to look up at him. "I am sorry I have made you angry or worried Bee, Please, can you trust me? Please? I promise you, I am not the serial killer you worry about meeting."

He's trying to lighten the mood and I feel disloyal questioning my new friend. After all, other than nature and our mothers' matching birthdays there is no other reason he should want to be friends with me really, it just kind of happened.

"Okay, I am sorry for assuming the worst James. I'm just overwhelmed, and I am not too great when I am not in control of everything, or surprises." I feel so feeble. "Hey did you say fairy pools?"

With that James pats my back twice in a friendly, buddy type way and we start to walk to the Landover while he tells me of the trip ahead, no more surprises. Turns out Sam is the Squadron administration sergeant whose uncle owns the cottage. She comes at least twice a year with her husband. She has been teasing James telling him the island is far more impressive than Vancouver, although she hasn't been to Canada yet. Sam is a diehard Scottish patriot and there is nowhere quite like home.

We set off in the rickety grey land rover, the gears crunch a bit when going through to second. Our bags rattle in the back as we go over cattle grates and bumps. We pass the three croft houses first, and then it is a long drive, about an hour until we finally stop again. We paused a few times, to look at the sea view, the birds and then when we headed inland, we stopped to watch the deer grazing. They are magical, such regal creatures wearing their antlers like crowns but, also so nimble and swift as they dart off. They'd be calm and elegant one minute then spook and dart off like lightning the next. When we park up, we see clear signs for the fairy pools, how cute is this, it's mesmerising. We are stood with views of mountains and a gravel path beckoning us to follow it, luring us like Hansel and Gretel. It takes us over half an hour to get to the pools, it should have been quicker, but we kept stopping, looking, listening, smiling. We talked all the way in the land rover but now we have just spent most of the walk-in silence, with James leading the way and looking back often to check I haven't wandered off. He stops to help at the river and the steppingstones, very much an officer and a gentleman. It's as if we have an agreement to be quiet here to take all this in, and just be here, absorbing the fresh air and freedom this place offers yet; we didn't discuss anything. I thought I grew up in a nice place but this, this is off the chart stunning. Purples, greens, yellows, birds squawking, crystal clear streams tinkling, it's like the backing music of a relaxation CD.

When we saw the pools, we stopped dead both exclaiming wow and how stunning it is. The mountains behind the waterfall that surrounds the fairy pool, look just like a sandy coloured Mount Rushmore, ten times smaller though. If we were in the USA, it would have faces carved out to celebrate the mountainous backdrop. I feel like a broken record, stuck with same words coming out of my mouth, it's this place, its hypnotic.

"We should have brought swimming kit, look at the water, it is so clear you can see the smooth rock underneath and how clean those pebbles are around the outside."

James is taken aback, it's not that warm out here. "Well I had no idea you'd be so adventurous, Bee. There's nothing stopping you stripping off if you are keen, we have a washing machine at the cottage to wash and dry your t-shirt."

I am so energised by the idea. "Sorry, I struggle to resist water; I have always loved it. I swam in rivers and pools on the moors at home most days, unless I was in the pool training."

At this point I realise I haven't given much away about me so far. The bare basics, answers on a postcard type stuff, I haven't divulged like James has. I am a private person, more so now, the guys in the RAF tend to think they know you and decide who you are anyway, and you are either to be ignored, made fun of or to be taken for granted generally.

That's it, I'm going in, it's a once in a lifetime swim and I am not missing it. I don't take my eyes off the water as I unzip my jacket and take it off, throwing it to my right, it lands on a boulder. I loosen my boots, kick them off and before you know it, I'm stood in my underwear and vest top walking slowly and confidently into the water. As the water reaches my thighs, my hands are wide either side, skimming the surface and I'm not taking my eyes of the enchanted pool floor and all the colours beneath. It's freezing cold, a reassuring reminder of my time at home. Dartmoor water was always freezing when you got in but if you just hold your nerve when it steels your breath, count up to five slowly, the cold passes and your breath returns. It awakens your sole, right to your core, and energy shoots through you, in just moments you feel you could take on the world and you want to swim as fast as you can. You need to slow it though, keep yourself calm to respect the water. James is shocked as he stands and watches her take on the cold water and the wilds.

After I'd swum to the end of the pool, I spin in the water to look back for James, the water falls off the rocks to form a picturesque backdrop.

"Hey James, come on, get in, it's freezing but it's great!" He's staring at me as if I am crazy. Shit, he isn't impressed. I wasn't thinking, I just wanted to be in the water.

"I'd love to, Bee, but it's too cold for me today, I'll save you from hyperthermia though when you get out, you can have my shirt." He seems serious. "Hey, you only have about five minutes Bee before you turn to frozen rock!"

I watch has he takes off his coat, he means it, he's taking off his polo shirt for me, God that's thoughtful and he's clearly not a wimp to the cold, maybe he's not keen on water then? Oh Christ, yes, he has taken off his top and Christ, he has the body of a god. He belongs on a billboard, or an aftershave advert, the tan, the muscles. I cannot stop staring at him, and he's just standing there, standing tall and proud, arms by his side staring right back at me. My gut tightens and I feel heat rising in me, the cold is long forgotten.

"A-Aaiiee!"

What was that. "Something got my foot!" The moment's gone and as James laughs at me, I swim as quick as I can back to the edge. James, the gentleman he is, turns away as I get out and holds out his top behind him. I quickly get his top on, my wet vest and bra off and crunched into a ball, leaving my pants on I struggle with my jeans for a few minutes as I keep glancing up at James. Even his back is masculine and beautiful at the same time, my eyes are starting to wander.

"Are you not done yet McBrien?"

I snap back to reality as James bends forward but away from me to grab his coat and put it on.

"Yep, two more minutes." I shove my bra and rung out vest top into my jacket pocket. "Yep, yep, all done."

James turns to look at Bee as she stands there in his top, hair wet, she is swamped by his top, but he could still make out her curves where the damp cloth sticks to her.

"You look freezing you need to get your coat on." He sounded almost like he was chastising Bee. She didn't understand, was she becoming a burden to him?

It was taking everything in James's power not to grab her and kiss her. No straight man finds it easy to resist an attractive hot-blooded woman wearing his top. James needed to remember Bee's reaction at the thought of any romantic ideas between them on the trip, she was horrified. He is sure now she only wanted to be friends and that was understandable really. She is about nine years younger than James, in his opinion she would be looking for someone at least five years younger than him, if not more.

It was a quiet drive; both were starting to tire a little and each eating a wilted cheese sandwich and drinking some water. Arriving at the cottage James caught a glimpse of Bee from behind and started laughing.

"Are you okay? Did you have a little accident Bee?" Bee knew exactly what he was referring to, she had wet underwear on when she put her jeans on and after sitting the wet patch is very noticeable.

"Alright there cowboy, at least I gave it a try." The mood was now reset to how it was before.

"Bee you better go and find something to put on whilst we wash your clothes. It's nearly two, and we are booked to fly back at nine, before the light's gone" James unlocks the door. Bee had agreed but, it was too much temptation not to quickly explore the cottage.

Straight ahead is a large picture window, the old cottage had been altered, removing an exterior wall and replacing it with glazing and it was breath-taking. The whole outer wall in the lounge looked out over the cliff to sea. The inner wall has a log burner and there is a large comfy beige sofa that blends into the room, a place to take in both the views and the atmosphere of the fire.

"Bee, I don't want to nag like your mom but, you really need to change if we are going to turn this around in time." Bee startled and got right to it.

"Sorry, yes, right away." Searching the cottage she found robes laid out on the bed, she grabbed one and went to the bathroom to change.

James called out from the lounge, "I'll put the kettle on and make a hot drink, coffee, okay?"

As Bee shouted agreement to the coffee James made busy turning on the stove and finding the washing detergent, checking the cutlery draws for the tools to cook dinner and finding the blue stoneware mugs. He is focussing on the tasks in hand to avoid his mind wandering anywhere it was unwanted. When Bee returns in the white robe carrying a bundle of clothes, she has no idea what to say and feels exposed in her new outfit.

Bee holds his top separate to her clothes. "Your top won't be able to go in the same wash as my dark clothes." James stumbles a little as he turns to see her looking vulnerable.

"Hey, no need to look scared, you are safe here. You look like a frightened kid? It's okay, the top is fine, here, I'll just put it back on."

Bee apologises. "I'm sorry, I feel a bit awkward that's all and, I didn't think it through did I, the swim, it seemed like such a good idea at the time." She worried, did he want to go somewhere else in their day and she blew it?

"No, not at all, it's fine. It was good to see you happy. Do you want to give me your clothes in exchange for the coffee?"

Bee tensed; she can't have him wash her things. "No, I'll do it, excuse me. The coffee is great though if you pop it on the table by the window."

James steps aside obligingly and takes the coffee as asked, he is just as keen to stop staring at her in nothing but a towelling robe.

When Bee joins James by the window he is standing and staring at the sea crashing on the rocks. He really wants to look at Bee more than the sea, he is intrigued by her, but he won't allow himself. She has an air of freedom that is the polar opposite to their force's way of life. James, like many others can spot a forces person in civilian clothes. He can also have a reasonable guess at what they do, and what rank they are by the way they carry themselves. Bee is totally different, and he would never guess she was forces. She carries herself well but relaxed, without boundaries. She doesn't apologise for being who she is and clearly hasn't tried to fit in, she isn't mirroring the fashions of the others around her, and she hasn't opted for the athletic look either. She's a tom boy with a natural beauty. Her carefree way of enjoying nature is beyond her years. James is bewildered at meeting a woman who seems so naturally herself it's a little unnerving.

James wakens from his thoughts and announces he will cook lunch.

"Can I help you with anything?" Bee offers out of British politeness. As soon as she has said the words, she hopes James say's no so she can stay staring at the sea and, also so she isn't too close to him. A voice in her head tells her to go easy on herself, it's natural to feel this way. Any right-minded woman would find James attractive and get a little giggly up close so it's okay, to not be okay with him being up close. In time, it will pass and hopefully he won't notice in the meantime.

Thankfully, James has no need for her to help so she sits on the sofa, knees up, robe tucked in to ensure she is covered and, knowing James is busy means she can relax and enjoy the view. Silence can be daunting to some, but in that moment it was serene.

Lunch was delicious and Bee appreciated the simplicity of the dish, and the flavours of Scottish salmon were complimented by the surroundings. Bee could never have imagined a trip so perfect and already knew she would never forget it. She didn't want to leave and at four thirty was already starting to mourn the passing of time.

"So, Bee, when your clothes are ready can I take you to the local pub, it's about a twenty-minute drive or did you want to just hang here? We need to leave at eight from either place to get booked in on time for our flight." James is hoping for the pub option as it gives them more to talk about when they get back and it is getting increasingly difficult to keep himself from kissing her in here and making a fool of himself.

"Whatever; I am happy here, but you're in charge." She looks at James in appreciation. "It's so nice here. I cannot believe you rented a cottage for a day but, at the same time I get it. It's beautiful, thank you for letting me tag along."

James wants Bee to enjoy the trip as much as he does and doesn't want her to get bored. Yet, she is happy here, and he gives into temptation. "There are books here, we could chill and read, and I'll make more coffee?"

"That sounds like a nice plan, I'll try and read but the view might win, I'll end up staring out." Bee is up and looking at the small bookcase that is by the front door, past visitors have donated their books for someone else to enjoy. "It looks as if there is mainly romantic novels and nature books here, how are you with Jane Austin?"

"Hey, don't knock it girlfriend, I love that Mr Darcy, he's so handsome!" James jokes and as Bee laughs, he chokes out a cough induced from him putting on a high-pitched voice, which makes Bee laugh harder.

"I think you need more work on your swoon voice if you are to convince anyone cowboy." James has joined Bee and they each chose a book.

"Hey, you worry that I am a serial killer yet, here you are, straight in with 'tales of the unexpected' books and trying to keep me away from public places." James looks around. "I think I need to know how to call for help."

"Ha, ha, ha, you are safe on this trip, my plan is foiled, I need you to fly me home." Bee hits him gently in the stomach with a book he has pointed to.

"I see, now I know the truth, you are the Queen Bee serial killer. I shall make sure I continue to foil those plans of yours, so you never succeed."

Joking subsides and they sit next to each other on the extra deep sofa facing the sea. Bee has her legs curled up; she is too short to sit comfortably any other way. They each read, look up for a while at the view and smile, read, look up…The pattern continues until it is broken with Bee falling asleep. It's been eventful, unexpected and restful for Bee, pure bliss.

James stops reading and is looking down, watching Bee sleep. She is leaning on him now, so he doesn't want to move and disturb her although he isn't comfortable. If he keeps look left at this angle his neck will get cramp. She is silent sleeping. Her lips are not fully closed, open just slightly and James is spending far too much time studying them.

She is beautiful, smart, funny, easy to be with. James knows hardly anything about her, but he does know she is the most interesting woman, and he wants to spend more time with her. In that moment of realisation James let's his head drop backwards to rest his neck, his eyes close, just a for a little while he will rest.

James wakes with a start and a crick in his neck. "Bee, wake up, we need to move. We'll miss out slot at the airfield." Bee sits quickly and remembers where she is. She had completely forgotten for a millisecond. James is already up and unlocking the washer.

"They're dry? Bee, I don't think they washed?"

"Yeah, they did I put them on a wash and dry cycle, it's a washer dryer."

James is relieved, he was worried she'd be travelling back in wet clothes right now. As he collects the clothes and turns to walk over to Bee, they meet with a bump and Bee squeals.

"Sorry Bee. Are you okay?" James grabs Bee to steady her and drops the clothes. He looks down at her, she is so fresh faced and wide eyed. He can't help but lean down into her eyes, he is drawn in to kiss her. At the last minute he manages to control himself and just pulls her in for a quick hug and a pat on the back. "Right, you better get changed and I'll pack up. We still have time." He is now wide awake and there will be no more mistakes.

Bee is agape, mouth just hanging open and she is a bit lost. She bends to get her clothes and scuttles off to get changed. Once she is in the safety of the bedroom, she sits on the edge of the bed to take a breath. She knows what nearly just happened was probably an accident, they had just woken up. She was looking up at him and must have accidently looked like she wanted to kiss him, which she did, but she didn't think it was obvious.

Back in the kitchen as soon as he heard the door shut James put his head in his hands and stopped for a second. He needed to get a grip. She was obviously not interested, she made it very clear, and he would be out of order to try and kiss her. He just forgot, it felt natural as if they were together. He told himself to concentrate as they needed to make the flight slot. He continued to pack the bags and they would soon be on their way. James felt anxiety and frustration at the situation brewing inside him.

They were soon on their way and there was an awkward atmosphere in the land rover. How could they be so close one minute and now it was so frosty. Bee thought to herself that she was an idiot. James had shown her respect and the curtesy of friendship, he had brought her all the way out here and she goes and offends him by nearly kissing him. It was her fault, she was convinced, and she owed him an apology so they could get things back on track or, at least before he flew them back. She could tell from his driving it was playing heavily on his mind, she didn't want it to be on his mind when they were in the air.

"James, I owe you an apology." She said it quietly, but James heard every word. They both stared straight ahead, James wasn't sure what to say. He was braced for a 'you're not my type but you are a lovely friend' speech and before he could say anything to stop her, Bee continued to fill the gap. "James, I don't know what I was thinking, I just woke up, it has been great spending time with you." James needed to act fast or she'd say it and he'd be mortified but he still didn't speak. Bee continued, "And then there you were holding my arms and, I just, I don't know, you were looking at me and I was looking at you and, I just wanted to kiss you." James was lost, it was all him surely? He still said nothing. "I am so sorry, I had just woken up, a little confused. I'm sorry, I don't want to offend you. James it won't happen again."

Bee is feeling so wrapped up in apology and embarrassment she hasn't stopped to realise James hasn't spoken yet. Instead of speaking James slams the brakes on and brings the land rover to a stop, unfastens his seatbelt as he leans over to Bee to grab her attention, he is overcome by strength and almost anger at getting it so wrong. "Don't apologies Bee, I wanted to kiss you. I did. I do. I want to kiss you." Bee is staring at James in shock, and he doesn't fail to take the opportunity a second time. He kisses her and slides his hand behind her head to hold her close. No easy task reaching across in the Land Rover, the gear stick is knocked and there is a crunching noise as they slide on the black shinny seats. Bee is captivated in the moment and fights against the slippery seats to be closer to him. When they stop kissing James is holding her with both his arms and they look deeply, intently into each other's eyes as their noses remain touching. It could easily go much further, the passion they feel is overwhelming, despite the inappropriateness of the surroundings. James interrupts. "We need to get to the airstrip." He needs reassurance from Bee. "Are you okay?" he asks, still holding her close. Bee nods a few little nods and then pulls away a little to signal James can let her go. The return to their seats, seatbelts on and stare straight ahead.

James doesn't drive straight away. He needs to focus and take stock. He places his hand on Bee's knee momentarily and looks over to her and smiles, then grabs the black snooker ball round knob of the gearstick and continues to drive them to the plane in silence.

Chapter 25 –
Blooming Ridiculous

So, flowers have arrived at my section. One of the guys, Jock Roberts called over to me from the other side of the hanger to go to the office as in Jock's words 'some soft bastard' has sent me flowers, the rough Glasgow accent makes it sound a crime. With a sprinkle of hangover on top, it has made me feel exposed so instead of smile like a girlie girl, I scowl a little. I have to blend in, be unnoticed to be safe. Otherwise, the attention that being different can bring, well it's too much of a risk. Like the time when I first arrived and I was pushed up against the lockers when I went into get changed, I was groped forcefully, with anger by some idiot who asked where my balls where, and he told me in no uncertain terms I didn't belong here. I dread what would have happened had someone not walked in. It only happened once, then my locker was moved to the ladies toilet. I said nothing had happened when I was asked as I was in the fear and shock of the situation. I could feel the undertone linger of just a one or two of the team who hated a woman disturbing their man only space. One telling me I was steeling another man's job. I am not different though, that's what gets to me. I am a standard, ordinary woman, to be fair I am masquerading in this RAF uniform as if I am a kick ass member of the armed forces which, most of the time I feel too inept to claim as my occupation. When asked for my occupation when registering for clubs and such like, I often feel a bit embarrassed to say what I do, like I am a fraud.

Straight after Jock's announcement there were cheers and hackles of further derogatory comedy showered on me as I walk across the hanger to the office to collect them. It's a real charm being in the RAF at times. Well screw them. I am kick ass, I am, or at least I can be. I passed the combat training didn't I for God's sake and, as for the engineering training, I showed the lads up most of the time by high scores and be having better practical skills.

As I get near Chief Roe, a towering Welsh rugby player of a man, carrying a few extra pint pounds is standing and staring at me. Chief is a fair man, he's from the farming area of Carmarthen in Wales. He is nature loving, and a sucker for the Scottish mountain rangers where he spends his days off, when Margaret his wife allows. She is definitely in charge, although must only be about four feet ten without her shoes, she is feisty and helps the pounds pile on with the delicious homemade cakes she bakes, she's like a pro and we are getting some sent to us once a month. Chief is respected, calm and as confident as a self-assured slightly aloof ginger tom cat, unless you call him Taff. Some young supply guy did last week, he exploded with tyrants and kicked him out of the section before finding out why he was there.

Chief calls me into the control office where a few of the guys are gathered to be nosey, desperate to find out more. They look like two keen spaniels waiting eagerly for a ball to be thrown. They are such gossips, honestly it is like they have no life at all other than to enjoy the personal news of others and spread stories. Just as you'd expect with Chinese whisper, the stories are usually unrecognisable from the truth by the time the gossip gets back to you.

"So Senior Aircraftswoman McBrien, you appear to have an admirer" – he takes a deep breath and stands tall – "may I remind you that you are an ambassador for this section. As such you are not to bring any disrepute to our door by fraternising with any males, females or random animals from other sections who are considered inferior to us. Which means pretty much all sections. Do I make myself clear?"

The Chief says this with a hint of humour, but I am acutely aware this is ninety percent humour and ten percent a serious warning to be careful.

"Yes Chief, I know. I am pretty sure these are from my 84-year-old great Aunt Mildred, to thank me for looking after her pussy cat, while she was in hospital recovering from a broken hip."

Good cover up from me there I think, although as far as thinking on my feet and quick quips I am still a novice.

"Now, now, McBrien, I think you are telling porky pies there aren't you? Do you have an Aunt Mildred?" Oh shit, I'm done for. "McBrien, I bet it is as likely you do have a great Aunt Mildred as it is that she has broken hip, did she fall on her recent skiing trip to the south of France?" The guys are giggling away now, so I can only flush red with embarrassment, and I am speechless. Chief coughs and, in his rich Welsh deeper more serious tone said, "Now McBrien, I think you owe me an apology for lying about great Aunt Mildred and her pussy, especially because we are only showing our concern for your pussy after all."

That's it, the guys are laughing so loud, some bent over gasping for breath as I grab the flowers, turn forthright to leave and show them the bird on the way out. How the Chief keeps a straight face I have no idea. I think given the tone has been lowered to such a level I'll get away with it, although I have never stooped this low before.

These flowers must be from James but, why would he send them? Surely, he'd know how much grief I'd get in the section? It doesn't end there, as I leave to walk through the hanger with the flowers to my locker, a few of the guys come over to quiz me and one grabs the little message card from the top and runs off with it. Little Jock Williams, a scrawny little blonde, a whippet long distance runner, dashes off to the centre of the hanger, jumps on a cable barrel and stands tall like a ringmaster in a circus, he announces that he has news to tell.

"Listen in, Listen in!" – A pause for dramatic impact – "I have here today news, that confirms signs of life in our dearest Bee."

The entire hanger stop work and start to walk very casually over to hear him. There are a few exceptions, two of the older corporals simply stop and look up to listen, saving the trip, none going further than the end of their generator they are working on.

"Hear this, hear this, a message for our very own Waffy, a dark horse she obviously is—"

He is interrupted by heckles from the tyre bay. "She's more like my little pony!" Another shout out, "a Dartmoor pony at that, a little wild and scruffy."

That is just great, it's a free for all at my expense. It is section etiquette that I stand still and take this crap.

Jock continues. "Who was aware she was dating?" Jock Williams looks around waiting for answers for a moment then clears his throat with a theatrical cough and opens the message card envelope as if he was announcing at an awards ceremony.

I hope to see you again very soon, hopefully we can walk the beaches on the north next time, J.

There are whoops and cheers, and Jock continues. "So, miss Bee, who on earth is J we ask, is it Johnny, our very own master of mechanics?" Everyone looks around to the small engineering bay to see if Johnny is in that direction and he is, he simply holds his hands up and says in his mockney Essex twang, "Not me guv, I'd not do the dirty in my own back yard your honour."

Great, I feel so exposed right now, what next. I keep walking, sod the card. The interrogation goes on without me and the team laugh and play like hyenas enjoying the sport, the embarrassment and intrigue. I'll put the flowers away in my locker and go out to do some servicing checks outside, get out of this circus.

James, what a prat, why on earth would he do it, I am so angry. So much for a private life, for some space. The guys will be all over this now for the weeks to come, seeking out new gossip about me and if they don't find what they are looking for, they'll simply make it up.

The day passes without any more hassle but at home time I am nervous about collecting the flowers and walking to the bus, I suspect they will all be there waiting to jeer some more and laugh at me. I really will give James a piece of my mind, such a basic mistake, was he trying to make life difficult for me? Heaven only knows how they will react when they finally find out he's a pilot. I could lose my job, get posted, get more grief than it's worth. In fact, I think I need to consider ending this now before they do find out. Yes, damage limitation. That's not a bad idea. If I end this now, whatever it is, before it's too hard, before anyone gets hurt, which let's face it is inevitable really. No pilot or any other commissioned officer for that matter is going to go out with a junior rank. Their career would be over, the shame they would feel. It's the same in reverse for me, reverse snobbery from the ranks and I'd be ostracised.

So, that's it, I'll have a think while I have a shower on how to end this silly stupid thing before it gets either of us into any more trouble. I can ask him to keep it quiet and we'll be both scot free. Yes, it's a plan. I feel a weight has lifted already now I have a plan and I can easy ride out the lads questioning me when I know I'm safe from them finding out anymore. I'll say it was some local lad from Elgin, they will assume it was the local beach we walked, they won't think twice about it, and I will say I won't be seeing him again. Someone else will mess up soon, be the new but of the jokes and this will all be forgotten. Yep, he's picking me up at nine after he finishes flying and I can tell him then, over dinner at his place, civilised and calm.

That's the bonus of a senior ranking chap I guess, he must be very grown up about this. He's quite a chilled out happy go lucky guy, he won't mind really, he'll be a little bruised, or maybe not at all. I'll make sure I get my head straight first then go for it. I'll wait until I get there though, not do it in the truck, if nothing else, my neck is killing me from lifting and shifting spare cables outside all afternoon. I think I have pulled something due to my anger fuelling my work efforts, slightly too overzealous lifting and shifting equipment. See, he is even bad for my health!

Chapter 26 –
Abrupt Endings

It's eight fifteen and I feel sick. I have showered, ate some chocolate, had three cups of tea, changed which top I was wearing several times and I'm now back to the one I started with. I have paced about a bit, checked my hair, and makeup. Although I wear very little make up, I don't know why I am bothering to check it. How about the 'it's not you, it's me' speech? I can hardly get away with 'I want to spend time devoted to my career', he'd probably laugh at me, all things considered. I'm only two ranks higher than the bottom and he's nearer the top of what ranks you'd find on a fighter jet unit and, he's a commissioned officer for crying out loud. Although I am on good reports so I might get promoted at some point soon, which means I get to go on my next course back in wet, windy Wales. New rules mean no gender is allowed on the paperwork just your number so, there is hope that I won't get held back now for being a woman. It would be almost a year-long intense course in return for a reward of a HND in electrical engineering, a new rank and a pay rise. I want it, mainly for the pay rise if I am honest but, I can't face training again just yet. It's a hellish place if you don't drive, you're cut off from the world. Maybe I should learn to drive, hmmm. I'll add that to the list. Okay, I'm struggling for ideas on how to do this. I guess just tell him I'm pissed off at being a laughingstock and want it to stop now before it gets out of hand. It may make me a bit of a wimp but it's the truth. Shit, I can hear the truck, what the hell, he's early and I'm not ready. Okay, go for it, time to get out of here before anyone sees us.

As I jump into Big Red, I say hi but stare straight ahead as I put my seat belt on, then I stay looking forward as I politely ask James how flying was, I can then keep him talking.

"Hey hold up, nice to see you beautiful, how about you slow down, take a breath, you sound like you are keen to get out of here?"

Okay, so with James saying that, my stomach turns over like I have hit the top of a rollercoaster, it's when I hear his voice and, what he says, the way he says it makes me feel special, even when he says little at all.

"Sorry James, nice to see you, I was just rushing about, you're early?"

He looks amazing, he makes my insides come alive and energy rush through my spine in a way I have never felt. He makes me feel light and I have a boost of energy, like I need to go for a run or something, which is odd as I hate running.

"Yeah, we finished the training early and wrapped up, it went well. The squadron team seemed happy we were back early so, they can get to the bar."

I feel like I will miss this. It's nothing is it, just talking but, I will miss it. I don't think I want to end this really, but I have to, and I have made up my mind already. I am not famed for changing my mind, when I make a decision, I am done. So, I'll turn to focus on the road ahead again. This is also needed to make sure I don't vomit all over him, looking sideways in a rumbling truck isn't a good idea, especially on a nervous stomach. There is a silence now between us, I don't know what to say and I am searching to think of something to tide me over until we get there, the atmosphere has suddenly become cold.

"Okay Bee, what's up? I can't tell something is on your mind. Did you get the flowers I sent? Were they okay? I don't know what you like but you mentioned your Aunt Rose so, I made sure there were roses in there." He is so thoughtful, and he can tell I am off. What do I say now?

"James, they were lovely. Thank you, and it's nice you remembered me talk about Rose, really very nice of you."

"Okay, so why am I feeling this odd vibe, what's on your mind?" I don't get this, how the hell does he know that I am pondering and not okay, I haven't said a word. It's like he can read my mind.

"It's nothing, it's just, look we'll talk when we get to your place okay? We are like a couple of minutes away, right?" He starts to look annoyed and puts the radio on by hitting the on button with the back of his hand.

"Why do I get the feeling this isn't going to be something I want to hear. If you are not okay; then I am not okay." – He is stern – "I can promise you though. Bee, we can sort out whatever it is that's on your mind, try not to worry." With this he reaches his arm over to my knee and puts his left hand on my leg for just a moment to reassure me. His hand is so warm, the heat radiates deep into my leg and the feelings spread to my gut. He just makes me come alive by one touch;

I remember the kiss in the land rover too. He is soothing yet so damn hot all rolled into one.

When we pull into a large farmhouse on the main road, I am a little confused. James explains he rents a small flat above a double garage from the owners of the farm. A nice forty something couple with teen kids and a retired sheep dog that he gets to borrow for beach walks as often as he likes. When we arrive at his place, he walks calmly around to get my door, looks at me a little annoyed, I had started to get out before he got there. It's habit, I spend all day fending for myself like one of the guys, and I am not used to being waited upon so protectively and with such respect in the way he treats me.

He does the same at the door to his place, we nip up the stairs and into the flat. James puts his keys on the kitchen side, gently, with control. He turns and holds the top of my arms and stares into my eyes and takes a deep breath.

"Okay, what is it? Are you okay? Has someone upset you?"

I want to kiss him, not dump him. I really want to kiss him; he is the most gorgeous man I have set eyes on, and he is so open to talking it out I am completely thrown. I am used to the awkward avoid talk of feelings British type. The type I have been surrounded by my whole life, just kids that grow up to be the overgrown kids like the ones I work with in the RAF.

"It is just, I got a lot of humour, banter about the flowers at work, it was a really bad idea to send them. I'd be in a whole heap of trouble if anyone thought we were seeing each other. I could even lose my job, be twenty-four hours posted, ostracised by the crew, your career would be over too, I think this is a huge mistake, we shouldn't get any closer."

Instead of replying, or arguing, his anger fades and he wraps me in his arms. His warm arms are surrounding me as my head rests on his warm inviting chest, he smells faintly of grapefruit and musk. James puts his head gently on top of mine and sighs. I think the hopelessness, the stark reality of the situation has sunk in, and he agrees. He is being so nice I think I want to cry, actually I know I do, but I manage to keep the water that is welling up in my eyes within the confines of my eyelids by closing my eyes and just waiting. It is so bloody unfair, it's like the dark ages in the RAF.

As James releases me he says nothing, he just guides me over the to the sofa and walks back to the kitchen, fills the kettle and switches it on. He stands with his back to me, with his hands on the counter, he leans heavily into it letting it prop him up. Without turning around James speaks quietly, "I'll make you some

104

dinner and we can talk more. If it is what you want, I will respect you obviously, but let's just take a little time to think it through first."

I feel numb, sad, lost and angry. I have already thought about it, I just need to wait for James to catch up, which I owe him, it's only fair.

*

As James stands holding the worktop, he feels the raw pain of rejection and disappointment which seems to physically stab him straight through the chest like a thud of a punch, and it leaves a residual heartburn that stings. He had no idea this was coming; he hadn't given it a second thought. He was always a free thinker and a life in the British armed forces was an odd match for him. It was his calling to fly fast jets, his childhood dream, and to serve others in some way that attracted him to join, and the strict military lifestyle was a chore. The lack of freedom it provided was always a burden for James. Not to mention the old-fashioned snobbery of the British armed forces. Hidden behind excuses for fighting order, he felt it was in the most part just the preservation of class divid-ing rules for the arrogant snobs to hide behind. James makes tea, he had bought Bee's favourite, Fortnum and Mason Chai. She said her parents buy it every Christmas. He has called the store and had it posted it up from London just like they do for her. Then he quietly starts to prepare Scottish salmon fillets, fried in little butter with gently boiled vegetables and a squeeze of lemon. Very healthy and served simply on a white plate. James thought to himself and pondered over his options while he cooked.

James

So, I can go along with this, politely say thank you and goodbye, drop Bee off at her barracks and walk away. That gives me my pride. She isn't normal this woman, she's different, a mystery in some ways but I see her. Christ, I have no idea, I hardly know her, but I like her, and I want her. I can't stop thing about her so, that doesn't sound like a good plan. The way she mocks me and calls me Cowboy. It is just too late, and I feel so excited before I see her, I am clock watching my way through the day until it is time. It's weird, she is making me weird, I think I love her, I think I did when I saw her on the first day. I'll tell her it isn't an option to quit now. Just to toughen up and we can do this. Or can we?

105

Maybe it is too much for her and I don't want her to be hurt or ridiculed by the crew. I could walk in there, right into her section and drop them all on their ass, what a bunch of immature idiots. Arghhhh…It's not my choice either is it? I can see how determined she is, if she wants this to end it will. I can't look at her, I just want to grab her and take her to bed, ignore this shit situation and somehow make it all go away. She has a point though, the RAF will put their foot down, it will be a constant battle. I don't care about promotion. I just want to fly and fly well, just do the job. Bee might want to climb the ranks though; promotion may matter to her? Of course it does, why else would she put up with it all, and this, this could kill her chances of promotion. I feel like I am at the last meal before my death here, none of which is in my control. I don't think I can eat, but my stomach will rumble like thunder if I don't, shit, I'm screwed.

James had already set the table before he left for work. It's a small wall hung fold out table, he made it look nice with a candle in a small glass, and a small group of purple heather flowers from his landlady's garden placed in a vase. He hadn't any of these things, his landlady gave them to him. When he knocked on the door to borrow the dog for a beach run before work, he couldn't help but tell her about his dinner date that night. She had them ready to hand over to him when he returned to hand back the wet happy dog that had been jumping in waves along the beach. James didn't light the candle though; he placed the filled plates on the table and with a kind smile and asked Bee to come over. He didn't sit until he had held out a chair for Bee and she had sat. Another sign of his good manners that would be missed by Bee. James asked if she liked the tea.

"Yes, it is lovely thank you, what is it?" Bee thought it tasted familiar but different and couldn't figure out why.

"It is your favourite, I had it sent up from London. I know how much you Brits like your tea." James thought it is odd she didn't recognise it, puzzlement showed on his face that she had not recognised the taste.

"Oh my god James." Bee laughed so freely she almost snorted, she also felt instantly sad that he had gone to so much trouble. It made her melt, and she is feeling very guilty now. "I was joking with you when you asked if I had a favourite, you were so intrigued. Any tea is great. I am not at all posh or fussy."

Bee stops laughing and started to explain. "My mum always buys it at home for when visitors come, but I am happy with any tea." James wanted to be annoyed at her, but he couldn't help but laugh. "Right missy, it better become your favourite now after the trouble I have gone to. I can't believe you, I thought tea

106

was such a big deal? My mum has a different tea for what time of day it is, breakfast, afternoon and so on. You got me!"

As James looks down to start dinner, gently shaking his head and smiling he remembers Bee's animated tone when they talked about tea, of course she was joking, how did he miss it. He raises his eyes, and they meet Bee's. Bee is smiling back, sheepishly looking up at James, she thinks it will be her favourite tea from now on, she is a sentimental soul. There is no mistaking the chemistry between them. The depth of care too that is there between them is remarkable after such a short time. Not like the cliché of feeling like they'd known each other years, just that they are a good fit. Breaking it up, walking away really isn't going to be easy. Maybe they will bounce back and forth leaving and returning before they finally do split for good. What is clear is that staying together in the long run is not an option, it simply isn't allowed by the RAF. What isn't clear, is just how long it takes to walk away and how messy this is going to get before it is finally over?

The silence returns and as they each tuck into the salmon, they each consider what to say to break the deadlock. The silence is prolonged and awkward so, Bee opts for complementing the food. She thought it would help but, it made it more awkward as James just said 'thanks'. No sentence, just a one-word quiet answer.

James takes a breath and tries to address Bee's statements.

"Bee, I am really sorry I have upset you. I had not given it a thought that you would be embarrassed, or that the crew would give you hassle, or that you were concerned about seeing me." Bee is stunned and James continues, "I hadn't given it any thought at all and I realise now that this was stupid. I'm sorry."

Bee stopped eating and stared at James. She thinks that this wonderful man, just as I as she is sometimes, under all his strength, rank and his worldly education. She can't speak now, she is mesmerised by James, his honesty and his total lack of hierarchy, no pretence and consideration for their difference in rank. He sees life so much more simply than Bee. Bee is a worrier, she's strong but, a worrier non the less. She has tortured herself with the pros and cons of every decision she has ever made. Except the odd life changing ones like joining the RAF in her lunch hour, or rebellious messing about with friends where she is quite the ringleader, or when she has needed to protect the underdog. She is not herself now though, the RAF has changed her, oppressed her in many ways. Bee has lost her voice and she now shies away from difficult times, especially when she must stand up for herself. She does have odd moments of free thinking and action but overall, the prejudice and experience joining the RAF has changed her. Bee is very aware of the class system; of British snobbery and how cruel people can be. Not just kids, the parents were the worst when she was growing up. Ignorant and cruel they enjoyed judging and labelling others, all of those memories flood back on mass to haunt her.

"Bee, are you okay? Are you going to say something?" Bee couldn't. She was unable to articulate how she felt, all those memorises from training flooded back right alongside the passion she felt for James, how wonderful she thought he was for not having such ugly cruel thoughts. She never took her eyes off James's as she stood up, left her side of the table and walked to his. She took his head in her hands and kissed him as a tear leaked onto her cheek. At first the kiss was gentle but as the electricity flowed through her veins, she felt the torment that had made her so broken leave her, the energy he gave her when she kissed him brought more passion and wanting from Bee. James had no hesitation in responding to Bee's kisses. He lifted her effortlessly as he stood, in one clean action of pure strength. As James kissed her, Bee wrapped her legs around him and he carried her to the bedroom, where no words were needed to confirm how they felt about each other. In the heat of the moment, the hopelessness of the problem they shared brought them closer than they had been before.

It's nearly 4.30 am and the birds are making what sound like war cries, gulls in droves squawking as they fly out to sea and the light is streaming through the windows, the curtains still open from the night before. Bee lay awake quietly stealing every minute she has with James as he lay fast asleep. He must be the first man who could sleep as silent as a baby. James sleeps flat on his back with one hand behind his head, a faint smile naturally falls on his face when he is relaxed. Bee is tucked snug into his side with his free arm wrapped around her. It seems so easy when they are together like this.

Bee moves slowly to sneak to the bathroom but is caught before she makes her escape.

"Morning beautiful, I hope you are not running away on me after taking advantage of me last night?" James is perched on his elbows wearing a bright smile as he watches Bee sneak across the room to the bathroom naked. As she closed the door, she answers him,

"No, I'll be back in a minute."

Shit he saw me. Now I'll have to walk back in there naked. I'll wear a towel, that will save me. But I will feel lame being so shy after last night. Arghhh I can't do it, the towel wins.

So, after washing her hands, checking her breath and splashing her face with cold water, Bee wraps the large green and blue hockey towel around her and goes back to the bedroom. Where is he? James has already got up and fetched two glasses and a bottle of juice from the kitchen, and he arrives just behind Bee.

"There you are, I have refreshments." Bee jumps and yelps with shock.

"Jesus James; don't creep up on me." She play hits his abs again with the back of her hand, as she laughs a little.

"Bee, why are you wearing my huge Canucks towel?" He has put his tight boxer shorts back on so he can't really talk about modesty.

"I can't walk around naked."

James smiles cheekily. "Yes, I'm pretty sure you can Bee, I promise not to complain."

Laying back on the bed, one arm returns behind his head again, he stares at Bee. She remains stood at the bottom of the bed, wrapped in his favourite colours drinking the juice he brought her.

"Bee, on consideration I think that would be a fine idea; I mean I think I may need to come and get my towel back."

Bee thinks about running playfully away; or dropping the towel in a confident move but, she freezes instead and just stares back at him. James takes the brief pause as an invite, without hesitation he is in front of Bee, and he removes the towel with both hands, like you would if you were unwrapping a gift; playfully raising his eyebrows and surveying her before he then pulls Bee towards him holding her tightly, he begins kissing her neck. Bee can feel the heat of his skin on hers as he holds her so tightly close to him. It's like he burns a temperature in comparison to her, so hot. His strong hold mixed with the gentle butterfly like kisses he showers her neck with make Bee relax her head back, close her eyes and groan with pleasure.

Once again, they are curled up in bed in the most relaxed state. Bee thinks it feels too good where she is to move or spoil things, but she is keen to ask James a question about his leg. The scar on his right leg looks like melted wax and is from mid-thigh to his ankle on the back and the outside of his leg. He has been in the RAF nearly nine years, has he been injured on operations?

109

The answer was not easily given. James looked torn and restless as he made ready to explain. He started with telling Bee that the scar was the reason he hadn't swam with her that day in the fairy pools, he'd wanted to but, he is very guarded and uncomfortable with people seeing his scar. He said that even in the height of summer he wouldn't be seen wearing shorts. Inappropriately Bee laughed a little, how was he so tanned then? Plus, this was north Scotland, there were nice days, but the cutting breeze meant she wouldn't be seen in shorts either. The light-hearted talk lifted James a little as he was struggling to open up, and he wanted to change the subject. Bee didn't allow any movement though, she waited and told him to go on. James hadn't needed to explain before, not even to past girl-friends, he kept them at arm's length. Most people were happy with him brushing it off as a childhood accident that he didn't want to talk about. If they pressed in any way, he was abrupt and didn't give any ground. With Bee though, he wanted her to know but he didn't feel ready to talk. The incident was locked up in his head in a little safe place never to be thought of, he may never be ready. He didn't look at his scars anymore. The guilt he carried was worse than any physical scar could be, and he felt he deserved the scar and much more for what happened that day.

James had been in a car with his parents on the way back from a celebratory family day out to Southsea on the south coast. They were all in high spirits until it was time for the ride home. They drove with the radio on but, as the day was ending James had started to become tired and grumpy. He didn't want the day to end and begged for them to stay on the beach just a while longer, he loved it all so much. He also liked his father's Ford Capri. Tomato red, a slick three door hatchback, shiny chrome bumpers and wheels, all his friends at school envied this car. Once or twice his father had managed to pick him up from school to James's delight. Not often but, enough for James to show off and feel like a cool kid.

His parents smiled at each other knowingly that day when James sulked, they understood James better than he did. It wasn't soothing, it made James feel pat-ronised by them. He decided he would spend the trip back home in silence staring out of the windows, changing from one window to another methodically, so de-termined not to fall asleep and prove them right. He wasn't tired in his mind; he just didn't want to leave, he wanted the day to go on forever.

As they came around a bend on a tree lined country road James screamed, he saw a dog in the road and his natural reaction was to scream for his dad. The quiet and relaxing drive home had been broken in such a shock his father swerved. He hit an oncoming car to avoid the dog, it was a split-second reaction. Their car flipped and finally after what felt like an age, landed the right way up by the side of the road. Petrol was leaking at the back of the car and a small fire started under the bonnet at the front. His dad was awake, but his mum was unconscious. James was disorientated in the back and scared, he started to sob, big fat tears poured out from his eyes. His father managed to get out of the car after pushing and kicking at the door. He told James to come across to his side of the car and crawl out too. James was frozen, he was too scared, and he wouldn't leave his mum, he wasn't sure if she was dead or alive, he could only shake his head and sob. So, his father ran around to get his mum out of the car first. Although, he knew she'd protest to this if she was awake, they had always put James first, he had no choice this time, she had to move she he could get to James behind her. All the time his dad was staying calm and reassuring James all would be fine. James tried to believe his dad but, the heat from the car was starting to sear on his face and he was starting to cough with the fumes, his eyes were stinging, and he was shaking uncontrollably. After James's father lay his quiet lifeless wife on the grass verge, he came back for James and pulled him out over his mum's seat. As his father struggled to walk away from the car with James in his arms the car fuel tank blew, and they were thrown forward. James isn't sure how far, but his dad was now face down about three feet behind him. His dad's clothes were burning. It was a second or two before James realised his own trousers were on fire too. A blonde man dressed in brown cords had now arrived, dazed a little, telling James over and over that help was coming. The man managed to put the fire out on James leg but, his synthetic jogging trousers had meted onto his skin by then. The man then tried to do the same to James's father's back, patting out the fire with his jacket. He managed to put the flames out. His back was a black shinny charred mess, the smell was unbearable, sweet and acidic. The man turned away from James's father as soon as he had managed this task and vomited.

James can't remember anything else; his memory of what happened stops there. All he knows now is what he has been told.

His mother regained consciousness in the ambulance, she had concussion, whip lash and a broken collar bone where the seat belt had been. James was taken to hospital and when there they assessed him. They then prepared him to go to theatre to have his melted clothes removed under anaesthetic.

111

His father would have survived they had thought, had it have not been for the extensive burns that covered his back, his buttocks and upper legs. Once he had arrived in hospital he started to come around. Staff immediately placed him in a medical coma to allow his body to heal and spare him the agonising pain of his injuries. He didn't regain consciousness, he died three days later.

James was eleven years old, and at that moment, on his eleventh birthday, he took on a guilt that a grown man would struggle to carry. A guilt that had shaped his life in one way or another every single day. James drove carefully, avoided night driving on quiet roads as there would be less chance of help should an accident occur. He didn't explain to anyone, he had excuses he had mastered to hide his driving nerves. Every car he owned was red, a nod to his father and their happy days together talking of the red arrows or travelling in his father red Capri. It was his silent way to mark that he would never forget his dad, and he would miss him always. James knew that if he had just got out of the car when his dad had first asked him, his dad would be alive. He knew it. His mother didn't. No one knew. He couldn't tell anyone before, and now he had told Bee everything.

James was quiet in hospital, he had three operations, but he never once complained or cried out in pain. His guilt and the emotional shock rendered him closed from what was going on around him. He thought he had no place to complain about his own pain and, he never has. He had caused it all. The crash and his father's death. James was a giving person without any selfishness at all and, this was in no doubt contributed to by this horrid event that scarred him forever both physically and psychologically.

As Bee held James he cried. Sobbing as he had that day in the car. She kissed his hair and held him, and he clenched his arms around her. Bee said what he knew people would say if they knew the truth. That he was just a child, it wasn't his fault but, he knew that this simply wasn't true.

Regardless of age, his actions had led to him losing his father. Robbing his mum of her happiness and leaving part of her empty forever. He lost the man he adored, laughed with and played with. They shared the love of planes, cars, sport and cowboy movies. Clint Eastwood was their favourite; John Wayne was a close second. He hadn't watched a western movie since his dad had died but he often remembered those days. The winter Sunday's he spent with his dad watching those films. Jam sandwiches, orange fizzy drinks and crisps lay on plates arranged on the orange patterned carpet of the living room floor where they set up their camp. Meanwhile, Mum took a well-earned rest somewhere else in the house, reading a novel most likely. She used to smile and laugh when she came back into the room to check on them. She'd see them playing cowboys, laughing together or just their eyes glued to a tense movie moment, right before a shootout scene.

He had not seen his mum smile the same way ever since they lost Dad. This saddened him as much as losing his father. A part of her would be gone forever. It took years before he lost hope she would be back to normal. She would smile again but, not in her eyes like she used to for Dad. When James's stepfather arrived on the scene, he hoped this would be when she regained her sparkle, yet his hopes were never fulfilled.

The first time Bee joked and called him cowboy, James smiled, because a happy memory of his dad calling him the same flashed brightly through his mind. A western style tumbleweed moment, just before an imaginary Dad and Son gun fight erupted. He thought about Bee's choice of words. No one had called him this since his dad. He was called Yank, American, Lumber Jack, Mounty and all sorts of other nicknames, but not that. James clung to all connections he had to his father in his life. Yet he didn't always realise he did this. Planes, cars, foods. His subconscious drew him in every direction that a vague link appeared. So, in all truth, his late father had played a part in his interest in Bee being ignited. His dad had brought them together and had introduced them just as effectively as he would have done if he were there in person.

Chapter 27 –
One Step Closer

After the time they spent together later that night and the peace of the early morning broke, the issues they had, were somehow overcome and were not mentioned again. No deep conversations about the future took place, no tactical plans, or considerations and no 'what if's'. It seemed as if an unspoken contract had been agreed. They both gained strength and a defiant will from the energy and closeness they both shared with each other. In lay man's terms, all caution went out of the window, and they got on with seeing how their unacceptable love affair would develop.

Bee felt the pull to call home later that day. She really wanted to tell her parents what is going on, but she couldn't bring myself to. Simply sharing her good mood would have to suffice.

"Hey, Mum. It's me…" her mum responded excited and as energetic as ever.

"Bee! How wonderful. Peter, it's Bee…your daughter."

Bee had no idea why she always said this to her dad, she was the only living Bee they knew. Her dad rolled his eyes as he clearly had no idea why she said this either. Bee also had no idea why she shouted this to her dad without moving the phone away from her. Every time she was struck deaf by the noise and every time Bee was unprepared for it, and so she became more annoyed each time she called. Bee's mum had a weird sense of humour so probably knew exactly what she was doing. Today though, she let it go quickly as nothing was going to spoil the relaxed, 'happy go lucky' mood, she was in.

"Bee, how come you are all Americanised now, what is Hey? You usually say Hi?"

How did her mum do this? How could she tell anything had changed at all without more than a hello?

"Mum, what are you on about, I just said Hi it's me, Hey, Hi, it's the same?" Bee was defiant and prickly, so her mum knew she was onto something.

Shouting again. "Peter you talk to your daughter first, she's becoming a grumpy American, there must be a boy involved."

What the hell, how come she can do this, I hate it. It's like she can see all, and it's so bloody annoying. Bee was infuriated but battled with her thoughts to stay positive.

Bee's dad stood up, walked over, and took the handset of the phone, he cleared his throat, stood more upright as if he was now on duty and asked Bee how she was.

"Hello Bee, how are you? Weather has been terrible down here considering. I see on the reports it's okay up there though, quite mild." This was her dad's way of letting her know he cared; that he was keeping an eye out.

Her mum in the background chipped in. "Ask her about the fella?"

Bee's dad didn't physically move at all when he replied to Bee, "Ignore your Mum, Bee. She has no idea what she is on about, are you okay?" This was Dad's code for Bee to say yes and ignore any talk of boyfriends, which Bee was relieved and thankful for.

Bee wrestled more with her thoughts. *I don't know why I can't just call home and tell Mum and Dad all about the most gorgeous person I have met. Maybe because I think it will end one day and then I will feel so embarrassed. It really can't last anyway, can it? I mean, yeah, here is me, all plain, clumsy and un-worldly, and then there is him. He has lived in two countries before he even left school. It was nice speaking with the folks, but I started the call all happy and I now feel like the end is nigh. Right, enough, think positive, enjoy it whilst it lasts, that is what Mum would say if she knew. I am seeing James again later at eight for a drink and I can't wait.*

Chapter 28 –
Cold Dinners

Where is he, come on James, it's not a good sign if you are keeping me waiting already. Is he going to distance himself now? I shouldn't have pushed him to tell me about his burns. It clearly was massive. It's nearly eight fifteen. Why is it that my stomach churns in this way, half in excitement and half like I am going to be sick with the fear he may not show at all. Yes, here he is, I love big red! I hear growling before I see it turn into the car park.

James is out of the truck and waiting, he looks worried though.

"Hi Bee, I am really sorry to do this and to ask but, can Bob come with us? He has had a really hard day, fell out with Cassie and he needs cheering up. I told him about us, and he is still in a bad mood."

I don't care at all, James is rubbing my upper arms gently as he talks to me, he could pretty much get away with murder with me right now.

"Yes, sure" – I may regret this – "erm, well do you want me to come along, or shall we cancel for today, you can see to Bob?"

Without hesitation James holds his hands up. "No way, I need to see you. Plus, I need all the help I can get with Bob today." He smiles and helps Bee into the truck.

Bob is handsome. He is dark haired, perfectly groomed, never with a hair out of place. He works out every day, sometimes more than once if he needs to. He is vein but, he also seems troubled, and the gym is his medicine. He has muscle definition that no one on station could rival and he shows it off as often as he can. Small shorts, tight white or black t-shirts, tight jeans. He has no problems attracting ladies when he goes out. He just walks in tall and proud, and everyone takes notice. He has perfected his charming smile and short one liner to raise a smile. Hey presto, he has never left a bar without a lady on his arm or at least their phone number in his pocket.

Bob has girlfriend after girlfriend. He never keeps a relationship long because if he starts to like them too much he moves on. He doesn't call it a day, generally he misbehaves until they can't take anymore, a coward's way out. He used to play rugby for the station, he's a strong sportsman until without warning he gave it up. He didn't tell anyone but, in truth he didn't feel comfortable with the closeness that the rugby team players had between them, all the hugging, messing around and team showers. Maybe it was the drinking? He didn't like to drink too much either, just a few beers. He was always on guard, always looking out and looking after James or whoever he was with. Maybe he didn't want to babysit an inebriated rugby team or be responsible for taking them home.

James knows Bob will mess up when it comes to women but, he will never mess up when it comes to work. Bob is one of the best Navigators in the RAF. He is the epitome of calm under fire. It's as if he can switch off his emotions and fear, like a computer. He gives calm, clear instruction to his pilot. James has the uppermost respect for Bob, and he relies on him completely to keep them safe in the air. James needs to fly, not be flown. He needs to be in control, and he needs instant intel from Bob to control the mission and fly well.

The pair had been chosen for missions that were delicate because of their strengths as a team, and collectively they had brought the finest results. Unflappable together and able to calculate risk perfectly. Their number one mission is not to succeed in the mission, but it is to bring the jet home. A fighter jet costs upwards of sixty million pounds and the UK cannot afford losses. Priority two is to succeed in the mission. This is probably one of the main reasons the RAF is considered one of the best of its kind. Precision and control bring great results from what seems like a very small stock of planes compared to many other countries. With less planes, they fly more missions than those who are plentiful with hardware, all due to their unchallenged accuracy.

James, Bob and Bee all head out to a pub overlooking the sea, the Skerry Brae. The plan is to order a bar meal and have some peace to talk. It was quiet during the week, despite the jaw dropping views, many local preferred to go out only at weekends. James heads up to the bar to order the food and drinks and Bee is left with Bob.

"Are you okay? James told me you are not feeling too great." Bee is polite and tries not to delve too deeply.

After a long pause Bob finally speaks, he doesn't want to, he can't contain his bad mood when he does. "I'm fine. You should be worrying about James, not me."

Bee wasn't expecting a snappy response. "I'm sorry Bob, what you mean. Is something wrong?"

"No Bee, it's fine, you carry on your affair with JJ and have your fun. Ruining his career as you go. No problem at all." Bob seethes as he speaks, his anger is showing too clearly, he really doesn't approve.

Bob's attitude towards Bee startles her. "Hang on a minute, I know you're in some sort of mood over your own love life but—"

James interrupts as he re-joins them cupping a triangle of drinks in his hands. "What's up? What's going on?" He looks at Bob first, guessing he has spoken out of turn.

"I can't believe you are talking about my relationships, when yours is a car crash waiting to happen." With this Bob realises that is the most thoughtless statement to use in relation to James. He knows the basics, that he lost his dad in a car crash, little more but he knows that. "I'm sorry James, what I mean is, you two can't carry on. It's not allowed, you know this right?"

"Bob, I don't want a lecture. Some rules are outdated, and no one will really care." James wants the subject closed; he can't afford for Bee to get anxious about it.

"What makes you think no one will care? I care?" Bob shocks them both and all three sits in silence, looking into their drinks.

After a moment, James is the first to crack. "Bob, I don't understand why you think it's a problem?"

"Your career is why I have a problem. It would be over." Bob snipes as if his patience is running out.

"My career, is that the best you can do? I am not going to have an outdated system tell me what to do when it has no bearing on my work." James is shaking his head. Bee wants to disappear. It's about her and yet she feels like she is intruding.

Bob looks out of the window and quietly said, "You just don't like the truth, it's inevitable you two won't last." With this, the food arrives, and James clears the air.

"Enough talk of this, let's eat and you cheer up. Maybe you are more smitten on this latest girl than you are letting on Bob?"

"JJ you enjoy your date and your disillusionment. You have no idea what you are doing and no right to talk to me about my situation, all things considered." With this Bob finishes his drink and puts his glass down. He stands and leaves with the food left untouched.

"Bob? What are you doing?" James turns in his seat, but he doesn't rise to follow him.

"I'm walking, that's what. It's what I do best." Bob leaves and starts his long walk back to camp with no comprehension of how deeply he has offended James. He is too busy wrapped up in his own anger and frustration. He ponders and talks to himself as he pounds the road, arms swinging to a quick his pace. Why doesn't James understand why his fling with a junior rank so off limit? All hell will break out, surely, he can see that? He may get grounded or posted somewhere grim. If James is posted, who will Bob fly with?

He loves flying with JJ. Ever since they were paired it worked, they operate like clockwork, as slick as any team could be. He enjoys JJ's odd accent and his Canadian behaviours. He is far calmer and easier going than any other pilot he has met. He doesn't judge anyone and it is as if he is content in what he is doing. The other pilots all seem eager to please their boss and gain promotion. The others are competitive with each other, whereas JJ isn't, he fathers the team. Bob suspects James would be relaxed in any situation. He doesn't realise that when they are flying, it is Bob that gives James the peace of mind to focus and relax into the task in hand.

Back at the Skerry Brae James apologies on Bob's behalf, as if you would when a spouse is out of line when out with friends. Bee, in complete British fashion reassures James that there is nothing to worry about. Together they reassure each other just enough to enjoy their meal and change the subject. It is remarkable how they both manage to ignore the concerns that have been raised and what hurdles that may follow. A resilience that is born more from first love's naïve blindness than from a sign of strength.

Chapter 29 –
Lost Property

Here we go, back to work and reality for me. Monday mornings bring shared news of weekend fun over a morning cuppa before work starts. Today was no different. Paul's wife wants to buy a house but, he wants to buy one in Manchester and rent it out, and she wants to live in it and therefore buy locally, preferably in Lossiemouth itself or Hopeman, a little bit along the coast. Paul is thinking the renter will pay the mortgage initially and they can settle in the house in another ten years or so when he leaves the RAF.

His wife Sarah is fed up with married quarters and the magnolia interior and sparse feel they all have, and so far, they can't find a compromise to suit them both. So, Paul is glad to be back at work as he's getting it in the neck. He doesn't understand the material nature of making a house a home. He thinks a home is anywhere his wife and kids are living. Sarah tells him he is wrong. She'll probably feel this way herself in decades to come. Paul appreciates her more than she realises.

Two of the youngest members of the section, Scott and Jason were out on the pull at the weekend and managed to have some success with the local ladies. We suspect that Jason having his own, and very shiny new car; even though it is only a white Vauxhall Corsa, may have given them the edge compared to the average skinny adolescent spotty recruit. We will await more news and gossip there, so we can poke fun at him.

After morning tea break, I head to the ladies before we go back out to the squadron. It's a small cold room at the bottom of the hanger, standard grey walls, blue woodwork and the window has that odd glass with a wire grid inside that never looks clean, the sparse concrete floor adds to the prison feel and the only hint of warmth is the cleaners red mop bucket slung in the corner with some pink rubber gloves laying on the radiator. We will be out in the van hours and nipping back to go to the toilet is always a pain. I didn't hear anything until the poisoned words appear in my ear as I washed my hands.

"Bee, I am so disappointed in your choice of friends these days. I think it's time you remembered who your true friends are don't you. You belong to us."

It's Shaun. The section charmer, he could blag his way anywhere and charm anyone, a natural salesman. He isn't bad looking I suppose, and he has piercing blue eyes but, he has a slight bullying nature to him that I have never felt comfortable with. He just takes every joke that little too far, everyone knows this, but everyone seems to tolerate it and just walk away if he gets too much. He is uncomfortably close behind me when he spoke into my ear, and I jumped and then quickly ducked for some reason as I started to turn around. I didn't notice him come in and have no idea how long he has been here.

"Shaun, what are you doing in here, leave, now!"

Within a second, I am being held up against the wall by my throat and all his body weight is pinning me, I can't breathe and the shock means I have no idea what to do. I don't know what is happening.

"Bee, Bee, Bee, I have heard you are giving out now, and I think you need reminding that you need to give to your nearest and dearest first."

What no, oh my god no, he is grabbing at my overalls, I only have underwear under these, they close with Velcro straight up the middle. As he is yanking them open, I start to fight as hard as I can, but I am flailing, I just can't breathe, and I feel so lightheaded. I'm struggling to move my head to try and get it away from him so I can scream. At the same time my mind is trying to calculate if this is real or a strange bad joke and any minute, he'll let go and laugh. I can't reach anything with the one free hand I have, my other is trapped behind me. I manage to kick the bin as Shaun undoes his blue trousers. Oh dear god please stop, please make this stop and make it go away. My arm is freed by his movements, and I reach to slap him across his head, I try and punch, but I can't get a swing in. I try to pull his hair but there isn't hardly any to grab it's too short. His height over me stops me from reaching his face.

"Stay still bitch, it will be much nicer for both of us if you play nicely." I am in so much pain in my chest, my shoulder where my arm was held pressed against the wall is excruciating, my head hurts and my eyes are blurred, I feel nausea sweep across me, I think I might pass out.

"McBrien, are you in there? What's going on?"

Oh thank God it's the Sarge, a forty something tall Irishman with pure black hair is bellowing into the room from outside the door.

"Say anything McBrien and I will kill you." Shaun has a venom in his voice and the snarl through his nostrils that makes me have no doubt he means it, I am paralysed. Shaun switches to charm mode in a heartbeat. "It's okay Sarge, I'm taking care of her. She's all upset because of that aircrew bloke messing her around. I'm just calming her down."

There is pause of silence as he releases my throat, and he stares at me threateningly to ensure I comply. Sarge bellows back into the room but without crossing the boundary.

"McBrien, get out here and get your arse out onto the squadron, and worry about your love life in your own time."

I manage to break away at this point a run out of the room, my eyes red and tearful, I must look dishevelled the Velcro on my overalls has joined automatically but not in a neat straight line as they'd started, as if I missed a button on a shirt and my collar is now much lower on the left than the right, I see the Sarge and Paul just behind him, Paul has come to find out where I am.

"Let's go Paul, now." I bark at him as I walk at pace out of the hanger and into the van. My heart is racing, trembling I can't make sense of what just happened and what could have been if Shaun wasn't interrupted. How could I have let this happen? For god's sake I am in the armed forces, I'm tough, I'm trained, how can this happen to me? Why wasn't I more careful? Why didn't I notice him come in the room? As Paul jumps into the van the door hasn't swung closed and he is already asking what's going on, perplexed at my odd behaviour no doubt. Without making eye contact, tears silently escape from my eyes I lock the door with my hands trembling, as my breathing starts to slow in the safety of the van, only slightly. I ask Paul to take me to the block, "Just take me home. Now, please?"

Paul knows there is more to this but instinctively doesn't push it, doesn't ask but instead puts his belt on, looks back momentarily at the hanger and then he drives me to my accommodation block on the other side of the airfield. When he stops outside my block my belt is already off in preparation and I get out the van and run into the block. I'm on the wrong side of the airfield now, we arrived in an airfield van and I'm in the wrong uniform, blues only to be worn this side of camp, not green overalls.

Paul doesn't know what to do so he waits patiently for thirty minutes, and then accepts I won't be coming back out. Paul heads back to the section to report in that I am ill, he really isn't sure what to say and although he knows something is wrong, he hasn't imagined the truth as one of the scenarios played in his mind. He thinks though the situation. This is unprecedented, Bee is machine like, she runs like clockwork, grounded and drama free, unlike his wife who can be volatile, especially when she is sleep deprived and worn out by caring for their teething twins.

Paul has decided to seek out Sarge in the control office. Sarge may have an answer. There is a few of guys outside waiting for paperwork, a list of checks to be done on some generators and servicing plans. Meanwhile, Shaun has spotted that Paul is back without Bee so hot foots it to control to listen in, just in case Bee has reported what has happened, he may need to think of a story to clear the air. Sarge sees Paul and looks over the three guys waiting to ask what's wrong, he senses too that something is amiss, but he has carried on with his day regardless, unsure of what to make of the scene earlier he thought best to keep calm and carry on.

"It's Bee, I'm not sure what's wrong but she is ill, I have erm, I've taken her back to the block. I don't think she'll be back today; she was in a bad way Sarge?"

The concern was in his voice and written all over his face, the Sarge knew for sure now that something wasn't right. Shaun interrupted swiftly; he couldn't afford for them to work anything out.

"See Sarge, women, unreliable, emotional…one argument with their latest boyfriend and they are off. This is why; I say women should never be engineers, or in the armed forces at all really." Shaun has got people listening to this radical stance so he continues, "They just can't be relied upon, and they bring their emotions with them. A bloody liability. I mean, I like Bee, and everything don't get me wrong; but this is what you get having bloody women in the workplace. Wasting time and making us run around after them, it's more like parenting children than it is having engineers around."

With this Shaun has the servicing team surrounding him so convinced, Sarge rolls his eyes and willingly takes this as the explanation, solving the nagging questions he has had. Further, he seems convinced by it all and feels let down by Bee and her behaviour.

Sarge had kept an open mind until today, about having a girl join the section. He is uncomfortable and shy around women generally but wanted to be fair and be progressive. He wanted to support Bee, until she put a foot wrong that is. A predetermined watchful eye, a subconscious bias born form being nervous of the change she brought to the section dynamic.

Sarge turned away back to his desk and shouts to the guys, without looking back at them to get on with their work. They don't disperse immediately, Shaun manages a few more quips, drawing them to walk with him, with tales of him and his sister growing up and asking if they too have sisters who played up and were a pain to be around when they lived at home. Asking how women bleed out once a month and yet don't die, isn't that enough of a reason not to trust them? All of these statements trying at humour now to gain favour but, also very damming in nature. He was too good at the manipulation, but Paul stood firm, he didn't join in, instincts telling him still that something wasn't right. He had never liked Shaun, but he didn't know why, so he questioned what was being said, and he had loyalty to Bee. One odd moment on one day didn't change his opinion of her, he thought highly of Bee and that respect was earned as he too started his time working with Bee with the cynicism, of a woman pulling their weight in a physically demanding job more than anything. He wanted equality or don't bother; he didn't want to pick up the slack and has a far more open mind than most but, he was still judgemental and a little negative to female engineers because of their likely lack of physical strength. Spending day in and day out in the van Paul found there to be no issue with Bee, a hard worker, a clever and grounded person to work with. He continued to watch as the men walked towards the centre of the hanger still snorting and laughing at Shaun's comedic rants, not knowing what had happened or what to do next but also knowing now was not the time to bother the Sarge further.

As Bee entered the barrack block, she shot up the stairs and, in the corridor, approaching her room she passed Gillian walking the other way. She didn't look up or acknowledge her. Gillian called after Bee.

"Hey, are you okay?" A very British question, it was clear from Bee's sobs and distress that she wasn't. Bee struggled to open the lock on her door, panic had set in, but she did somehow and no sooner had the door flung open, it had slammed behind her. Sinking to the floor by sliding her back down the back of the door, Bee sobbed holding her knees to her chest, almost rocking as her heels dug into the floor and her toes lifted through her anger. The RAF was a place for good people, for those who work in teams, helping others with, for integrity yet this lowlife monster charmed everyone around him, and she knew not only has he just assaulted her, but it could also have been worse, he was trying to rape her, and he was probably covering his tracks by slandering her as she was sat there trying to recover. It's just what narcist do, always undermining other's reputations and playing hard done by victims when they are caught out. When perpetrators play the victim, many won't see that they are guilty, a clever, overused but effective trick of the natural bully. She hadn't really met any narcissists before, such that she'd noticed but, she remembered learning about them in school, she took psychology class, and it was all starting to make sense. Shaun had always made her feel uncomfortable, so she naturally stayed away from him without giving it much thought.

Her feelings were raw and passed like a flashing light from disbelief to anger, what could she do? She could rip her room apart, scream, sob but nothing would undo what just happened. As Gillian knocked on the door, pleading to come in, Bee suddenly thought she could cover up what had happened, pull herself together and put a brave face on, yes, that is what she could do. If she didn't say anything, it didn't happen, a good plan she thought, this way it meant she had some sort of control. Bee felt ashamed, the most powerful emotion in that moment, a huge wave of shame. There is no sound logic that can adequately explain why this happened but, she didn't want anyone to know due to shame and guilt, and for the fear of being talked about in such a small community as theirs. She decided to open the door and pull herself together, tell Gillian it was just a bad day, and all was fine, she'd smile and then she could hide away for the rest of the day. She smoothed her clothes and trembling she opened the door.

"Bee, what has happened? Tell me so I can help you?"

As Gillian spoke, she was surveying Bee like an airport scanner up and down for more clues.

"I'm fine, just a bad day, that's all. Now I have a migraine coming so need to sleep it off."

Gillian didn't hesitate. "No, that's not it, Bee? Let me in and you need to tell me, trust me? Maybe I can help?"

With this, Bee was shaking her head. "Help? How can anyone help, you can't help me? No one can help."

"Bee, I have probably been in your shoes, there is not much I haven't seen in my time."

With this thought, that it might not be isolated to her, Bee broke and sobbed. Gillian caught her and ushered her into the room. It took over an hour to explain the bare minimum of details of what had happened, Gillian patiently stayed, not pushing and she waited. Once Gillian saw that Bee was exhausted and couldn't say any more, she told her to get into bed to rest, she got her a drink that she knew Bee would not drink, Bee would likely fall asleep in a shot. Gillian said her goodbyes and said she'd drop in later to check on her. As soon as she left, Bee was up, locking the door behind her, placing her chair under the handle before returning to bed where tears fell silently and eventually, she succumbed to asleep.

Paul couldn't rest and drove back over to the block, maybe he could catch someone going in and ask them to check on Bee. He could see she was okay then and find out what had happened. He saw a lady coming out of the barrack block, it was Gillian, so he had timed his return perfectly.

After a brief moment of hostility from Gillian, she realised this was the guy who brought Bee back to the block, not Shaun the nasty peace of work who assaulted her, and Bee clearly trusted Paul. Gillian apologised, hands on hips, furious in her stance she looked like she would explode. Paul offered for them to sit in the van where they could talk without anyone hearing. After all, this wasn't going to be a short chat and standing outside wouldn't work, he could sense it and, Gillian knew it.

Paul had no doubts this was a true account, he hit the steering wheel repetitively in despair and swore, the horn of the van went off a few times and Paul ranted about beating the low life Shaun when he got his hands on him.

Gillian told him to calm down, she bluntly but calmly told him that this isn't the first time something like this had happened on camp to a female in the RAF, she assured him it was far more common than he would want to know. This stopped Paul in his tracks, he was worldly wise, yet he had never suspected anything of the sort had ever happened on an RAF base. He was aghast and didn't know what to say or do. He was now quiet but, more stunned than calm and therefore ready to listen.

"Paul, we need to handle this carefully, it can backfire for Bee and become so much worse."

Paul nodded and listened; Gillian sounded like a seasoned pro? Paul was worried she spoke from personal experience, but he didn't dare ask, more as he couldn't bear to hear it if she was. "No one wants to believe this so this can be easily covered up. And maybe the right thing for Bee is to do just that, cover it up."

Pauls startled back into the conversation with this last suggestion.

"No fucking way, no way. Something has to be done, that wanker cannot get away with this, no way, no. Just no fucking way OKAY!" Unaware he was now starting to shout, Gillian speaks quietly,

"Paul, first thing is first, Bee told me in confidence and here I am telling you and I have never met you. We must do what is right for Bee and she may not want to tell everyone. I don't know Bee very well, but she seems nice. A bit quiet even. Who is she seeing Paul, can we get her fella here to comfort her and take the lead in sorting this guy out?"

Paul explains about James and between them they decide he was the best person to call. Unlike some, he would probably be very official in sorting this out too given his rank, which is sensible. They decide the average RAF bloke would likely plot a physical revenge, a good kicking behind the hanger or some such. Making sure Shaun would think twice before even looking at another woman. So, an Officer was a good call on both the emotional support front and the official. He'll have him charged, posted or jailed in Colchester. He may even be kicked out of the RAF for this, actions unbecoming of an airman.

James is called into the control office; he is wanted on the phone. James picks up the receiver and answers, "Flight Lieutenant, Jamieson." The usual telephone answering protocol, short and to the point.

"Sir, I mean James, this is Gillian Bridges, Corporal Bridges here" – she carries on – "there has been an issue with Bee, Beatrice I mean. You are needed, erm, sir."

James is dumfounded. "Has there been an accident?"

Quick to reply Gillian says that Bee has been assaulted and he is needed at the Women's block. They will wait outside to brief him. James puts the phone down, calmer than most and he tells the Controller to remove him from the flight plan as he had to return to the mess due to unforeseen circumstances. The Controller had been listening into the call and as soon as he had heard James asking of there had been an accident, he expected he'd be leaving. So, although he was desperate for more information, he nodded and turned to remove his name from the white board and re-schedule the flight plans in front of him. James left straight away, he didn't stop to tell Bob who was playing pool against one of the engineering Sergeants in the crew room without a care in the world.

Once Gillian and Paul had briefed James, he was unnaturally calm. He wanted to go to her room, a forbidden act to enter female accommodation unless when accompanied by a female non-commissioned officer or higher, Gillian could be considered acceptable. Gillian stressed she would always stay outside the door. James would not be left alone with Bee, not that she believed him the be a threat but, because it was the rules that protected them both from any criticism. Nearly two hours had passed since Gillian had left Bee, all the talking and planning had taken longer than they had realised. It was odd that the squadron hadn't wondered where Paul was and radioed to check on him. As James and Gillian walked to the block Paul felt a weight had lifted, James would sort this. Paul would stay outside a while before returning and saying nothing of this to anyone. He'd given James his name and extension number should he be needed and assured James that he would do anything asked of him, which he appreciated. He knew Bee thought highly of Paul and strangely it was nice to speak to him and feel the same sense that Paul was a good person, that she had a good friend in him.

Chapter 30 –
Knowing Wright from Wrong

When James leaves Bee, he told her that he was heading back to work to clear his diary for a few days. He'll just organise a couple of days leave and then he will be back to collect Bee and take her home, to his place where she can feel safe, and he can take care of her. Bee has insisted she won't talk to the RAF police and there is little evidence, a bruise on her shoulder and forearm is all there is. Bee still feels shaken and she is too tired to go through it all over again. She knows the bruises will be explained away by Shaun, that no one saw what happened and that he is just too glib and charming he is sure to get away with it. Meanwhile, she will be the one who always accused a guy of assaulting her in a work scandal. The rumours will grow into bigger fictional stories, and she will have it hanging over her for the rest of her career. *Ah, is that girl that is just posted in the one who ruined that guy's career?* Or *Did that girl get promoted to shut her up?* And so on. No, a formal complaint just wasn't an option.

James had meant it, he meant he would go to work, sort some time off and take Bee to a safe place and never let her go. But he missed out the fact he was going to the Ground Engineering Flight hanger afterwards to sort out this mess.

When Gillian had asked what the plan was, James was disconcertingly relaxed. Gillian called Paul after James had left to say his calmness worried her. James had simply said was going to 'sort' everything out, whatever that meant. Was he going to charge him, or speak to his boss, what? If he charges him, under what Queens Regulation (QR) did this come under? This isn't a usual insubordination charge or lateness. No sooner had Paul got off the phone in the control room, he saw James walking into the hanger. James was walking tall, determined, and heading directly to the offices.

Paul stayed still, thinking James was coming into the office to find the Sarge but, James asked for the Boss. Flight Lieutenant Wallace, suspected to be the shortest and oldest junior engineering officer in the RAF at five feet six inches and in his mid-thirties.

James was directed to the Boss's office and Paul knew he had to quickly get hold of Sarge to go in there after him. By the time they get out of the control room and into the corridor to walk to the Boss's office, the door of the Boss's office had swung open, and the Boss was calling for the Sarge.

"Sergeant Murray, in here now!"

Sarge walked forward and closed the door behind him leaving Paul stood outside, nothing was said but he stood there waiting to be called in for questioning.

"Sergeant Murray, where is McBrien?" The Sarge looked shocked and caught out. "Well Murray, where is she?"

James was restless on his feet, he was pacing backwards and forward behind Wallace, his right hand on his hip and the other clenching to his hat, which was now looking like a rung-out dishrag.

"Sir, McBrien isn't well, so she has returned to the barrack block to recuperate; what seems to be the problem?"

James couldn't take it any longer, he should be following protocol and let Wallace lead the investigation and sort out this issue, this incident happened to his team, in his hanger, on his time, but he couldn't hold back any longer.

"Unwell, She's not unwell. She has been assaulted in your hanger, right under your nose by Shaun Wright. In fact, you interrupted the assault earlier and did nothing about it and, if you hadn't of interrupted it would have been rape! Did you not think to look after her and, well, to do something?"

Before Wallace could interrupt, Sarge had lost it, he knew this now made sense and he was angry. Deeply disturbed, he didn't think twice. It all fell into place, he recalled her overalls looking odd on her, how she was upset, he hadn't felt comfortable with it and yet he fell for the explanation given by someone he wouldn't entertain a beer with. He was complacent and therefore compliant. He had sisters, a wife and he had daughters. The thought of this happening to them allowed a rage to build and escape. Instead of answering any more to the Boss, he turned and grabbed the door and flung it open, it knocked a picture off the wall as it flung back, a picture of the squadron framed in glass, like a school class picture but, of their section sat in front of a plane. Glass flew everywhere and no one seemed to bat an eyelid as Sarge screamed, "Sean Wright, get in here now!" The section document clerk, an overweight sixty something widow, poked her head around the corner in shock and Paul said he'd go find him. But the Sarge barked to stay put with such bitterness, he was scared to move. When minutes later Shaun walked down the corridor towards the Boss's office, he knew what it was about, he could see James waiting in there. All three stood waiting, unheard of in RAF terms.

Normally there is such pomp and ceremony. You knock, you wait, you are greeted by a boss sat behind a desk, an immaculate desk at that, you walk in and salute. You remain stood to attention and await to be addressed, all regardless of the reason you are in the Boss's office, good or bad.

Arrogantly, Shaun thought he could handle this and talk his way out of it, as he always did. He'd been in similar situations before, not in this hanger or in work but all the same, this had not been a one off for Shaun. The Sarge grabbed the door as Shaun approached the room, and he stood aside to let him in, which seemed to Shaun to be polite, only for the Sarge to slam it shut the moment he entered with as much force as he had opened it, and the handle flew off on the outside of the door landing three feet away.

Paul, still waiting outside felt really worried for what was about to happen and stayed, as ordered, glued to where he was, albeit he was tempted a to pick up the handle.

James felt his chest tighten and an anger inside him that he wasn't sure he could contain. Sarge took no time to lay into Shaun first. "Did you touch her? Did you fucking touch her?" Poking Shaun hard in the chest with his index finger, as he asked the second time he was asking through gritted teeth, furious and there was barely any space between them as Sarge was eye balling Shaun up close.

Without any hesitation Shaun stepped back a bit to address everyone in the office and replied, he had mastered the facial expression of an innocent baby animal, vulnerable and scared. "Sarge, I don't know what you mean, touch who?" Shaun held his arms open, to signify his innocence, waiting to be told more of the story and he glanced momentarily over at James.

That glance was a big mistake. Just as Wallace was starting to recoup his officer command and urging those in the room to calm down, and to hear out both sides of the story; James launched forward like lightening and punched Shaun so hard he flew backwards and landed on the floor with his hands still wide open and palms up. He was like a toy soldier falling over, he hadn't seen the punch coming.

131

"Get up and I swear I will kill you. If you EVER touch Bee again, or look at her, or so much as breath the same air as her, and I will finish you. Do you hear me?"

Oddly, Sarge and Wallace hadn't interrupted. James's actions were not the actions of a commissioned officer, and it took them all by surprise. Sarge looked at Wallace, Wallace looked at Sarge, they moved left to right a bit on their feet like penguins, lost for what to do next. As Shaun came around a bit, Wallace brought his hand up to his chin. As he rubbed his chin, he changed his feet to rock front to back, he had a thought, raised his head back enlightened and took control.

"Flight Lieutenant Jamieson, I think you had better make your leave now. We know where you are should we need to contact you, don't we Sergeant Murray?" Murray nodded and mumbled a 'yes'. James straightened, and more due to the adrenalin coursing through his veins than agreement, he left the room at a fast pace. As he did, he slammed the door shut behind him, and now the handle had fallen off on the inside too.

Murray was keen to assert his authority and control, so he shouted at Wright to get up and stand to attention in front of his commanding officer. As Shaun was rising and fumbling, Sarge lost it again and just screamed at him to get out, that he was too disgusted to look at him.

Wright was keen to make his leave, he moved to the door and then he saw he had no way out. Sarge Murray had spotted this before Shaun, and it made him angrier that he was still in the room. Sarge started to boil over again.

"Wright, you are a fucking waste of space, you are so far not right you should have been named Shaun fucking Wrong. I said get out!"

Shaun looked at Murray confused, then looked at the door again, Shaun daren't speak, for once he couldn't talk his way out of this, so he looked at Wallace, the Boss for guidance and to help. Wallace stood tall for his size and remained silent, he just raised his eyebrows at Wright. Wright chanced the obvious question. "But, the door handle…"

Wright didn't get to finish his sentence. Murray had walked over to the window, swept the memorabilia that was neatly displayed off the windowsill onto the lounge chair. He then opened the window, Wallace didn't move an inch, just placed his hands in his pockets and continued to roll back on forth on his feet as Sergeant Murray screamed,

"I said get out, there is a window here, get the fuck out of it before I throw you out of it." Sarge took a quick sharp breath that fuelled another tirade. "Get your saggy arse of an excuse of a body back to the block and stay in your room until I send someone to come and get you. You do not speak a word of this to anyone, you fucking lowlife wanker!"

Sarge managed to raise the tone to yet another decibel as Wright hadn't yet moved. "DO YOU HEAR ME?! Until we know how far we are going to take this, you stay quiet, and you stay put!" With this Shaun clambered out of the window without any finesse and legged it. He was gone, red faced and shaken, he managed to run quickly.

Shaun thought it sounded to him as if it wasn't a done deal and that he may yet get off the hook with a warning. After all he had been careful to ensure there was no proof. He always made sure he had a way out of any accusations made. None of his actions had been spontaneous. If they knew that, he certainly wouldn't be in the limbo of awaiting his fate as he was now.

Sarge sat on the edge of the comfy chair now cluttered behind him with RAF photo's, shields and paperweights and put his head in his hands. 'Sir, I am so sorry', is all he could say.

Wallace remained calm. "Murray, who is the chap stood outside the door?" Sarge gently and slowly looked up, his hands slid down and were still holding him under his chin. "Wilson, sir, Paul Wilson, I think he knows something about it all. I think I do too."

Wallace saw the look on Murray's face, bereft that he had seen signs and not understood them, nor followed it up. Wallace calmly walked up close to the door. "Wilson, could you be a good chap and go and find some tools to fix this door? Shouldn't be too taxing for a young engineer like yourself."

Wallace was trying to lighten his tone. A higher pitched voice than usual came from Paul.

"Yes, sir. I will, back in a tick, just stay there."

Wallace smirked, the irony of staying put wasn't lost on him.

"Oh Wilson, make sure we are left alone, no one is to be lingering in the corridor. Can you see to that?"

Again, another high pitch replies from a little further away, Paul hadn't wasted time in picking up the handle and walking to get tools.

"Er, yes, sir. Will do."

Wallace confirmed back. "Good man Wilson, Good man."

133

"Sir, what are we going to do? I think I interrupted this incident earlier, but Wright set us off the scent. I could tell McBrien was dishevelled and upset, I should have delved deeper."

Wallace was quick to comfort Murray but also remind him this was not as straight forward as it once was. "Now, now, Murray, you had no idea this sort of thing had happened. Right in the middle of the day, and here in the hanger, who would have believed it? No, it is certainly not on you. However!" The tone of the last word was serious and followed by a long pause in which Murray stared at Wallace patiently. "However; a commissioned officer just burst into my office telling me this news and then punched one of my men. This is not the actions of a commissioned officer Murray. Furthermore, why was he so involved anyway? I don't understand. He could be in a lot of trouble, more than that rotten scally-wag Wright for a start!"

Murray knew, he had put two and two together and knew James was dating McBrien.

"Sir, I just found out today, McBrien is dating an officer, that was him no doubt."

Wallace quickly looked at Murray in surprise. "What? Are you sure? Oh, right, this only gets worse. Ranks are not to fraternise! In responding to save a woman's honour, he may lose his career. Is he a pilot? He was in a flying suit with wings, wasn't he?" – Wallace left no time for Murray to answer – "it simply won't do, Murray." Sarge Murray is a quick thinker.

"Sir, Wright won't tell anyone until I go over there, so we have some time. In these circumstances may I recommend the SWO, sir. He is head of discipline and with his years of service must have seen it all. He will offer a way through this, quietly and appropriately."

Wallace isn't so sure, he should escalate this to the head of the engineering wing and the SWO, albeit respected, the SWO is not senior to him in rank.

Murray sees the concern on Wallace's face and said, "He is also a personal friend, sir. He will be discrete and of course any actions pertaining, whatsoever, would be yours to decide and for you to take the lead." With this Wallace is content that he is in control and won't be criticised. There is some time to play with and Murray calls his friend the SWO. Explains in very few words that there is an urgent delicate matter and requests his quiet attendance soonest.

The SWO is the head of station discipline and facilities management. He is the Station Warrant Officer. Known as SWO, like you say snow, but you say 'swow'. As well as being feared, he is also much respected for his experience in discipline and counselling through difficult situations. From bereavements, family situations and administration nightmares, he is second to none. He is not the only Warrant Officer on the Station; every section typically has one of those at the helm but, he is 'the' Station Warrant Officer. He can make things happen. Organise the unexpected, and he can fix pretty much anything. Yet, the one thing he most certainly cannot do, is arrive quietly.

The walk from the Hanger door to the office for the SWO takes all of three to four minutes and in this time, the entire section has noticed. Not least because of a pacing stick that is tucked under his arm, or his shinny peak hat he is yet to remove, nor his clickity clacking shoes with metal heals and toe tips that methodically note him marching across the concrete floor like Fred Astaire. He holds a ceremonial presence that would stop all going on around him, and he probably scares small children and animals. By the time he has arrived in the corridor, the whole section is wondering why he is visiting and who is in trouble.

Two hours pass by, it's nearing the end of the working day when the SWO materializes from the office. All three men seem in agreement with their plan and calls have already been made to inform the senior ranks and Personnel department at RAF Innsworth, in order to mobilise the recovery.

The Station Commander, Wing Commander Jeremy Biggleswade, was called, even though he was on annual leave Skiing in the Swiss Alps with his long-term friend, and best man George Clarke. He is not shocked but, he is disappointed and agrees to the plan, giving the go ahead to call RAF Innsworth.

In a bizarre twist most of the discussions were about James, his career, his acts unbecoming of a commissioned officer, and the honour of the Queens Commission that must be protected.

They talked of retaining control of the ranks, keeping the incident quiet. Hardly any time at all was spent discussing Wright and how he would be disciplined, and even less time on seeing that Bee was okay and taken care of. While no doubt existed that all three men thought they were doing the right thing, addressing the matter appropriately and with the highest integrity, what they in fact were doing, was sweeping it under the institutionalised carpet, just as the men before them had on occasion had done.

The upshot was, Wright will be sent to Stornoway in the Outer Hebrides first thing the next day to service all general equipment, and then take an inventory of all airfield equipment. This should take him at least six weeks. Upon return he will be escorted to pack up and he will be posted as far away as possible, no leaving drinks allowed. No one will suspect then as he will have been given notice of a posting whilst away. They were careful not to move him immediately, as it would indicate a problem. When staff are moved without warning it is always known to be linked to a scandal. So, the works placement will throw them off the scent and protect the section's reputation.

Wright will be told to not speak of the events to save all involved and that if he does at any time, he will be formally disciplined for his actions, likely facing time in detention at Colchester Barracks and a dishonourable discharge from service. No question Wright would agree to this, as the boss will add a sweetener and tell Wright that there will be no mention of this formally on his record if he complies.

Shaun will fall for this but, in truth a discretionary black mark will be placed on his record with no explanation other than 'administrative incident'. This will ensure he is never promoted, and he will not be given an extension to his service contract when it expires in just short of two years' time.

James will be called in by his boss and talked to, told to keep quiet and finish his relationship with Beatrice McBrien. After all, it is an improbable and forbidden romance that is sure to end anyway, may as well use this event as a catalyst to have this discussion and call it a day.

When the Station Commander returns, he will see Flight lieutenant James Jamieson and remind him of his personal support. The support offered to a long-standing Officer in the Queen's Royal Air Force, and most importantly because he is a highly respected and decorated fighter pilot. This should help ease the situation where they want it to go.

For Bee, she will be sent word to take the rest of the week off and recover from the 'flu'. Bee will be told part of the plan and reassured that she will never see Wright again. Promised that Wright will be severely dealt with but, for the sake of the Section's reputation, and the Unit, the Royal Air Force and, of course her own anonymity, that it would be best that this terribly shocking incident is kept quiet. Bee will be sent away too. Though they will tell her in a week or two, not straight away, so it doesn't seem to be obviously connected. They all think if Bee is sent on a four-month long detachment it would help James clear his mind, and he would focus more on his career. Definitely, this would put paid to any chance of the relationship rekindling.

Of course, for McBrien's sake she could do with time away, they discussed this as an afterthought. Nowhere quiet though, McBrien would only brood they thought. So somewhere busy they thought best, an active war zone was decided to be the best place, it would put things in perspective. McBrien would have no time to think or dwell. The next rotation at her rank is due in six weeks. She would go to the gulf and help with Air Operations in Iraq. Not only is that busy when she arrives in post, there is pre-deployment training to do in the meantime to ensure she is prepared, and that will also keep her mind off things.

For Junior Technician Paul Wilson, the early news of his promotion to Corporal. The promotion board is due to be ratified the following month anyway, he was already selected, and a nod to keep quiet is all it will take. Paul is a rule follower and a good man. One talk from the Boss and the incident box will be closed tight. The three men all seemed satisfied with the plan when they left for the day.

The next day after Paul had been given his news, it was all playing on his mind. If the plan was that Bee was knocked off her feet with severe flu, then he should help cement this. He'd go to the medical centre to pick her up a flu pack, a standard issue bag of flu goodies, throat lozenges, paracetamol and such.

He did just this and took it back to the section to be seen with it at morning tea break. He sat in the crew room, feet up on the low tables, a coffee in his hand, with the radio and the flu pack sat next to each other on the coffee table. Paul was a bit more spread out than he would normally be as he was bound to be asked what it was or to move up a bit when the crew room got busy. There were rarely enough seats at tea break, he was banking on it.

When he got his cup of coffee, he took time to chat to the guy behind the counter, he is one of the biggest gossips the section had, so he slipped into the conversation that he was working alone today as Bee was home unwell, that he had worked hard and deserved a bacon sandwich. The guy behind the counter didn't hesitate to dig deeper insisting he had heard Bee was upset after splitting with her fella and had wimped out. Paul was annoyed but he didn't show it, pleased he got to set the story straight, albeit the new story is still a little wonky.

"No, No, you don't listen to that Shaun and all his bollocks, do you? He's winding you up. She's still with her fella, she just puked everywhere, embarrassingly so, and needed to get back to the block before it happened again." – Paul could see the guy thinking this through so kept going, – "which, by the way, we didn't make it. I had to pull over at the bottom of the runway to let her puke again, right in no-man's-land." He saw him falling for the story so he continued, "Christ, I thought we'd be in trouble, the lights might have changed to red, and we'd be sat there at the bottom of the runway with two GR4 tornado's coming at us if we didn't shift." He's got him, he is falling for it and laughing at the predicament. "I nearly puked too with the fear of it!"

As they both laughed it off, Paul didn't feel any guilt for lying. He was still angry about what Wright had done and had decided, much against his usual self, that this was a much-needed white lie and that he owed it to Bee to do what he could. He wanted to do more to help and, being unable to help her was stressing him. The prop of the flu pack was great, a few more guys asked to move his stuff and he managed to get the story retold the way he wanted. To his surprise, some of the guys who joked along with Shaun and his version that day were fickle, and they were quick to criticise Shaun for his ill-mannered humour. Paul wasn't feeling forgiving, they had started, with very little encouragement that day to doubt Bee, and to cast her out as a waste of time. In that moment of clarity, and unable or unwilling to take responsibility for this, they blamed Shaun. Only a few wiser older characters stayed quiet, some shaking their heads slowly, pursing their lips as they drank. Paul suspected this was because they knew only too well Shaun was a loser, and they hoped that in time, these young lemmings would wise up and start thinking for themselves.

Over the coming days the Sarge and the Boss crossed paths and nodded with a sadness and acknowledgement of their burden. They felt bruised and forlorn as if they themselves had been through the hardest times, that 'dreadful business' that it was now referred to, was only spoken of if paperwork to confirm movements, plans or letters needed to be processed. Least said, soonest mended.

Chapter 31 –
Coffee and Counsel

When James arrived at Station Head Quarters to meet the Station Commander, he knew this was linked to what he had done in hitting Shaun Wright. His boss had already given him a dressing down about it, how they were embarrassed, how they were placed in an awkward position and so on. James hadn't held back then and spoke his mind; he was on good terms with his boss before this and that stood him in good stead to get away with being outspoken. The Station Commander was different. He was strait-laced, hardly smiled when he was seen around station. He was known as a hard authoritarian, punishing minor offences harshly, James was right to be nervous.

James was told the Station Commander was ready to see him. So, he put his hat on, stood tall outside the door, took one deep breath to steady his nerves, and then he knocked on the door three times.

Inside his office Wing Commander Biggleswade, affectionately known to his friends as 'Biggles', was dreading the meeting ahead. He had heard what had allegedly happened and somehow knew there had been no mistake. Upon reflection, he could have stepped in when he got back from leave and dragged the offender Shaun Wright back to base and had him charged but, that would undermine all that was done in his absence, and it would look like he had no control over his unit. Wright losing his career without knowing it would have to serve as a punishment. It troubled Biggleswade that Wright might not realise it was punishment, that he'd think his contract terminating would be just a coincidence? This weighed on his mind a lot. The thought of Wright thinking he had got away with it.

Then there was the relationship between one of his best fighter pilots and a junior rank. He knew attractions outside of the rules happened and sympathised but, rules were there for a reason. He had sacrificed his own relationships for his career, as many before him. If he hadn't, he would not have reached Wing Commander, or been placed as Station Commander at RAF Lossiemouth, and he hoped for promotion further still to lead at Strike Command.

"Come in." His voice boomed with authority; the meeting commenced.

James walked in, stood to attention, saluted. "Flight Lieutenant Jamieson, sir."

"Yes, Jamieson, stand at ease. In fact, take a seat." His tone was already showing signs of disappointment to James.

"Thank you, sir."

"Jamieson, may I call you James?"

"Yes, sir." James is feeling more anxious now, this is less formal than he had prepared for. He had prepared to stand tall and hold his ground.

"You may call me sir." Maybe James wasn't so wrong after all. "Terrible business this James. Really terrible."

"Yes, sir."

"What a toe rag that Wright is. His career is over, I want you to know this. He will be carefully watched moving forward." Biggleswade is nodding at James hoping for some sort of agreement. James sits quietly and still. "However; we are in a tricky predicament with you Jamieson, I mean James." James stays silent and it's awkward. "We simply cannot have our finest commissioned officers hitting junior ranks, it simply won't do James."

"No, sir."

"No doubt about it, the little scallywag deserved it but, that is not the point. You hold the Queen's commission, and you must not act in this way."

"No, sir."

Biggleswade was becoming bored of his own voice already but knew he had to push on.

"Now James, as much as I understand what has happened there is one other thing, we must not ignore" – Biggles was dreading this next bit – "your relationship with a lower rank, which if truth be told, one has to ask if this contributed to this incident?"

"No, sir. I don't think it did? Wright is a nasty piece of work and is a danger to women, regardless." James was angered at the inference that Bee's choice of partner contributed to the attack.

"You may say that James but, in my experience, these Neanderthals have triggers for their behaviour, and your prohibited relationship likely provided that trigger."

"Sir, why is he still in his job and not locked up in Colchester?"

The Station Commander was angered by this remark, how dare he question what has happened when he was the one who complicated the issue.

"Why indeed Jamieson. Because you hit him and I am determined, that given your exemplary service, to save your career! Had you not of hit the toe rag, then we would be able to lock him up and throw away the key now, wouldn't we?"

James felt a blow to the chest as if he had been hit as he realised that this was the case. It's his fault that the scum Wright was moved on quietly. He should have kept his cool, dealt with this properly. Although Bee wanted it all to go away and taking the formal route that would not be the case. Everyone would know about it once it all went on record and bee would not have forgiven him.

"I'm Sorry, sir."

"Well James, it is time to put this behind you. We must consider the future and all it holds for you." James wasn't sure what was coming next but had a feeling he wouldn't like it. "James, you are a very valued fighter pilot, a squadron team player and a leader, given your outstanding capability and your grounded nature, you have a lot of support both on the Squadron and indeed with me."

"Thank you, sir."

"This relationship with SAC McBrien, it isn't a safe one, we already know this. Isn't this a good time to call it a day? For you both to move on?" The Station Commander seemed genuine, as if he knew it wasn't easy but that he really thought it was the right thing to do. James was thrown by it. "Hasn't McBrien been through enough James? The ranks will never accept you two together and it would be an end to your career, just as you are ready for squadron leader. You know how difficult this is James. There won't be a happy ending I'm afraid."

It was silent for a moment. Biggleswade couldn't gauge what James was thinking so, he thought to wait for his speech to sink in.

"Sir, I appreciate your understanding and your advice."

"Good man Jamieson. I knew you would understand."

"Sir, I joined the RAF to become a pilot and to serve. I have no interest in being promoted out of the pilot seat and into an office."

Biggleswade was envious that James felt this way and was wise enough to know it. He himself had missed flying and the knowledge he would never be operational again now he was a Station Commander saddened him.

"Sir, I have strong feelings for Beatrice. I will take on board what you have said, and we will discuss it but, I don't think we will be ending our relationship, sir." James felt he was taking a chance being so upfront, he couldn't think of what they'd do to him or Bee. Would they post one of them to split them up? He would find a way around that. His mind was racing now and wandering to consider all the possibilities.

"Jamieson are you telling me you are prepared to give up on your career and put you both in the direct line of criticism and harm? Are you considering McBrien, or are you letting your own needs get in the way?"

"Sir, I am saying I won't give up on Beatrice. I will talk to her and let you know our thoughts."

"Jamieson, I wish the RAF was different for you. The establishment is slow to evolve, if it ever will in this regard, I don't know." Biggleswade is genuinely saddened. "There is method in the madness of rank and order. I hope you have a long think about that. Do let me know after the weekend what your thoughts are." Biggleswade stands at this moment to signal James is to leave. James stands quickly and steps back to apply his headdress, salute, and leave.

Chapter 32 –
Calling Home

Biggleswade had promised to call his wife with news of the meeting, and he did so straight away. His wife was his most trusted confidant and, she was one of the few people who would understand why he found this situation difficult.

"Hello darling. Is this a good time to talk?"

At the other end his wife told him cheerfully it was always a good time to talk. She asked him to hold while she closed her office door.

"Jamieson has just left. It didn't go as I'd hoped."

"Oh darling, tell me more. What happened?"

"Well, he came across as a good fellow. His record speaks for itself. I expected someone career focussed having read his file, but he isn't."

"What? What do you mean?" She was confused. She had no understanding of people who didn't want to keep moving up the ranks.

"He said all he wanted to do was be a good pilot and serve. He has no intention of ending this romance with the young girl."

"She has a name Jeremy. It's McBrien and she is not a young girl, she is an engineer."

"Yes Darling, sorry. I did my best to explain why it was such a bad idea. I can't imagine what lies ahead for them if they don't see sense and end it now."

"Yes, you do Darling, you can imagine it very well. You also know it will be just ghastly."

"Yes, it will. I told him to go and think about it and come back to me after the weekend. Hopefully he will see sense by then. I told him to think of McBrien. Surely, she has been through enough. Pulling at his conscience you see."

"Yes, yes, well done Darling. Look, I must go now, call me next week when you have more news. Keep me posted. Enjoy your weekend Darling."

*

Bee called home, after all that had happened, she didn't want to tell her mum and dad and worry them or go over it again, she just wanted to hear the normality and, she thought it was time she told them about James. The last week had felt right between them, she felt she would go on seeing James and see how it went, regardless of the outcome. She is in too deep now; she adores him and can't give him up.

"Hi, Mum. It's me."

"Bee, hold on…Peter, it's your daughter. He's in the kitchen, he'll come through now." Bee can hear clattering and noises in the background.

"How are you, Mum?"

"We are both good, aren't we Peter, your dad say's we are both okay. No American accent this time Bee? Ditch that fella, did you?" Bee isn't annoyed as she would be usually. She is laughing and she is pleased her mum has given her a way in.

"No, I haven't he's fine, James is fine." A long pause until Bee's mum comes back to her.

"I knew it Pete, she has a fella, an American, I knew it Bee, why did you keep him a secret, is he ugly then?" Her mum's humour is so predicable to Bee.

"No, Mum. He is not ugly, and he is not American. He's Canadian."

"Peter, he's not even a real American, he's a fake, he's from Canada."

Bee is laughing now, her mum is trying her best to be outrageous and upset her sensibilities, but she has somehow found a new resilience. "Mum, he is not a fake and he is English, but moved to Canada as a kid, so a bit Canadian, look I'll explain another time. What matters is, I am happy."

"Peter, it's worse than we thought, he's a mongrel, a half breed." Bee's mum cannot stop herself laughing now, she is impressed with her own humour, her dad is telling her off in the background and Bee is laughing too now, shameless. It's a good job she behaves in public, that she puts the filter back on. Bee knows she doesn't mean it, but some would think she's a bigot, a racist or something.

"Mum, you are insufferable." Bee is light toned, and her mum is pleased she has found humour.

"Bee honey, we don't care who you fall in love with. So long as you have good looking children."

She's set herself off laughing again, a one-woman comedy routine.

"I'm kidding, I'm kidding. We don't care as long as you are happy and, I notice you are laughing so, he must make you happy then, this James?" For all her joking she hasn't missed a trick.

"Yes, Mum. I am happy, you'd like him."

"What does he do then?"

"Same as me, Mum. He's in the RAF."

"Same as you, an Engineer then." Breaking away from the handset for once to shout to her spouse,

"That's good. Isn't it, Peter. He's an engineer, we can draw a list of jobs for him to do when they visit. They'd like that as much as we would I suspect."

Her dad is beside himself with embarrassment and shaking his head, not finding it funny at all, Bee bringing a man home. He isn't ready for that yet.

"Really, Mum. You must be joking now, you do want me to come home for a visit, don't you?"

"Sorry Bee, do you want to speak with your dad?"

"Sorry, I need to go, I'll call back. I love you, Mum."

"Love you too Bee, look after yourself." Her mum was adding something else on the end, but Bee put down the phone. She wanted to speak with her dad, but she felt too emotional. He might be able to tell something was wrong, he might know it wasn't all good news and she only wanted them to hear the good stuff.

Chapter 33 –
Back to the Day Job

When Bee arrived back to work, she was nervous. She was concerned everyone would know what had happened. She had no idea what was to follow. James reassured her that no one knew. She dreaded walking across the hanger floor to the toilets to change so she got in early before anyone else, only the two-duty crew were in. That way she'd be safe changing and be sat with a mug of tea in the crew room before anyone arrived. No one could make a scene that way and she could tackle any issues the guys had one at a time as they arrived. It wasn't a chore going in early, she hadn't slept well the night before.

She'd insisted that James take her back to the barrack block and she spent the night there, just like normal. Her time off that week with James had been intense and wonderful. She felt cared for, protected. She had laughed and cried. They had enjoyed time alone, walks on the beach and snuggled up watching movies. She didn't want it to end but, she needed to get back to normal as returning to work was starting to be a bigger emotional task to overcome with each day that passed.

"Hey, hey, Buzzy Bee! I hope you have stopped puking up now, it's not always fair to share my lovely." Sid had arrived first at the crew room. "You owe Paul an apology, he was really pissed at cleaning your puke out of the van and doing all the Squadron work on his lonesome last week."

Bee was so relieved, Paul what a star. She really did own him. "Er, yep. I will apologise and no doubt I will have to do it all myself this week while he stays in the van."

Sid sits close beside her even though it's an empty room which, unnerves Bee.

"So Buzzy Bee, we hear that your aircrew chappy isn't too bad after all. Apparently, he marched in here last week to tell the boss he was dating you and that he'd do right by you, fuck the rules." Sid raising his eyebrows waiting for a reply.

"What?" Bee was lost for words.

"Yep. That's right. Don't get me wrong, I think all Aircrew are just stuck-up overpaid drivers but, that has to be a first. Sarge said he could almost hear 'love lift me up where I belong' tune in the background. He was quite the officer and a gentleman. Quite a scene I am led to believe." Sid looked ahead now nodding. "Maybe he isn't as bad as the rest of them after all?"

"Erm, I had no idea. Are you winding me up?"

"No, not at all. I tell you what, I'll give him a chance Bee but, if he puts one foot wrong towards you mind, we'll come down on him like a tonne of bricks." Sid got up to leave. He'd made himself awkward with showing Bee, albeit in a funny way, that he cared about her welfare.

Bee was taken aback and could only think of how ironic it was that they would be upset if anyone hurt one of the guys or girls from their section. When it was Shaun who could and had done so. Bee knew James had been in meetings about the situation. She knew Shaun was sent away and that he wouldn't be back. She knew James had seen the Station Commander and refused to end the relationship which she felt guilty about. She didn't want to hold him back. Sid had given her some hope though that it wouldn't be as difficult as she thought coming back, or for James to be accepted by the lower ranks.

A few of the guys came in next, young ones who had welcomed her and said it was hilarious hearing about her puking in the van and getting stuck in between the lights on the runway. Adding that Paul hadn't stopped going on about it like an old fish wife. They said they were glad she was back, so he'd stop moaning and so they thought they would mark the occasion, they had a gift for Bee. One of the guys ran out to the hanger and brought back to the crew room a pair of ear defenders. They were her ear defenders, and they had been vandalised. Each ear-piece was now black and yellow stripped with bee faces on. Shit, she was touched as they called her 'Buzzy Bee' and there really are worse nicknames but, she was worried she would be in more trouble, defacing uniform. It's a chargeable offense. Shit, the last time this happened, a guy had announced he loved women's breasts so much he put modelling clay nipples on his ear defenders and painted them pink, they looked hilarious, but the Sarge went ballistic. She had better go an approach the Sarge now she was back, she could mention that someone anonymously had decorated her ear defenders and ask if she could go over to stores to get some new ones, in a hope he wouldn't shout at her, she felt she'd caused enough trouble.

"Morning Sarge, I am here to collect the service sheets for today." As good an opening as any. What else could she say.

"McBrain, feeling better, I hope? Fighting fit?" Sarge studied her for signs of fragility.

"Yes Sarge, I am. Sorry about being off."

"Not your fault McBrien. Are you okay to be back on Squadron duties?" He assumed the plan had worked and that James and Bee had decided to call it a day.

"Yes Sarge, no problem."

"Okay then, here are the sheets, not much to clear this week. Just four generators and a hydraulic rig to find and bring in." He passed her a wooden board with the list clipped to it.

"Erm, Sarge there is something else."

"What is it McBrien, spit it out?"

"Someone has decorated my ear defenders Sarge, erm, like this." She held up the buzzy bee ear defenders waiting for the shouting to start.

"Very fetching McBrien. I am sure we'll spot you a mile off in those, very safety conscious."

"But Sarge…" confused by the lack of issue with them she isn't sure what to say next.

"Are you still here McBrien. Make sure you wear those with pride, someone has gone to a lot of trouble to make those for you, it would be rude not to show them off."

Bee shakes her head and laughs. "Okay Sarge, if you insist."

They have cheered her up and she feels a hundred percent part of the team. It's the exact opposite to what she was worried about. She fretted all night for no reason. She feels her day will go well, she is sure of it now, and she is seeing James after work. Not for long, James is night flying this week, so he needs to go to work. He's picking her up at six at her barracks.

The only part of the day she is dreading is changing. That room now gives her the creeps. She rushed getting ready and changed inside the toilet cubicle. She was getting more stressed the longer she stayed in there with flash backs of what happened the last time she was there. Although Shaun was gone now, she felt as if he was still in that room. Bee knew it was illogical and held onto hope that it would pass with time.

Chapter 34 –
Pick Up

Bee watches out of the window for Big Red. She should feel tired, no sleep, a physically hard day at work, yet she wasn't. She was excited to see James, and this made her flourish with energy. When she saw Big Red pull up, she flew along the corridor, down the stairs and out of the main door so fast she almost skidded on the path to stop at the truck. James was already out waiting and greeted her with a huge hug and kiss, lifting her gently from her feet.

"Hey gorgeous, I have been looking forward to seeing you all day."

Bee felt the same and jumped in the truck. As usual James had opened the door and Bee jumped in with her usual lack of finesse. Once James was back in his seat he hesitated before putting his seat belt on. "Bee, I wasn't sure where to go for dinner. I was stumped a little. We only have just over an hour. We can't go to the Officers or Junior ranks mess obviously, and the only places to eat at night on camp is the NAAFI club which, is junior ranks only." The reality was starting to sink in, of the small obstacles they would face. "Anyway, I brought something with me, we can eat in the van like teenagers. What do you think?"

"Ha, ha, ha, yes, that sounds great. We can talk and catch up. I don't care where we are."

"Well, I do so, I am driving us to the beach, we can at least have a view down by the harbour."

"Okay, that sounds perfect, let's go."

As they drive away, James asks how Bee's day went.

"Yes, it went really well. Paul has been amazing. While I was off he was telling everyone, he had to clean up my vomit and all manner of illness related details. Nobody suspects a thing. He was brilliant." Bee was beaming.

"Wow, I am not sure if that is pure genius or pure weird. But I'm glad you feel better about being there. What did Paul say to you about last week?"

"Nothing as he isn't in. I can't thank him until Wednesday. He took a long weekend. He's been promoted so he went home to Manchester with his family to celebrate. I'm guessing they'll be house hunting too as he is posted after his promotion course. They want to buy something. Great news isn't it."

"Yeah, that's great news." Of course, James already knew but, he didn't want to explain how. His Boss had told him the plans to keep the incident quiet. James had thought keeping it from Bee was a good idea, given Paul was to be promoted anyway, it's convenient more than related, but he wasn't sure now. He wanted to be open with Bee. The twist was Paul's posting afterwards was not part of the original plan. Their boss Wallace had managed to swing a posting near home, commutable to Manchester. He felt Paul was owed something for his loyalty and discretion.

"You don't sound so happy? James, are you okay?"

"Yes, sorry. I have something to tell you that's all."

"What is it? Should I be worried?"

James was turning into the beach road and seemed to be concentrating hard on the road, he was frowning and leaning forward onto the steering wheel. "It's about dinner. I confess I can only cook salmon, steak and ham with eggs. None of which would do for dinner in the truck."

"You had me worried then. What's the problem, are we eating jam sandwiches?"

"Actually, I did rather well all things considered. I have a flask of your favourite tea." James smiled and Bee laughed as they pulled onto the Harbour car park. "I also have another of your favourites…Tad dah…Pasties." They were both happy and as carefree as children, just pleased to see each other.

The hour went quickly, dinner was perfect although there were flaky pastry crumbs scattered all over the truck. James did have something a little more serious to discuss with Bee. He told her about his meeting with the Station commander and how he'd hoped to take her to the Officers Summer Ball. That the rejection of the idea by the Station Commander was annoying him. After all, his Navigator partner Bob hasn't even met yet who he will bring. It'll be whichever girl is on his arm that week. Bee understood and reassured James that she didn't care as much as he did about it. It was a small issue given the last few weeks with all that had happened. She just wanted an easy life right now; James couldn't help agreeing. A nice quiet time, with no drama or upset would be great and, things would quieten down. People would get used to them being together and hopefully soften their stance over time.

The following weeks went smoothly, just as they had hoped. Time away from work was spent away from camp at James's place or having lunch in country pubs along the coast. When news of Bee's detachment came in it was taken well. Bee saw it as a fact, inevitable as she was expecting to be called forward and go somewhere, either that year or early the next year, she suspected nothing untoward. She was concerned at going to the gulf though. She hated extreme heat and it would be forty-five degrees at times, maybe more. She had limited knowledge of what was in store, but the training would prepare her.

When she told James, her eyes glazed over, but she didn't cry. It's four and half months away and she'd miss him. James worried for her and held her close. He couldn't look after her when she was away in operations. It was dangerous out there, he knew first-hand Iraq airspace was unpredictable. He respected that she knew her job, that she was military trained as well, if not better than he was but, that didn't override the protective feelings he had for Bee. He had never been so comfortable with someone. Bee had become his best friend, his lover and his motivation for adventure. He was planning trips together, mostly outdoors, they loved nature and seeing new places. He thought about their future together and couldn't help getting carried away. James knew Bee was his future already and although he hadn't told Bee, he assumed she felt the same. Some of the trips he planned would change to accommodate the short timeframe they had together, and some would have to wait until Bee got back. He was already worrying about what to do for such a long time without her. Bee would be busy, limited days off, he had at least two days a week, mostly at weekends. His family weren't close by and everything he thought of doing with his time he knew would be so much better if Bee was by his side.

Chapter 35 –
Marriage Guidance

The Station Commander was exasperated after the meeting with James. It's only Monday and he can see he has one hell of a week ahead. He'd call his wife Joan to let off steam, she could always calm him down.

"Hello darling, It's me. Do you have time to talk?"

"Of course, Darling, wait one while I close the door." Joan closed the door to her office and sat down to listen to her husband's woes. Regardless, the same opening greetings and response were a tradition for the couple.

"Darling I have just had Jamieson come back to me and he won't call off the relationship with McBrien."

"Oh dear, that is a worry." She rolled her eyes, sat forward and fiddled with a pen she was holding.

"That's not the end of it Darling, he only asked if he could bring McBrien to the Summer Ball."

"Which one Darling, what do you mean?"

"Our one, the Officers Mess summer ball, why which one did you mean?"

"Never mind, I'd forgotten about the ball. How many weeks away is it?"

"Four Darling." Jeremy Biggleswade was becoming exasperated, the call was meant to reassure and calm him.

"Right, I had better look at what to wear. I'm thinking of a change and a bright coloured gown this year."

"Honestly, Darling is that all you can say?" Jeremy now rolled his eyes; they were more like twins than husband and wife.

"Well, what do you want me to say?"

He refuses to be side-tracked any further. "I told him no, of course. What was he thinking?" Biggleswade snorted in the shock of it all and was shaking his head and Joan was not impressed.

"Darling, listen to me, and listen carefully. I have met some very undesirable women at these summer functions over the years. It appears it is perfectly okay for an officer to ask some girl he met just two weeks ago at the local pub, a barmaid, or a stripper no less, and bring them along, no question."

"What is your point Darling?" Jeremy Biggles was truly lost.

"My point is that McBrien is a pillar of the community, serving in the Royal Air Force as an engineer, willing to fight for Queen and country and somehow Jeremy, she is deemed not good enough!" Joan was livid. "You know it and I know it; this is just ridiculous. I am sick and tired of the rules that make little sense. I have simply had enough."

"Darling, darling, Slow down, I am sorry. I didn't mean to upset you. Please don't be upset. Are you alright? I haven't even asked you how your weekend was? Darling, I am sorry." Jeremy hated hearing his wife upset, she was usually so upbeat, so cheerful. Her never ending positivity was one of the attributes he liked her for most. She kept him going, hearing her like this was torture for him, it hurt.

"Ignore me Darling. I just wish it would end. Cinderella should go to the ball darling. It's just so unfair. You of all people know this?" She pleaded with a softer voice.

"I know Darling, I do." Jeremy knew what she was implying.

"Then do something Biggles, make a stand, make a change. Tell Jamieson he can bring McBrien. I would love to talk with her, and I'd make sure she won't be left stood alone."

"Darling you are such a kind and fair soul. I will think about it I promise. You know how delicate this situation is. I do promise you, that I will think about it though Darling."

"Very well, I will leave it with you. Just think what a difference it would make if small changes were made, baby steps darling. This could be a very large and monumental baby step towards change." With this she said her goodbyes, her voice was cracked as if she were going to cry, so she left the conversation before she did. Joan felt depressed, she sat silently in her office contemplating all she had given up for her life in the RAF and all the rules that had gotten in the way and restricted her own happiness.

Chapter 36 –
Sharing Is Caring

James had an interesting conversation with his mother. She wasn't pleased for James, that he had found someone to care about. She seemed anxious and she showed signs that she did not approve of the relationship already. James was sure that it was because she had a vision of her son climbing the ranks and having an outstanding career. James was angered by her attitude, she of all people should understand that family matters, people matter, jobs belongings and titles are all nice to haves but, not as important as people. James's mother was coming to the UK to visit him, she was visiting other family down in the south of England, flying into London. She wanted to know if James could come down to London to see her to save her the trip up to Scotland. James agreed, he was willing to do this but told his mother he would be bringing Beatrice with him. This didn't go down well with his mother, she was hoping to talk some sense into her son when she saw him. She didn't want James to have any adversity in his life.

In her mind James had already been through enough. She hadn't managed to leave behind the hard times, the difficulties of losing James's father. She loved her new life but, she still ached for the one she'd lost. She mourned not just for the loss of her husband, but for the pain their son had endured in the following years due to losing his father and coming to terms with so much change. This made her keen for James to avoid any adversity, loss or hardship. She felt he had his share of hardship already and at an incredibly young age, and she couldn't bear the thought of any more bad times for him.

James hadn't considered Bee when he told his mother that he would come to England to see her, and the rest of the extended family. He had assumed Bee would be very happy and excited to meet his family. James had an aunt and uncle he was particularly fond of. They lived near Southampton in a place called East-leigh, an hour south of London. His aunt reminded him of the Queen. She was always polished and held perfect etiquette. She never spoke badly of anyone, the perfect lady and forever calm. Her quiet strength was a huge support to James when he lost his father. She radiated a sense of certainty when she was in the room. He remembered they exchanged a knowing glance at each other in the days following his father's death that made him feel as if he would survive this pain. That he must accept what had happened and have faith life would go on. It was a lot to communicate in a look, but she had that expertise and presence.

James started to be excited, London wasn't too far from Cornwall. A place he had put on his imaginary list to take Bee. He thought it would have to wait until Bee got back from the Gulf. If they flew to London and then he hired a plane, he could get them to Cornwall and back in a long weekend. Hoping their few days of leave would be approved he started to look at flights and hotel bookings.

When James saw Bee that evening, he was so excited to tell Bee of the plans, focussing his mind on sharing Cornwall, he didn't consider that Bee might not be ready to see his family. They had only been dating a short while in the big scheme of things.

"James, slow down, I can't keep up. Your mum is visiting London and you want us both to go to see her. Where does Cornwall fit in? Are you wanting to go to the Southwest to see my parents? They are in Devon, not Cornwall, it's a different county?" Bee was trying to make sense of his plan, it seemed very old fashioned. A trip for meeting the parents.

"No, sorry Bee. Before I knew of my mum's visit, I knew I wanted to take you to a place in Cornwall. It's special, I used to go there as a kid before; well with my dad." James paused and realised he hadn't thought about Bee's parents or that she wouldn't understand his connection with Cornwall. "Bee, I am sorry. I should have thought. We can see your folks if you like. Maybe hire a car. I know I haven't told you of this place yet but, it's special." James sighs and looks down, he was getting carried away and now realises how ridiculous the plan is. "It was where my happy kid memories were made. Where I got to spend time with Dad in the holidays, and I just wanted you to see it."

Bee is so touched that he wants to share this with her and sees how fragile he looks when he mentions his father. For a split second it is like looking at a young 11-year-old James. She walks over to where he is sat and wraps her arms around him to hold him. "James, this is an amazing idea, and not at all crazy for you. Hey, on our first day you flew me to the fairy pools, so anything is possible." Bee laughs as she lets go of his shoulders. "Meeting your mum and family though, are you sure you want me to meet them or just meet you in London afterwards?"

James stands to take her in his arms and kiss her. When they finally stop and release each other he looks down into Bee's eyes. "Bee, I want you to meet everyone. I am so proud to be with you and I want you to know them, and I want to share everything with you."

"Okay, give me the dates and when I go in tomorrow, I will ask for the time off."

"Are you sure?" James watched Bee nod enthusiastically. "That's fantastic." Lifting and swinging Bee around, in that moment James felt such a rush of happiness he couldn't imagine life could get any better.

Bee, conscious of time, said, "We only have a few weeks left cowboy; let's make them count."

"Well, funny you should say that I have big plans." James laughs. "What do you think, if this weekend we go down to Loch Ness and search for the Loch Ness monster?"

"James, you're just a big kid really aren't you." Bee is laughing and wondering how she will keep up. As doubts flash through her mind, Bee starts to worry about when this bubble will burst, and all this happiness will come to an end. It's just too nice and they had both managed to work around all that the RAF had thrown at them so far. It was almost going too well.

"Bee, what's the matter?" James has noticed the mood change.

"It's nothing really, I just can't help thinking about going away, that's all."

"It'll be fine, it will pass far quicker for you than me. You'll be so busy with work you'll hardly miss me I bet." James jokes with Bee, trying to make her smile.

"Don't say that. That's not true. By the time I get back you will probably have forgotten me and moved on." She is fretting and serious. "I'll come back, and you'll be dating some tall leggy blonde that Bob has introduced you to." As she looks at James, she realises that comment hasn't gone down well, she meant to joke but her tone was way off, it sounded like an accusation.

"Are you kidding me, really? So, I am just another bloke who messes people around, Thanks a lot. I thought you knew me, Bee. Obviously not." James grabs his keys. He is so angry he needs to get away from Bee before he says something in retaliation. He has just shared how he felt about his dad and told her he wants her to meet his family and she comes straight back with a critical lack of trust that he does not deserve. James is hurt and angry, he would never do that, he wants Bee.

"Where are you going?" Bee is shocked and instantly regrets her comments.

"Out!" James's mind is now torturing him, wondering if Bee feels the same as he does.

"How long? You are leaving me here at your place?"

She realises she has spoken out of turn but surely, he realises she is insecure because of her own demons, she thinks so highly of him, she doesn't think she deserves him. Why is he with her anyway, it's crazy? Bee is just waiting for the end, any day now she thinks he could wake up and think she isn't worth it. That he'd prefer an easier life, less attention, less hassle, more prospects of promotion. James never replied to her, he just left. Was this their first argument? Or was this to be their last, Bee felt sick to her gut.

After an hour sat on her own, two cups of Chai tea later she realised she had been completely out of order. James had given her no cause for doubt, only the opposite. But surely, they could have talked about it? It didn't bode well that he left so quickly. Bee heard Big Red grumble onto the drive at the farm and her stomach flipped over again waiting for those last moments for him to come back to the flat.

"Why did you leave?" Bee comes across a bit strong, annoyed even but she wasn't. She had just gotten herself into a bit of a worried state.

"I didn't want to say something I'd regret." James looked at her. How could he be annoyed at her. She had hurt his feelings showing such little trust. Time out had made him worry more in case she wasn't as into him, and he was her. Would that be why she assumed they wouldn't last and that he'd be seeing someone else before she returned? "I am sorry Bee. I think we need to talk."

"Talk? Okay, that sounds like a one-way conversation. What is it? Are you dumping me already, to save waiting until I'm gone?" Adrenalin is running high, and she is standing confrontational in front of him.

"Are you out of your mind? No, I am not dumping you. Is that what you want? Have you had enough already? Fuck, I don't believe this." James raises his hands to hold his head at this point, he has no idea what is going on, bloody hell.

"Is it what you want? I wasn't the one who stormed out?"

"Obviously it is not what I want. I just invited you to meet my family, we were making plans to go away for Christ's sake."

This point is not lost on Bee, it's a valid point. But what if Canadians are more liberal and meeting family means nothing? Except his family is English and yes, this is a big deal. What if she doesn't want to meet them, it's too soon. If he can walk out so easy like he just did, he might do it again. She can't cope with it, her emotions are in pieces over what, she isn't even sure why they are arguing.

The pause that came from Bee thinking, albeit at lightning speed was enough for James to snap out of his confusion and grab Bee and tell her he loved her, and he kissed her before she could argue any more. They would leave this argument right there. No more words. No more stress. Bee wrapped herself around James and forgot the whole debacle. As they tore at each other's clothes in the lounge, they remembered that although they had known each other for such a short time, it was clear they fit together perfectly in a way that was beyond words.

Chapter 37 –
Sealed with a Kiss

It was near ten o'clock when they woke from a nap curled on the floor of the flat. James showered Bee in kisses on her forehead. "Please don't doubt me. I am not going anywhere."

"I'm sorry." A tear threatened to leak from her eye. "It's just been a lot to take in. Being with you is so unexpected. You've taken me by surprise Mr Jamieson." She smiled now, and her eyes now twinkled, she was trying to lighten the mood and avoid any more confrontations.

"Hey, it's okay. I am sorry too. Can't we just accept how we feel and not question it all the time?" His logic was hard to falter but was it enough?

"Yes, but—" James interrupted.

"But nothing Bee. Please don't try and find something to worry about."

"I'm not. It's just that I haven't been like this before." speaking quietly, she felt vulnerable.

"Me too and I am a hell of a lot older than you. If we examine it all the time we will miss out on just being happy. Can't we just be together and be happy?" James was tired and really didn't want to argue so he held her cheek gently, stared into her eyes and kissed her before she could find any more problems. His kisses made it feel as simple as it was. An problematic relationship, but a solid one, nonetheless.

Bee decided to stop questioning, worrying. She had thought this before but doubts crept in. Now though, she had decided and a promise to herself. Enjoy it all, throw the doubts aside and put her faith in James.

Chapter 38 –
Bedruthan Steps

Sarge approved Bee's leave pass. It was short notice, and they would have to make do, many were on holiday taking their kids away. He wanted Bee to have a break and she was only extending a weekend by three days; she wasn't being greedy. She and Paul would have to go to RAF Prestwick near Glasgow when she returned, to service and collect some equipment that had been shipped back to the wrong location. He let her know this as he approved her leave, so she would come back prepared for the five days away when she returned. Paul could cope on his own on the Squadron without Bee for a day or two, he had proved that already. Whenever he looked at Bee, he still felt guilty for doubting her and he wanted somehow to make amends, signing off her leave pass, requested at short notice, was a good place to start.

James and Bee flew from Inverness to London Gatwick with a cheap airline. Then took a car to his Aunt Susie and Uncle Richard's house in Eastleigh. It took over three hours from landing and they were both shattered. They had managed to get the flights at short notice, but they needed to be at the airport for six in the morning. James booked them into a nice spa hotel nearby in Winchester to compensate. Plus, he was sure his aunt and uncle wouldn't allow them to share a bedroom and he was not willing to be apart from Bee if he didn't need to be, they'd be apart for many months soon enough.

His aunt and uncle were wonderful, kind, funny and relaxed. His sister Monica had come along for the trip, she loved the UK and her heritage intrigued her. She was a passionate young lady, keen to talk about animal welfare, the environment and global warming. She had so much knowledge of global matters that Bee felt ignorant and humbled by Monica. At her age Bee barely knew what was going on in her own house let alone around the world. Bee really liked Monica and all her energy, zest and moral opinions. She had a cheeky sense of humour too, sarcastic but not too heavy, pretty much the sort of things that went on in

Bee's head, Monica said out loud with no filter. It was a shame Bee didn't feel the same about James's mother, Margaret. She was aloof and didn't want to engage, and she kept her conversation short which made Bee feel very unwelcome. Luckily James's aunt and uncle were socially adept and took over so that Bee was included, and they soon kept Bee at a distance from the coldest conversationalist in the room. James had noted his mum's frostiness but had politely not challenged her on it whilst others were around. Monica had too, and to compensate she had showered Bee with encouraging compliments and asked Bee about her engineering career, citing girl power and all manner or clichés.

What was it with James's mum and her hostility? In time Bee may understand, she was sure James would find out what was going on when the moment was right, although it seemed there wouldn't be time on this trip.

They left to head for the hotel after eight that night and popped in after breakfast the next day. The second visit James's mum seemed on edge, and she could not even look at Bee. Words had obviously been exchanged with Monica, maybe even the aunt and uncle had stepped in? James told his mum that he'd bring Bee out to Canada when she returned from detachment, either spring or summer, and he said he'd call her soon. Bee knew not to make a big deal of hugging and saying goodbye, she left after big hugs from Monica and some kind words wishing them a good trip from Uncle Richard and Aunt Susie.

James and Bee drove back up to Gatwick to collect a small plane that they charter to get to Cornwall, all perfectly arranged. On return they only had to drop the small plane off and head back up to Scotland on a connecting commercial flight.

They were soon in the air again, this time in a small four-seater propeller plane. The weather was glorious. James had warned Bee she would be hot in flight. Bee was so excited, she had not seen her home counties from the air. They would follow the main motorways and roads to where they were to land, flying right over where she grew up. She'd called her folks, and after talking to them had decided to skip a visit this time. Her parents were sad but supportive of Bee, despite the digs and dry humour, her happiness was all that mattered really. They were pleased she was being treated well and doing something fun. With only a couple of days off they wanted her to spend it well, not rushing around like a postman to so many houses, visiting too many people. They would see her as soon as she came back from detachment and meet James then. Until then, they'd continue to speak to her every week on the condition that she promised to send an updated photo of her with 'this fella James' she was dating.

Bee was so in awe of flying and the views at two thousand feet meant you saw it all, it still felt so close beneath. She had been terrified when they went on the commercial flight but, she had hidden it well. To some this would seem illogical but, to her it was rational thinking. Commercial flights crashed if they lost power, small planes could glide their way down and still land safely. Commercial planes were too technical, there was much more to go wrong. Lastly, there was the RAF, the little plane was looked after by the best engineers and she had the best, an RAF pilot in James. She had no doubts he would get her there and back safely, her respect for his flying capability was given without question.

James was in utopia flying with Bee sat next to him. He was so excited about the trip, and he felt he had so much to look forward to with Bee by his side. "Are you doing okay Bee?" He wanted to check but also, just to let Bee know it was okay to talk over the headset as they followed the M5 motorway south.

"Yes, I love it. It's so beautiful James, I don't think I will ever be bored of this." Bee's smile reinforced just how much, she was beaming.

"Me too, and I've been flying for years. It's so relaxing, I think it's heavenly really in these small planes. You just float along." James wanted her to know what it felt like, to be in charge of the plane. "You know you should learn to fly Bee, then I won't struggle to explain. It really is hard to put into words what it feels like."

"No way, I think I'd be too nervous and all those dials, I wouldn't have a clue." Bee laughed off his suggestions as ludicrous.

"No Bee, it really is easy, because they teach you it all slowly, it's just simple engineering. Why do you laugh like that, you could do it, easily, really easily?" James was sad by how quickly Bee laughed the idea off as unachievable. Why did she think it was such a crazy idea?

"James, until I met you, I'd never been in a plane. The idea of me actually flying one is too surreal." Bee tried to explain without sounding underconfident. She hadn't come from a privileged background; she had never thought of flying or a whole host of other hobbies as attainable, so she hadn't given it a glancing thought. It must cost a fortune as well, it was for posh people surely, not for normal people.

"Bee, I will teach you one day. Promise me you will keep an open mind? I really would love to share how this feels. I think you'd be hooked, and I think

162

you'd be a great pilot too; you can fly me around next time we head up to the islands."

He jokes now but his intent is serious. He would love nothing more than to share everything with her that he values, and he is so grateful he can fly. There really was no other hobby or job he would rather have. Bee was quiet, this was all too much to imagine, she stared at the dials and controls and was unsure she could ever understand it.

"Hey, Bee, promise me you will try when you get back from Detachment?" He was serious now.

"Okay, I will try it. If I can't do it or I hate it though, you promise me I can quit? It looks scary as hell." They both laughed at that, although James was confident, she would love every second behind the controls.

"I think you'll love it, holding the controls at two thousand feet, on a nice day is like a form of meditation; time stands still. It really does. Just promise me?"

"Okay, okay, I promise, now let it go fly boy, I said yes!" James nodded in satisfaction. Bee started to think about what it would be like, such a crazy idea. Maybe he would forget by the time she came back. Four and a half months apart can make you forget a lot.

As they reached the counties of the west country, they started to point at the beauty it held from the sky. Bee was excited at recognising places she had been. When they neared RAF St Mawgan on the Cornish coast, Bee fell quiet again. It was stunning from the air, just breath taking. James kept glancing in her direction and took pleasure seeing her transfixed on the views, smiling and eyes wide open. James felt so lucky, he couldn't do this with any other girlfriend. Bee was different. She was outgoing and as an engineer didn't freak out at popping here and there in a tin can aircraft, not much larger than a family car.

When they landed, they were given a lift to a hotel on a clifftop in a nearby town of Mawgan Porth. Bee found it a stark reminder that they were different ranks when all the RAF staff they met called James, 'sir'. Also, they were professionally distant and polite. Had she have landed at her rank, well she'd have been engaged in conversation for a while, full of banter and been called 'mate' or some endearing yet sarcastic nickname like 'fly girl', or 'Birdie'.

The hotel looked just like a white box sixties motel, nothing special from the road just utilitarian but, once you were inside you understood why the front of the hotel didn't matter. The hotel's envelope hides its blossoming beauty; it holds cinematic views and a vibe of relaxing acceptance that brings out the best behaviour of all who cross the threshold. Families laugh quietly as children beam in pure joy, and grandparents watch with the upmost pride as if their lives have led to this very goal; that they have accomplished in making the warmest memories. Every room possible had floor to ceiling glass windows overlooking the sea views. There were lounges, cocktail bars, children's playgrounds, swimming pools and restaurants all facing out to the uninterrupted clifftop views of Mawgan Porth bay. The soft golden sands and the ocean crashing against the rocks are mesmerising and hypnotic.

"You came here as a kid? Really?" Bee had no idea people had holidays in such places. She had gone to the beach on day trips. They had soggy sandwiches and she returned home with sand scratching every crease of her body after haphazardly dressing behind a towel on the beach. They didn't stay for a week in a hotel full of things to do and views, just a few hours and she hadn't known of this other tribe of holiday makers.

"Yes, this is the place. We always stayed in a family room facing out to sea. I got us a standard double, it's all they had left at short notice, sorry." James was proud of this part of his childhood.

"Wow, James you were so lucky to have this. What else have you been up to as a kid?" Bee was worried her life would seem bland and inadequate.

"Nothing, this was it, Dad brought us here every summer for a week. There were no other holidays, we used to go to local places on day's off from time to time, but we just waited for our special holiday." James was smiling from ear to ear. "It was better than Christmas." James was excited when he talked. He knew he had been lucky having those times. His friends went camping or to traditional holiday camps, and yet he went to this magical place that no one knew of, relaxed, happy, spoilt with time and such fun, it was a hotel but, a hotel with a difference.

Bee was bowled over yet again by James and how much he loved all the things that she considered precious, time, nature and the things in life that cannot be bought. They had two nights together here to explore, enjoy and make new memories. The type of memories that last a lifetime.

To start with hot drinks and a seat with a view in the main bar. The fire was glowing and crackling behind them, even on this hot day. Surrounding them people read or chatted quietly. Bee looked at the seagulls and black birds diving and soaring past the cliffs. There were a few homes on the cliffs that joined them, they had odd Dutch style roofs iced with moss. The small mound of rocks that seemed to have broken away on the beach drew her eye. These rocks are the Bedruthan steps, and local legend tells that they are simply the stepping-stones for a friendly Celtic giant called Bedruthan. The sea around them captivated Bee, and as the water crashed and diverted around the steps to seek land, she gazed and followed the tide coming and going.

Then they took their bags to their room after drinks so they could unpack and get ready for some time in the spa. The task should have taken ten minutes but, once inside the room, one look at Bee as she stared out of the window in awe of nature, made James come alive with thirst for her. They entwined into a hot and passionate embrace with the view as a backdrop and the noise of the sea crashing onto the rocks next to them. The light was fading when they finally decided to move. Their plan needed to change and divert to the Wild Café bar for sustenance before they could head to the spa.

Later, the large hot bubbling pool surrounded by candles and sumptuous loungers were bliss. There were fresh jugs of water and silver carafes of hot herbal tea in the centre, offering refreshment. Hugging a silver mug and smelling the warmed tones of hibiscus and green tea helped them relax and recover before they retired again to their room.

James and Bee grew closer with every passing moment they were there. They hardly left the hotel, too content in their surroundings.

On the last morning they agreed they needed to walk down to the beach. It was a steep walk down to the beach following the slim private pathway, lined in wild blackberries. It was chilly in the tidal breeze, they had set an alarm to make sure they got to the bottom at sunrise. They had brought a blanket from the room and sat at the bottom of the hill, wrapped together in their wool cocoon.

"Bee, I don't want you to freak out on me but, I need to talk to you about something." James was nervous but he was steadfast that he needed to do this.

"What? What is it? What's wrong?" Bee had found a happiness that was so precious, no matter how much she tried, she was on constant guard, worried it would be taken from her.

"Okay, it's simple really" – James took a deep breath – "When you get back, I want us to move in together, I want to be with you like this, not just here and there in between shifts. We can wake up together every day, it feels right." There he had said it. He knew Bee felt the same so why was she so quiet. "Bee? Say something?"

"I don't know what to say. How? Where? My head is spinning."

Bee felt euphoric but also totally bewildered that this was all happening. She had been a sceptic about relationships ever since she was an early teen. She had been the one to comfort her friends when they had sobbed, break up after break up. Always due to the same pattern. The boy and girl would meet, apparently be in love overnight, they'd then have sex together. Then the boy got bored and moved on, and it was devastating for the young girl who thought her life wasn't worth living after such a fickle and foreseeable rejection. Was she falling into this trap at twenty? No, this was real, grown up real and far more perfect than she had thought possible.

As Bee stared at James, barely taking it in; James asked her again and reassured her he would take care of it all while she was away. He'd find a flat close to Station. It would give him something to focus on to stop him brooding about her too much. With the confidence and openness of James wants and his worries; Bee threw caution aside and said yes, showering James in small, excited kisses as she repeated her acceptable over and over.

Chapter 39 –
As the Penny Finally Drops

Bee was sent off to Prestwick as planned the day after they returned from Cornwall. James was happy remembering Bee in his arms and the closeness they had shared, but the time away from Bee gave him too much time to think. The RAF rules gnawed away at him. Bee had said she was okay with not attending the summer ball; he wasn't. Bee wasn't a passing fling, she was who he wanted to be with, and James hoped and expected them to be together in the long term. He was serious about Bee and the Ball was one of many occasions she would be banned from. He needed to fight this; he could chip away at the boss so he would be on his side. He'd show them he was serious. Then with support he could take it higher, change had to happen surely. They were all led to believe without question that change wasn't possible, that the rules were stuck solid, but it isn't true.

Bee was one of the first women engineers, well the only one to stick it out past a year so far, she was tough. The RAF had female pilots since the second world war, not operational pilots, reservists helping on engineering missions at home. Then recently, in 1990 there was the first female operational fighter pilot, and James knew her, she was good, damn good. So, change was possible, it just took exceptional people to make a stand and prove it was worth it. He tried to speak to Bob about it, but Bob was adamant that James should not be with Bee, let alone that the RAF should relax the archaic rules to condone their affair. James was angered by Bob's reactions. Why was he being so bloody ignorant and old fashioned. Was Bob jealous of James finding something much deeper than Bob's indifferent and fleeting hook ups? Bee wasn't a lesser being because of her job choice. The snobby hierarchy held in place in the RAF was encouraged and nurtured by the few upper-class uptight officers, but Bob wasn't from that ilk? So, why was Bob so annoyed and opinionated about them being together? Why couldn't he at least count on Bob to be at his side, to cover him just like he did in the sky. The injustice and betrayal he felt by Bob reacting this way ate away at him. It made him more determined he would do something about it and fight. He decided to request a meeting with his boss, and then to take it all the way back to the Station Commander. When he tells them about her, about them living together and building a future, they would surely have to give Bee a chance.

It wasn't going to plan. James's boss was dismissive. He told him that he'd been seeing McBrien for such a short time. How could he possibly know they had a future together?

"James, listen to me, I have been married to Sarah for five years, we dated for seven years before that, and I still have doubts we have future together every time I try to find anything of mine in the bathroom." He sounded exasperated as if James was asking for something he would later regret. "Honestly, give it some more time. Maybe next year if you are still together it would be worth taking the risk?"

The risk, James heard the word risk as if he were contemplating a fool hardy mission, outnumbered by the enemy aircraft seeking to destroy him while under constant ground to air attack to increase the odds of his demise.

"I don't think you understand, I'm a grown man and I know what I want. Can we ground ourselves here a minute? It's a function, not a mission. Bob will be bringing some girl he probably met last night, and he won't know the first thing about her."

For a few minutes no one spoke, the only noise was the boss's tapping pen on the table and the humming sound of a jet taxing outside. No one could argue that Bob probably would bring someone unsuitable to the ball and it wouldn't impact on the RAF sensibilities or Bob's career. The boss sat forward and reached for his desk phone.

"Squadron Leader Gray here, could I speak to the Station Commander please?"

James was on the edge of his seat, his elbows on his knees and his hands clasped together, he sat perfectly quietly as minutes passed by. This was it; his boss was behind him.

"Sir, I am sorry to disturb you, sir. I have a delicate matter, sir. And I would appreciate your guidance."

"Of course Gray, how can I help you?" Biggleswade was lifted by a call for help. He loved the chance to guide and support his Officers. It was rare they asked him and, like a proud father he was keen to help.

"It's Jamieson, sir. I have him here with me and we have a predicament, sir."

"Oh Good God, Gray, it's McBrien again isn't it, she isn't pregnant, or something is she?"

"Oh no, sir. Nothing like that. No, it's just Jamieson has put forward that they have a long-term future together, sir. He expects this relationship to go all the way, sir."

"Right, understood. That is unfortunate news Gray." Biggles eyebrows raised and he exhaled though his nostrils loudly, he wasn't sure how he could help with this one. He was really hoping the call would give him a chance to show how useful he could still be, even though he was bound to his desk by politics and policy. He knew James was a courageous fighter pilot which meant he probably wasn't going to back down.

"Sir, Jamieson would like to bring McBrien to the summer ball and he makes quite a good argument that this should be considered." The boss knew he was pushing his luck, Biggles wasn't one for change and could bite if someone was pushing their luck.

"I have already told Jamieson that it is not going to happen. It is simply not allowed. It isn't my rules Gray, it's just the way it is." Biggles was restless in his seat and stood, hand in one pocket to stop him gesticulating as if he were conducting an orchestra.

"Yes, sir." Gray waited, he knew there would be more to be said by the traditionalist Station Commander and thought better of pushing any further.

"Gray, it is simply not an option, what case has he put forward that made you think it was possible? Come on now, tell me as I really don't see what he could possibly say to you to warrant you escalating this to me."

"Well, sir, the thing is, many of the young chaps will bring a local girl they have only just met. Just to have someone on their arm, sir." Gray was about to continue but Biggles interrupted sharply.

"And what has that got to do with it Gray? That is of no consequence, none at all."

For some reason Gray had forgotten to retreat and care for his own relationship with the Station Commander. "But it is, sir. It is exactly the point. We let it go, brush it aside if someone totally unsuitable is brought to our mess. Some leaving before midnight due to drinking too fast or, falls asleep in a corner and snores as we see in the day with our champagne breakfast. We don't hold it against the Officer who brought them, it is laughed off and the girl in question is never seen again, sir. It's not even an issue."

"Listen to me Gray. I have no problem with a lady we will never see again letting herself down and being the laughingstock." Biggles raises his voice to the level of authority that a Churchill speech would command. "I will not have one of my airmen in the same position. McBrien has had no formal training for such an occasion, and she has to resume her duties afterwards. She must do that without our judgement and with her reputation intact, do you understand Gray? I will simply not take the risk of such a discord."

"Yes, sir. Understood, sir." There was no goodbye, the Station Commander had put the phone down on him as soon as he heard Gray agree. There would be no room for further discussion.

Gray replaced the received gently and looked at James. "James, he is really pissed. He put the phone down, it's not what you think."

"Then what is it then? Why is it such a problem for him?"

"It's about protecting McBrien." James scrunches his brow, wondering what from. "I think the Station Commander thinks McBrien would be risking her reputation if she attended. She would be put in a place of judgement and scrutiny. You know how some people can be, especially some of the wives."

"What do you mean? I don't follow you. What are you trying to get at?" James is angry and his tone isn't received well by his boss. Gray had just challenged the Station Commander for him, he could show some acknowledgement of this at least.

"She has to go back to work James, after whatever happens in the mess. McBrien has to go back to her day job and pretend she wasn't quaffing cocktails with us all. She must Salute, be subservient to us. It's not healthy for her. Have you stopped to consider her James? Don't you think she been through enough?" As soon as Gray said those last words he regretted them. It was a low blow.

James was wounded by this and felt instantly deflated. He didn't want to remember what had happened to Bee. He carried a misplaced guilt that she had been a target by the lowlife who had attacked her because of them being together. "Thank you for your time."

James got up to leave but before he went through the door, he turned back he spoke formally to his boss, so as not to lose the friendship he had gained from working with him.

"We need to change, sir. I understand but change needs to start somewhere."

With this John Gray nodded at James, he knew that although he had convinced James and himself that change was not happening today, and for all good reason, he knew and agreed that it was nonsensical to judge lower ranks as fragile, lower class or irrelevant. He thought they were world class and highly capable, and this played on his mind until he returned home to his family. Soon after, playing with his boys had taken his mind off his day and it would all be forgotten.

Chapter 40 –
An Angels Love

The Station Commander secretary, Sergeant Claire Johnson knocked on his office door and announced that his wife, Squadron Leader Joan Biggleswade had arrived. She was currently signing in at the main gate. A few moments later she arrived full of energy into his office to deliver a double cheek kissing embrace.

"Darling, Darling, so good to be here." After she released Biggles, she looked him up and down like a mother. "Have you been keeping well Jeremy, you look a little tired my Darling."

"I'm fine, just a little tired. It's been a busy time preparing reports for Strike Command. I also have this blasted airfield resurfacing to organise Darling, it's tedious. It feels as if we only just completed the last resurfacing a little while ago, when will it stop?" With this he returns to his chair whilst his wife Joan looks around and takes off her coat.

"Jeremy it really does feel like the smallest office possible, it's a cupboard. How can you be expected to work in this place? What is it, three meters by three?" Her office in Wales by contrast, is at least four times the size and includes a sofa area which came in very handy at times. She was hoping for the hard work to reach the top would bring rewards of grandeur. "Is there really nowhere else you could make your office?"

"It's fine Joan, really. I hardly notice." He secretly favours a smaller office, as then he isn't expected to hold meetings here and hardly anyone bothers him. No more than one or two people at a time can fit in. Anything more would need a meeting room to be arranged in advance which, often was too much trouble and, if he did go to a meeting, he could leave at any time. His approach forces general issues to be sorted without bothering him but, this is an accidental bonus; his primary reason is he is fearful of being trapped anywhere and always needs an escape route. Boarding school was a tough time for him, the discipline was tough. The hard work didn't bother him, being locked in the cupboard in nothing but his grey underwear did, and it remained his most feared demon that held him, only because he had never told anyone about what happened, not a living soul.

"Don't be silly darling size always matters, on this we can agree, can't we?" they both smiled. "How is George by the way? Did you enjoy your trip together?"

They both started to chuckle and nod. "Yes Darling, we did. And how is Chief Tech Griffith? Wasn't it such a coincidence that he was in Bath the same weekend as you?"

There was a knock at the door and tea arrived on a wooden tray, a white pristine porcelain tea pot and cups and saucers laid out neatly and a silver spoon. They always used the nice crockery when the Station Commanders wife visited. She was a popular, uplifting woman with much zeal for life. She had authority about her even in civilian clothes and she often taken an interest in the staff at HQ, even though this wasn't her station. She encouraged learning and courses mostly, after all as an education officer it was her passion, she loved to see people grow in confidence and become happier for it.

Now sat and enjoying a garibaldi and tea they talk about the summer ball.

"I have a rather gorgeous dress for the Ball, but I also brought my mess dress uniform with me Darling, which do you think I should wear?" Joan is keen to please her husband.

"Either is fine Darling, you always look lovely, and you are the only woman I know who could pull off wearing a black sack and still look divine." Joan smiles at Jeremy, he does adore her, and she knows he means every word.

"Jeremy, I have been meaning to ask, how is McBrien and our lovely Jamieson, still together? I looked up his records, he's quite a dish isn't he. McBrien has done well." Joan means to be cheerful, but her husband looks forlorn.

"Yes, yes, they are. It's quite a situation Joan, I don't think this is a passing fling." Jeremey Biggles looks so troubled, as if he is the one expected to sort it all out, as if it would reflect badly on him if he can't make it all go away.

Joan leans forward and places her saucer on the table but, remains leaning forward to address her husband in a serious tone. "Jeremy, I want you to listen to me. It is time you sort this out."

"I know, but what can I do, I can't stop them if they are determined. I can't lock them up for heaven's sake." Jeremy is anxious and exasperated, it had clearly been playing on his mind.

"That is not what I mean Jeremy. I mean it is time for change. Don't you think it is time?" She remains forward and stares Jeremy in the eye, a stare without any blinking, it was almost threatening.

"Are you completely mad Joan, what are you saying? You know it's not possible. It would degrade the respect between the ranks."

"No Jeremy, that is utter nonsense, and we have hidden behind that sort of hogwash for long enough."

"But Joan—"

"No buts Jeremy, haven't enough lives been ruined? Haven't enough people sacrificed their happiness for the RAF, for us to know it wasn't necessary." There was a pause but, as Jeremy was about to speak, Joan upped her campaign. "When does it stop? When? Do we, and all the others tell the truth when we retire? For what? For our friends to abandon us because we lied to them for years?"

Jeremey was floored, he didn't know what to say anymore, Joan had made it personal, he could no longer detach from the situation. "Jeremy, we have lost years, and I love you with all my heart, you know I do. You are my best friend and I can't live without you. But I should be able to be with Callum, and you should be with George. Proudly, without hiding." As Joan raised to her feet Jeremy was aghast. "Jeremy, you must take a stand now, and if you do, change will come. Maybe not in our lifetime but, it will come." Joan reminds him with flared nostrils. "You are well respected, and no one will think any less of you, quite the contrary." Joan stood still, staring at her husband.

She hated hurting his feelings, or any confrontation. But she needed things to change, and she needs to be part of that change. She had sacrificed the life she should have had. She had wanted Callum's children. She had wanted it all, and only continued with their sham of a marriage because she had promised Jeremy before she knew Callum that she would always be there to cover him and support him. A promise made that she could not bring herself to break, integrity of a promise is the backbone of the RAF and it the RAF is who they are.

Jeremy had known this and carried the guilt with him for years, he loved Joan and wanted her to have her happy ending. He too wanted his life with George to be open but, he couldn't for a single second ever dream of it happening, so he hadn't given it the head space to grow into an issue.

As Joan stood there, she felt frustrated to the point she may cry. They stared at each other but, no more words were said. Joan, holding her car keys in both hands in front of her nodded a little and turned to leave. She was an accomplished actress after all these years, she was jolly and charming to the staff on her way out of the building, no one saw how much she was hurting, normal service was resumed. In her head she thought to herself, *right, the dress, I will wear the dress. Tonight, the uniform doesn't own me.*

Back in his office Jeremy sat still at his desk, and when there was a knock on his door, he told them he was not to be disturbed without even looking up to see who it was. He needed to recover from what Joan had said to him. He felt deeply sad that Joan was hurting, the pain it gave him seeing her like that was too much. He pondered, had he been too accepting of the rules, he asked no questions as to the suitability of the rules. He certainly hadn't thought of himself as someone who could start a wave of change, no matter how small. He was a born rule follower, not some sort of trailblazer. He was far too reserved and stuck in his ways to do anything of the sort. Ever since school he'd been that way, where he had learned painfully to do what was expected of him, or he'd be back in that small dark place again, he was conditioned to comply.

An hour past and he was still thinking, and he hadn't moved. His mood had changed from sadness, to feeling infuriated by the system. He had passed through various feelings along the way, bereft for Joan's inability to have been a mother. Stupid for not considering what would happen when they retire and, bewilder-ment. Joan was right. He wondered how on earth could they come clean without causing such a fuss amongst their friends, that would have to remain a puzzle he couldn't solve. He was incensed that the rules had ultimately led to McBrien being a victim. If there were no boundaries, that lowlife bully Wright wouldn't have had a weakness to exploit, she may not have been attacked by him.

He finally stood and started to pace the office, over and over thinking of the reasons why the HM Forces rules governing relationships, some formally writ-ten, some not written, were now unwarranted and damaging. You can't be gay or bisexual, you can't love someone of the wrong rank. You definitely can't be single, that was a career killer if you wanted promotion past Squadron Leader and, just as much taboo as the other ridiculous rules. He picked up the phone to call 617 Squadron and speak to Jamieson's boss.

"Squadron leader Gray, it's Wing Commander Biggleswade here."

"Hello, sir. How can I help you today, sir?" The Squadron Leader started to worry, the station Commander only called with bad news generally, a threat level had risen, an urgent deployment or one of his team had messed up.

"I have been giving it a lot of thought Squadron Leader and my wife, Squadron Leader Biggleswade has been bending my ear. She has a very solid career of her own down in St Athan, don't you know?"

"Yes, sir. I was aware, she is very well respected I hear." Gray was confused by the Station Commanders familiarity.

"Well, the matter is, I have decided McBrien can come to the Officers Mess Ball. We must support such decorated officers and our troops, not divide them."

"But sir—" The Squadron Leader was desperately trying to tell the Station Commander something.

"But nothing Gray, I have decided it is time for small changes to occur to show our boys and girls we are not outdated ogres stuck in the past, and we are here, in the now and we are right behind them."

"But sir, if I may?"

"No, you may not Squadron Leader. Do you not think our boys and girls, who go to the most horrid places, and to all lengths when we ask of them, deserve our support in such small ways?"

"Well yes, sir, I do." Gray needed to tell him it wasn't going to happen.

"Good, then I will leave you to break the news to Jamieson."

"It won't matter, sir. I was trying to tell you she isn't here. She is in Prestwick until Monday, she will miss the Ball, we thought it was best, sir. That she was out of the way." The Station Commander without any hesitation lost his temper.

"Prestwick, that's not outer Mongolia or Australia Squadron Leader. Get her back here. Get her back here right now, today."

"But sir—" Gray pleaded.

"What now Gray? Have I not made myself perfectly clear?"

"Yes, sir, only, it's hours away, sir. If we send a car now, we probably won't get her back today, sir."

"This is the RAF Squadron Leader, not the blasted girl guides. You can't get her back today? What is wrong with you? Have we lost all of our helicopters on 22 Squadron, send a bloody Sea King to search and rescue her if you have to. Call the Squadron now and tell them I have given the order to seek and extract McBrien today."

"Yes, sir, erm, what shall we call the trip, sir, for the paperwork?"

"I don't give a flying hoot what you call the bloody trip Gray, you can call it Operation Cinderella for all I care, just get it bloody done! I want her dropped back home to base today!"

The phone is now slammed down hard. The Squadron Leader cannot aggravate him anymore with any trivial nonsense. Jeremy can't sit, his adrenaline is throbbing in his temples so he grabs his hat and decides to leave for home where he can tell Joan what he has just done. He has done it for her, for his Joan, he had taken a stand.

Chapter 41 –
Flying High

At the other end, the Squadron Leader opens his office door and calls for his Chief to be found and sent to him straight away. He is annoyed at the Station Commanders tone and misuse of resources but starts to fill out the paperwork, for Operation Cinderella. He will pretend he thought the Station Commander was being serious should he be pulled up on this name debacle afterwards. In the moment, he was totally unaware of the level of attention the code name Cinderella would attract across the station and beyond.

After briefing his team and calling 22 Squadron, he called the Ground Engineering Flight to inform Bee's boss, little Willie Wallace, that McBrien would be extracted from Prestwick in style and offer to drop in a replacement engineer should it be needed. Finally, he remembered to tell James. Who was stunned by the unexpected turn of events, and after telling Bob, he went to find out where to meet Bee so he could bring her home.

The Sea King helicopter was in the air in under twenty minutes and word spread across the until about Operation Cinderella just as quickly. At the Ground Engineering Flight, Bee's team came to an outright stop and they all gathered for an impromptu tea break to dispel any rumours. Sarge had arrived with the Boss to give them a briefing to calm them down and get them back to work.

The Sarge had asked them to listen in, but they continued to gossip and mutter, there was an electric energy in the room, anticipation. He needed to shout to get them to concentrate.

"ATTENTION!"

The room sloppily brought themselves to stand to attention as directed and the Sarge added,

"QU-I-ET!"

The room instantly obeyed, and stragglers had now caught up.

"You are all no doubt wondering what is going on and you have heard of an operation ongoing at this time." Sarge couldn't bring himself to say the code name Cinderella.

"The Boss will address you now and answer any valid questions." Adding and emphasising the word valid to warn the team to behave and not act childishly.

The Boss, Wallace stood as tall as he could, which wasn't the most towering stance considering his size, he then addressed the team.

"At ease men."

The room relaxed their stance.

"The Station Commander in his generosity, has decided to provide discretion to McBrien and her ongoing relationship with an esteemed pilot of 617 Squadron. Furthermore, he has ordered that McBrien is extracted back to base urgently so she may attend, as a guest, the Officers Mess Summer Ball."

As soon as the words were out the team murmured and started to talk amongst themselves again, Sarge had to shout once more to gain their attention and bring about rightful order.

The Boss then continued with a standard closing comment. "Right, are there any questions?"

A broad Scottish accent carried over from the back of the room. "Aye, is she pregnant then? Is that why we are good enough for you lot now then, eh?" Luckily the owner of the voice could not be seen, the Boss replied swiftly.

"No, she is not pregnant and there are to be no rumours of any kind." – He cleared his throat as if he was embarrassed to say – "Just to be perfectly clear to you all; you are ALL good enough and, it has never been a question of that sort of thing, never."

He held them in his stare and the belief evident in his voice.

"You horrible lot are the finest engineers in the world. The rank system is just about keeping order, nothing else, do you understand?" A few mumbles of 'yes' were heard but not enough for the boss, so he raised his voice and repeated "DO YOU understand?"

"YES, SIR!" A united crowd confirmed, and the boss nodded and left. Laughter was heard as he walked away.

The Boss hadn't been held with much respect amongst his engineers to date. They thought he was too unassuming, and he kept himself to himself. They were shocked at his quick reply and his praise, and it gave them a lift that he seemed to have a glimpse of humour. Some joked, "Aye, if we are the best there is, then we are all fucked now eh lads." The atmosphere was euphoric. They decided to meet Bee as she got off the flight and headed over to the squadron in one of the workshop vans.

Sid took charge of the plan, they'd have airfield clearance in a squadron van, with regulation flashing lights on top and a radio so the tower could contact them. They wanted to be part of getting their Cinders to the ball. They piled in, squeezing more than a dozen of them into the van and they set off to 22 Squadron, no consideration for where Bee would fit. They'd wait in the Squadron until they heard on the radio which bay the helicopter had landed at and then they'd pounce.

Chapter 42 –
A New Start

Joan came out of the kitchen where she had been staring out of the window whilst waiting for the microwave to ping. "Jeremy, why are you home already? Are you felling alright?"

"Not really Darling, not really." He looked edgy.

"Is this about earlier? I am so sorry Jeremy, I didn't mean it, I didn't mean to upset you."

"I hope you did mean it Darling, as it's all done now." Jeremy slumped heavily into a floral sofa that sat inside the mint green front room of the station Commanders house.

"What's done Jeremy? What do you mean?"

"Are there any staff here, can we talk?" He looked over his shoulder as he asked.

"No, no one is here, do you want tea and then you can tell me?" Joan British to the core, believed that if in doubt, make tea.

"No Joan, a whiskey. This needs somethings stronger." He got up again and walked over to an ornate globe drinks cabinet and lifted open the lid. Joan sat down, she was perched on tenterhooks. She asked him to bring her a whiskey too, she had a feeling she may need it.

"Joan, I have given permission for McBrien to come to the Ball." He drank a large gulp of dark Scotch whiskey neat and then needed a sharp intake of breath to recover.

"That's good of you Jeremy." Joan sounded flat, confused, and was beginning to feel more concerned for what he just said.

"You don't sound too happy about it, Joan? It's what you wanted?"

"I am darling, I am. I just didn't expect it, Jeremy. It's tomorrow, the Ball is tomorrow, there is so much to do before then." Joan's mind was ten steps ahead as usual.

"What do you mean lots to do? The staff have my mess dress ready, and you said you have a choice of what to wear?" She's lost Jeremy completely as her mind spins into action.

"Darling, McBrien won't have a stock of ball gowns hiding in her closet or a remote clue of the etiquette of the ball. If we don't send some help, she may turn up inappropriately dressed at such short notice or worse, not turn up at all."

"Great, it's a bloody disaster already. Not to mention that the imbecile of a Squadron Leader Gray over at 617, only went and called it operation Cinderella!" As he looked over to Joan, he realised he hadn't told her everything. "I'll get you another drink darling, I haven't told you the best bit yet. My career may be laying in tatters when Strike Command finds out what I've done."

Joan laughs uncontrollably when Jeremy tells her everything, and by what means it all unfolded. She has a knack of always seeing something positive and turning a poor situation on its head. Joan reassures him that with his impeccable leadership record, he can easily convince anyone who questions his actions that the mission was to boost station morale. The squadrons had been back and forth on missions constantly to various desolate places. They were over stretched it had notably impacted upon station morale, resignations were up, and the Station Medical Officer had informed them that there had been a rise in mental health issues amongst the unit staff, with nearly sixty of the five hundred staff now downgraded and unable to be deployed due to depression or similar. Joan said they would applaud his investment and support towards his people and, she was later proven to be right.

*

When the powers that be expectedly challenged the Station Commander, they left the conference call in awe of his ingenuity. Joan had prepared him a list of other initiatives to improve health and wellbeing of his staff, that would in turn increase operational capacity. Such as rugby matches, functions and charitable expeditions. After the call the collective of high-ranking officers at Strike Command praised Wing Commander Biggleswade as a forward-thinking leader, an investor in people. They were so pleased with him they recommended he be considered for an award by Her majesty the Queen in the New Year Honours list.

It was a mystery to Jeremy why he was so easily recognised, and repeatedly so, year after year to become Station Commander. Yet his beloved wife Joan, the true inspirational leader of the pair, was so easily overlooked.

Chapter 43 –
Incoming

News came over the radio in 22 Squadron control, the helicopter was on approach. Squadron Leader Gray came into the room and asked the bunch of greasy engineers what they were doing there. He knew, but he was enjoying asserting his authority.

Sid spoke up for the team most respectfully. "Sir, we are here as part of Operation Cinderella, sir. To collect the package, sir."

"Well then Corporal, you and your team seem to be in the wrong location." Squadron Leader Gray enjoyed delivering this message, he was smiling and trying not to laugh. "The direction from upon high was very clear indeed. The package was to be returned back to base without delay, so we are delivering directly to Ground Engineering Flight Corporal."

Sid was stunned but worried. "But sir, we have no room for a Heli to land?"

"Now Corporal, who said we were landing? Package Cinderella will be dropped by cable." He laughed as the engineering team seemed to realise in unison what was about to happen.

Sid jumped to it. "Shit, fuck." Thinking quickly, he pointed his whole arm and hand like an arrow to the exit. "Right boys, you heard the Squadron Leader, move out, NOW!"

The excitement was clear, everyone on Squadron watched them leave and as they drove away, they radioed over to their own control office to inform them what was going to happen. Those who had stayed behind in the office, shouted to the others in the hanger to spread the message, then they rushed outside to witness Bee arriving.

As a crowd had started to form outside, the screeching of breaks was heard and the van with its flashing lights, tore around the corner at speed, nearly toppling over with the weight of a dozen grown men squeezed tightly inside.

They tumbled out and assembled, they heard the loud cat purring sound of the helicopter approach and they cheered. As the Sea King came above them it hovered at eighty-feet, not much higher than the hangers they had their back to, they felt the warm powerful downdraft wash over them and their overalls flapped around their bodies like struggling kites.

A member of the aircrew opened a side door of the aircraft as the pilot kept the helicopter steady, he waved with his whole arm to those below and they cheered and waved back. Bee was inside being hooked onto a cable, she was being told how to unclip when she reached the bottom and, they told her sternly to do this quickly in case the aircraft moved in the wind, she could be dragged on the tarmac if she wasn't quick. Bee was so excited, she wasn't scared, she was itching to go. She hadn't really understood what was going on at first, she was told she was ordered to return to base and go the Ball and that she was getting brought back to get ready. Until the helicopter arrived to get her, she was convinced it was all a practical joke.

It wasn't until she was onboard strapped in, and an aircrew helmet plonked on her that it had really sunk in and, at the moment she realised it was all true, she said a few 'shits' quietly to herself; only to hear some laughter in her ears, and the crew reminded her that with her helmet on she was on comm's with them all.

Bee was guided to the open side door where the noise of the propellers became lounder, the cable was attached to her front, and she was asked to step out. She looked up to the arm of the winch and without looking down, she did as she was told. She had complete faith in what was happening, without question and she started her decent. When she started to look down, she saw the team below and she smiled and laughed.

Down on the ground the broad Scottish accent of a mature balding man said to a younger engineer, "Aye, she's making a good job of that Son, Tom Cruise will be worried."

"What do you mean, what are you talking about?" Replied the fresh-faced newcomer.

"For crying out loud, yah wee numpty, Mission Impossible? Tom Cruise?" – he shook his head and added – "fucking Muppet, just forget it."

On the ground Bee did as she was instructed, she unclipped as soon as she could and held up the cable above her head. The aircrew that was hanging out of the door above gave a thumbs up with both hands and reversed the winch to retract the cable. As he did the helicopter raised higher and the aircrew waved to below to a roaring response. Bee was then swamped by her team and lifted into the air in celebration. The seniors looked on and after a second or two turned together and returned indoors. Sarge shouted over to Sid, telling him to make sure that Bee returns the flight equipment, and then return her to barracks. Sarge was pleased the morale of the team was bolstered, but he couldn't help thinking aloud to himself, *Operation Cinderella, for fuck's sake, whatever next?*

As the team were asking Bee what it was like and calling her Cinders, Sid noticed Big Red had parked up next to their van. James stood, hands in both pockets leaning back onto his steadfast truck. He loved seeing the welcome Bee had received. He didn't want to spoil it so stayed patiently out of the way. Sid shouted to Bee that her prince had arrived. "Albeit he's a bit fucking late to the party to collect her." The team open up and direct her towards him, Sid taking the helmet from her and her harness. They both start to walk towards each other now laughing at the hilarity of the situation and as soon as they come within two feet, Bee rushes and jumps into James arms. Regardless of them both being in uniform, he takes no hesitation at holding Bee and kissing her right there in front of them all, and the team cheer them on.

Chapter 44 –
The Ball Drops

Waking up together was, as usual, blissful. They lay together talking, they had set an alarm for eight thirty as James promised to take Bee shopping for a Ballgown. He told her it would be fine, but he was worried that an on the day purchase may not be successful. It was only ten to eight and the landline phone rang. James runs to answer it swiftly in case it was an issue at work, a call out maybe. "Hello?"

"Is that James, Flt Lt Jamieson?"

"Who is speaking please?"

"Oh, I am so sorry James, it's Joan here, Station Commanders wife. Apologies for the early intrusion on your day but, there is no time to lose, the early bird catches the worm." Joan spoke as if she was about to issue orders for a new mission.

"Is everything okay, ma'am?" James was confused.

"Yes, yes, listen I am sending a car for you and your lovely lady at nine hundred hours. They will take you to the Tailors office on camp."

"Okay, ma'am." James is following what she wants so far but, he doesn't understand why and looks puzzled as he looks over to Bee.

"Jamieson, a lovely lady called Sarah, our tailor will meet you there and provide you with a selection of dresses to choose from. McBrien is to pick one and, Sarah will tailor it for her, so she is ready in time for the Ball you see." Joan was more excited than she had been before any function, not even her own first officers mess Ball was this much of a buzz.

"You may still need accessories though; can you arrange for those as needed James? No pearls are allowed. Shoulders are to be covered at dinner and, hair is worn either all up or all down, no in between styles. No garishly loud lipstick or nail polish either James, for McBrien, not you, obviously." She chuckled to herself, and the list went on. Silence on the other end of the phone led her to realise it was probably all too much for James to take on board. "Do you understand James? Never mind, I will send a list to help."

"Thank you, ma'am. This is very kind of you and we both appreciate it very much." James was looking over to Bee who was looking back at him bemused. James was completely shocked by Her kindness and thoughtfulness.

Before Joan closes the call, she adds as serious closing address, "We are very much looking forward to you being there this evening. We will make sure you are both well looked after."

"Thank you, ma'am." James exhales a huge sigh of gratitude; he isn't sure of what else to say.

"Oh, and James, please call me Joan, not ma'am."

"Thank you, Joan, really. Thank you." James started laughing as soon as he put the phone down and runs back to Bee, jumps on the bed excited to tell her what had just happened.

Afterwards, James and Bee talk about why the Station Commanders wife was being so kind? Maybe she was a hopeless romantic. Maybe they just wanted to be sure Bee was dressed appropriately, so she didn't let anyone down, or let her husband, the Station Commander down so he wouldn't regret his decision, but James and Bee decided it was kindness and support they felt.

The Station Commander's car had arrived to collect them, they were out for three and a half hours and returned with a gown and accessories along with a note. The note was simple and explained the straightforward mess rules that would normally be formally explained during Officer training.

Bee didn't need to keep the note, but she wanted a reminder of what a woman whom she didn't know, who had written with the most eloquent handwriting, had thoughtfully done to support her. She knew none of it would happen without the Station Commander too and she felt humble by the support. She became more nervous as time passed by but, thanked her lucky stars she had been to Hairdressing and Beauty college, she thanked in her thoughts her mum for being so set on sending her there. There was no need to search for a last-minute salon appointment which, on the day of a Ball at short notice would be fruitless. She just needed a quick trip to Elgin to pick up some hairspray and some nude nail polish and she would do the rest herself. Bee decided to get ready in the barracks to save picking up her things and adding more trips back and forth to an already busy day. They agreed James would pick her up from the block at seven and they would take the short drive to the Officers Mess together.

Chapter 45 –
Ready, Steady, Go

Bee came out of the showers in the barracks carrying her bag of toiletries and as she walked back to her room, she saw Gillian coming the other way. Gillian was pleased to see Bee and very excited for her. Word had spread and everyone on camp knew what was happening, Bee was going to the ball, she was representing them. Standing in the corridor talking Gillian's voice was so loud and high-pitched others came out of their rooms to see her. Bee was swamped with good wishes and hugs; Bee was overawed by it. Some of them she hadn't met, they were on shift work normally or just rarely home. She managed to prize herself away back to her room to get ready, but her nerves were now at a stage where she couldn't hold a steady hand to apply her nail varnish. Bee hated attention and now she was known to everyone and yet she still knew only a few people herself. It felt terrifying to lose her anonymity overnight. She coached herself aloud. "*Get a grip, come on, get a grip.*" She had a few hours left, so she could take it slowly and take her time.

Only two minor mishaps, complete with a full-blown swearing outbreak, and she was back on track. Nail polish was successfully on her fingers, toes and half the carpet; that would cost her a fine when she handed her room back. Plus, she had a slight burn just in front of her ear where she had been using hot hair irons. She had also spent a good ten minutes on her hands and knees searching her room frantically for an earring she'd dropped. She only owned one pair so she had no other choice but to continue her search as long as it took, and just then the reality of how hopeless she could be made her cry.

What the hell was she playing at going to this Ball? She told herself she was an idiot getting into his situation. She had a dreadful fear she would let James down. Her stomach was rumbling and churning, and she was bewildered as to why all this faff was supposed to be fun or romantic. She hadn't felt stress like this before, never, not even in basic training. Just yesterday she jumped out of a helicopter and soon she would be off to a warzone in the desert, yet it was this event, with all the pomp and all it meant, that had her the most stressed and worried than she had ever felt. She knew James would be by her side for the most part, but she felt so alone.

Facts were facts, Bob was barely civil, and many wouldn't approve, and she knew it. She may be going to the Ball, but Bee wasn't expecting it to be a fairy tale evening. She stood in her underwear and shoes in a masculine posture as if she was on a starting line of an obstacle race. Every aspect of her was ready bar putting on her dress, she glanced at her clock checking the time again, and then composed herself by staring at herself in the mirror and hearing her mum in her mind, giving her an imaginary pep talk. She must put her dress on at the last minute. There had been enough mistakes, she could not afford for anything more to happen. She heard big red had just arrived outside, it was time. She told herself one last time in the mirror that she could do this, nodded and then stepped into her dress.

Outside James stood waiting in his mess dress uniform. He looked taller, even more handsome than usual. He seemed more authoritative standing there than his usual easy-going self that Bee knew of him. As Bee came out of the barrack block, she flinched a little as some of the girls were hanging out of the windows cheering. Mocking the pair affectionately as if it were a royal wedding, waving homemade union jack flags on sticks. When she saw James, she stopped still. The magnetic look between them stopped all noise and nerves. James gave her strength and confidence when he was around, he believed in her without question, and she found his belief gave her courage and energy, such was her trust in him.

James was thinking slightly different thoughts. There she was, looking royally beautiful in the long blue gown. He almost didn't want to share her tonight and would happily sack off the Ball and drive her straight to his place. Passion was a powerful force between them but, there was also a depth and connection that pulled them towards each other, a rare connection needed for longevity.

Bee moved first, she walked towards James as he stood still. He was hoping his thoughts of sex would subside without notice. As Bee walked forward, she noticed a group of guys slowly walking past, they were staring at her, all in jeans, each with one or two hands in their pockets. They were not there by chance. It was some guys from her section.

Shouting over, "Looking good there, Bee. Shouldn't you have a black and yellow stripy dress though mate?" The others laughed and one more added.

"We are not here to see you, we are just off to the NAAFI for a beer, just fancied a different route today." They all nodded and shouted yes in agreement with each other. One said quietly amongst them, "She scrubs up alright really" – paused and then due to embarrassment added – "for a waff like."

Another chipped in. "Glad she isn't letting us down eh, she'll do." Another added, "She's not my type of course, but she has put in a good effort, looking good…just saying." None of them could openly give Bee too much praise, only back handed compliments. But they all smiled and waved as they passed by. One turned just before they were out of sight and ran back over to them.

"We need a picture of this for the lads, just so we can take the piss out of you next week Bee, obviously."

This made Bee and James laugh and certainly helped ease the nerves she was feeling. The guy with the camera was beaming, he looked like a proud parent of his daughter heading off to a prom. He knew the guys would all want a sneaky peak at Bee in a dress. As James and Bee came together to pose for the picture he added "Not you mate, just our Buzzy Bee on her own. You could be anyone for all we care mate." Those watching laughed at the cheek of the cameraman, and James honourably stepped out of the frame.

After he took the picture of Bee, he looked at James and added "Alright mate, go on then, if you must" – he looked at James – "come on now, a pic of you two together." And signalled them to stand for a snap. As the photographer ran back to the guys who stood waiting with embarrassment, he shouted back, "Be good, Bee!" When he arrived back in the pack he said affectionately to his team, "aye, he's not bad that one really you know…for a fly boy wanker."

Chapter 46 –
Champagne Upon Arrival

Arriving at the Officers Mess they both looked perfect for the occasion. Bee's nerves heightened a little as they entered the Officers Mess through the front door, something that wasn't allowed by lower ranks in normal circumstances. They were immediately greeted by mess staff smiling and offering them a glass of champagne. A blonde stewardess in uniform winked at Bee as she took her glass from the silver tray. She couldn't say anything to Bee due to the mess rules, yet she wanted Bee to know she was happy she was there, and that she was rooting for her. As for all, they were ushered forward to have their photograph taken as a memento and afterwards led into the main hall.

The ballroom was decorated with hundreds of white sparkling light curtains, and tall opulent silver candlesticks on each of the tables that complimented the chandeliers hanging from the ceiling above. The theme for the ball was based on food, and this year the theme was Italian. Silver platters were walked around by white coated staff offering Italian smoked sausages or cheeses, little sticks with tiny Italian flags standing proud in each of them. Coloured lights twinkled outside and peeked through the large oval windows of the great hall, tempting you to where an old-fashioned fairground had been set up. It was only sporting two rides, the dodgems and a rodeo horse. There were stalls for shooting and yellow duck hooking, candyfloss and coconut stalls, it lay unused and deserted. No one had ventured out there as it was not acceptable to do so until after the closing speeches, when the Master of Ceremonies announced formally that it was play time.

When James and Bee walked into the hall it was already more than half full. They had hoped to be earlier than the majority. Bob wasn't there yet and although Bee worried about his frostiness towards her, if he were there, at least she'd know just one more person.

Some couples who were gathered in small groups looked up, drinks in hand they stared at them and then returned to talk amongst themselves. Maybe they were not talking about them but, Bee felt self-conscious. Just like the little yellow hook headed plastic ducks outside, she felt she didn't belong in there and that there would be many wanting to pluck her out and cast her aside.

Just as James was about to tell her she looked stunning, for the fourth or fifth time, a couple came behind them and interrupted.

"Jamieson, James, I am glad you could both make it." They turned and it was the Station Commander and his wife. "McBrien, you do look wonderful, and we are most pleased you are joining us this evening." The station commander was every bit the gentleman and it was appreciated. Bee glanced towards his wife Joan; she was dying to thank her for all she had done, when she was dumbstruck. 'Ma'am?' Is all she could say. At that moment she realised the lady who had helped her was her training officer from Wales. She had no idea; she knew so little about her. She never would have guessed it was her and she had no idea her name was Joan.

"Ah, McBrien, may I call you Beatrice, do call me Joan this evening." As Bee looked back and nodded still a little dazed, Joan filled the silence with pleasure. "Oh, you do look stunning Beatrice, you picked the blue one, I loved that dress, I wore it to my first Ball too, many years ago." She was smiling and her eyes drifted upwards as she remembered. "I had it specially made you know, I was so in awe of Princess Diana, a huge fan of her style I have to say, I literally took a picture of a dress she wore to the station tailor and begged him to make it for me." Joan had her hand on her chest as she leant back and laughed nostalgically about it.

Bee thanked Joan for everything, she couldn't be more appreciative. Joan gracefully replied apologising to Bee they should have asked her to attend sooner, not sprung it on her last minute. She had been dying to hear everything about how Bee had been since she left the training school, and she went on to tell Bee that she had kept her ear to the ground every now and then. Inconspicuously of course, that the Chief at St Athan, a good friend of hers would call Bee's Chief at Lossiemouth, a good friend of his, and casually ask about her somewhere in conversation. She was pleased she was doing so well at work and that she had everyone's respect as an engineer. This was news to Bee, she had no idea anyone cared or that she was thought highly in her own section. There was absolutely no sign to give this away day to day.

The Station Commander and his wife spoke with them for a good fifteen minutes, smiling and laughing and as planned by Joan, it did the trick. There were many eager, career focussed officers, desperate to have time talking with the Station Commander, that they approached them and joined in with the conversation. The ice was broken. If the Station Commander was pleased with them, then they would be, in the most part. They would soon accept James and Bee and be gracious about it too.

There were a few who refused, mainly wives of officers who wouldn't lower themselves to talk to Bee. A couple of the wives stood nearby critiquing Bee's choice of outfit. As one claimed it looked as if it was a cheap high street dress and that it lacked class, Joan enjoyed bursting their toxic bubble. From behind them she interrupted to inform them it was indeed a tailor-made dress of the finest material and, that it was indeed her dress. That only the best would do for an RAF world class engineer you see. Then, swiftly she bid them good evening and left them to it, knowing they would likely fret that they had upset the Station Commanders wife, panicked at how this may impact upon their cherished husband's career.

Joan wondered If any of them were bright enough, that they'd understand the dig she had made at their lack of worth in comparison to an RAF engineer. Joan was a passionate advocate of her trainees, she believed they were simply the best you could find and brimmed with pride if she ever had a chance to mention them. Serves them right if they did, she thought, there was always one or two wives who thought their husband's hard-earned commission was given to them to abuse and use as a form of snobbery. It used to appal her when she witnessed such vulgarity; in recent years she had developed a sporting appreciation for an opportunity to put them back in their place. She would love to frankly remind those few poisonous wives, that they had only earned for themselves a place in the Officers bed, and not at their table. She knew that satisfying moment would never come, it would have to remain her daydream.

During dinner Bee was strategically sat next to Joan and they talked almost constantly as Joan got slowly sloshed on the wine. The staff paid attention to the Station Commander and his wife, ensuring their glasses were never less than half full. Joan indulged and her quirky humour started to show openly. Meanwhile, the Station Commander Jeremy stayed alert and hardly drank a drop. It was a sacrifice he needed to make it as a leader but, more so to conceal his relationship with George. He simply could not afford for anyone to see so much as a passing glance between them that could give the game away.

Joan asked Bee about the lovely amber ring she was wearing.

"That is a stunning piece Beatrice, such a large and clear stone and so unusual?"

"Yes, my Aunt Rose gave it to me. She had it made for her many years ago. I am not sure if it is a yellow sapphire or what it is. She designed it and had it made when she lived in Africa."

Joan was delighted. "Oh dear lord, I think it is yellow sapphire, look at it. Do you have any idea how much that thing will be worth? I hope it's insured Beatrice. You are probably wearing tens of thousands of pounds right there." Joan marvelled at the design, it was divine. Bee's family seemed to be so unusual, she wanted to know more.

"Well, I have no idea how much it is worth, and I'd never sell it. My jewellery is pretty much all I am wearing that is mine. I can't thank you enough Joan." Bee smiles and adds, "Oh and my underwear of course." As Bee say's this Joan howls with laughter and Bee fears she has said something inappropriate and lowered the tone. When she is composed, Joan leans closer to Bee to explain, "Bee Darling, I gave up wearing underwear under these dresses years ago. It's hard enough trying to take a pee as it is, squeezing into those cubicles, wrapped in a circus tent sized dress."

Bee couldn't hold herself she was giggling to the point of tears. Bee found she could hardly breath for laughing when a moment later Joan calmly leant forward again, holding her wine regally up in front of her and added an apology. "I'm so sorry, I should have added that to the list I sent you, poor you." Joan knew she was dry witted, and she had expert delivery of her puns. She loved to find people with a shared sense of humour. She loved it even more if her dry wit fell on someone who didn't.

Joan would share stories and recall such accounts fondly with Jeremy after such an evening laughing all over again at any poor victims shocked responses. It provided Jeremy with countless dinner party stories to recall, of how his wife shocked or put in their place some stuffy righteous snob. They had class and integrity as a couple, but they were not remotely snobbish.

After dinner there were speeches and thanks. The Station Commander chose his words carefully. Describing the challenges they had faced in their duties, at home, and abroad in war torn places. Either fighting drug or arms smuggling or,

195

when they were undertaking the delicate and heart-breaking search and rescue missions. He asked for respect and thanks to be given to all those who kept them operational, the vital cogs in the wheel of the machine as he called it. He asked for all to support their ground staff and engineers, who made it possible for them to operate in the sky, without whom they would not be effective, nor later return home safely.

There were enthused claps to his speech and some, a considerable amount of the attendees, looked over to Bee. She saw one nod in her direction. She was touched. It wasn't about her personally, but she was the only one in the room who could take the compliment and thanks that they all felt. She had not realised that Officers valued support staff this way. They led and, some Officers were protective of their section yet, she hadn't thought that they were appreciated for what they contribute.

Speeches finished at half ten and they were then dismissed to dance and have fun, as well as permitted to head outdoors to marvel at the fun fair. Much of the stiff and formal atmosphere had disappeared with their dinner plates. Many Officers and their guests were now loud, raucous and gregarious.

As the hours passed, Joan checked in on Bee often as she passed backwards and forwards, pleased all was well.

At one in the morning, James stole Bee from conversation to go out to the fun fair, sneaking a fleeting kiss in the dark where they could. James was careful to not spoil the elegance she naturally held by acts of unbecoming public affection. He was so proud of Bee and how she had braved the ball, aware of the pressure she had been under and the unwanted attention it brought her.

Watching the dodgems cars together they laughed freely as some of the pilots form the squadron had decided to try formation dodgems, pretending to be spitfires attacking just one of the drivers who was given a red flower to hold in his mouth to distinguish him as the enemy. They had ordered that the music was played loud and proud. It was the Dambusters tune, and it got everyone's attention, giving away that this was 617 Squadron's game. Spirits were high, one driver had a large cigar out the corner of his mouth, and another wearing black swimming goggles shouted in wartime English, "Onward to defeat the enemy chaps, CHOCKS AWAY!" The antics made most laugh as the overgrown children played imaginatively.

A short, heavily tanned, grey-haired man in a tuxedo came and stood next to James, they hadn't met before. With a drink held purposefully high in one hand, exposing his glistening diamond incrusted Rolex watch, he put his other arm around James's shoulder, it looked more like it was needed to hold the short and slightly inebriated man up than to be friendly. "So, you lucky fellow, I hear you have gotten yourself a 'waff'." He looked over at Bee and eyed her up and down slowly and then raised his eyebrows at James. "And what a fine waffy she is too, you lucky bastard."

James wasn't comfortable with this guy leeching at Bee, nor his choice of words and his temper started to rise. He said nothing in return only moved closer to Bee and slid away from underneath the man's arm. He apologised to Bee as he started to lead her away. The short portly man wasn't going to let James go that easily, so he shouted after them making a scene. "Come on now chap, I am just saying you're a lucky fellow to be bedding that piece of totty; top notch I say." He snorted with tasteless laughter and raised his glass in toast to James's achievements. James squeezed Bee's hand as a red mist descended. He went to turn to go back, he wanted to shut him up and have him apologise to Bee. Bee simply squeezed his hand in return to cause a moments delay. Many stopped to watch, including Joan and the Station Commander. They looked on to see how the unfortunate incident would unfold. The lewd, alcohol fuelled man stood arms open waiting for James to return, begging him for a fight. James looked back at Bee and as soon as their eyes met, he knew they needed to walk away to keep her honour.

Joan asked her husband loudly who the wretched man was. A single sentence that ordered that his card was marked. The fact he appeared to have been wandering around alone, a social outcast, confirmed that the ban he would receive preventing him on enter the Officers Mess ever again, and the dressing down he would receive to boot, would be well placed.

At five in the morning and as tradition, staff excelled as they continued through the night to serve and cater for the guests with pride and excellence. A bell sounded for those still awake and present, to return to the great hall where a champagne breakfast was to be served to them. It was daylight and Bee, and James were in fine spirits. They had watched the sun rise over the formal gardens, talked with so many lovely people and managed to spend some time alone, just sat having a warm drink and a rest at around four o'clock. Bob was nowhere to be seen. He was there briefly, he argued with his date shortly after midnight and they left. He didn't speak to Bee when they were momentarily together, only nodding an unspoken hello, James was deeply disappointed.

Alone, over their hot drink in a quiet side room, James told Bee he loved her again and he meant it. She was strong, brave, fun, caring and she made him happy just by being next to him. Once again, he never gave her a chance to respond as he had kissed her, and the bell summoning their return to the great hall had disturbed them.

After breakfast they arrived at James's place, it was just before seven. They took no time heading to bed, tiredness overtook them, and they were soon sleeping like an entwined romantic picture for the rest of the day.

Chapter 47 –
Ritz or Blitz

The long journey didn't manage to make Bee's heart ache any less. It took a day and a half to get to the airbase in the Gulf via a quick refuel in Cyprus. Bee noticed the intense heat as she arrived and that the sand surrounding her was a remarkable pinkish orange, very unlike a beach scene. Was it even sand she thought, or dried clay? She smirked a little as she could hear her dad's voice in her head making jokes and telling her it wasn't a holiday, that she'd soon be home. Bee was shattered, desperately in need of some sleep. She had managed little in days and it was a welcome feeling to be overcome with tiredness.

A lone driver in a Land Rover picked her up to take her to her tented accommodation. The team had all arrived the same way and it was understood she would be exhausted. She could sleep, settle in her tent and they would collect her for dinner later that evening.

As they arrived at the tented area, she saw a familiar face. Before she had a chance to say anything, he had spotted her.

"Bee!" He walked over to her with long strides.

"Adam! Oh my god, it's so fantastic to see you." Bee noticed he was wearing a dog collar under his combat uniform. "Oh shit, sorry. I mean, it's really good to see you, sir." Adam laughed, and they soon chatted as if they had not spent so much as five minutes apart.

Bee was fortunate, she had a tent to herself. A whole luxurious eight feet by ten feet of peace. The guys were not so blessed, they shared four to a tent, so had worked out a rota to ensure each tentmate had a different day off in a week to relax on their own. As Bee sat on her flimsy camp bed she put her watch, wallet and welcome notes on a large steel box that doubled as her storage and furniture next to her bed. The sounds around her were unfamiliar, no birds or wildlife, only crunching of boots on the hardened ground and mumbling of male voices. Pungent smells of cigarettes wafted in the air as the chefs walked past talking of what supplies had arrived on the plane and how they would substitute for the missing garlic with peppers and chilli powder. Bee lay back on her camp bed and her thoughts left the industrious noise behind. It was Sunday and it was only around nine in the morning back home. As Bee placed her forearm across her eyes to black out the light, she had visions of James lying in bed, waking sleepily as he had done beside her so many times now. Her chest physically ached for those days to be back, and a tear silently rolled down her cheek, and a pain in her throat stifled her cries. The first glance at James in the morning was the happiest part of her day, in that moment is her bliss.

Chapter 48 –
Contact Wait Out

After several weeks Bee had acclimatised to the heat, the altitude, and the waves of aching sadness of being away from James and all she loved back in the UK. She had laughed at her cheeky comrades from her section as they made fun of the situation or joked sarcastically about the wonderful weather they were having. British, American, and French sorties were flown daily, some to gather intelligence and some bombing insurgent strong holds or convoys of weapons when spotted. There had been attacks on their base before, but none in recent months. This left an air of expectation. Many speculated that a big attack was imminent, that the lack of attack wasn't a winning sign, more a calm before the storm. Although, nothing had prepared them for what happened next.

At oh four hundred hours flares shot up and lit the sky red overhead and the siren to make ready for incoming attack screamed through the ears of the sleeping, bringing fear and panic. Training and practice had paid off with everyone up and armed in minutes but, there was nothing left they could do to prevent incoming fire, only time to take cover and fight back. Rocket propelled grenades flew around the camp, it wasn't clear at first from which direction, but it seemed to be from within the boundary on the east. The Jets were deployed to get them away from the area, each two seated asset worth tens of millions were precious, both financially and to keep the conflict at bay, which they did most of the time. The comms tower was hit, and screams echoed in the compound accompanied by the noise of gunfire and explosions. Bee could smell the injured charged flesh and needed all her resolve not to vomit, the stench almost unbearable, but knew she had an important task before she could see to them.

The diesel tanker was parked up just forty-feet away, next to the engineering huts, medical centre, and mess. It needed to move away from there, it was a sitting bomb where it was. She had no idea what idiot had parked it there, it was against the rules to be there. She was determined to move it. They keys would be in the ignition she thought, where they were trained to leave them. She crouched down as she ran to the cab trying to avoid fire and managed to climb up and get in the cab so far unnoticed in the dark, as she opened the door, she had banged her helmet off the door window and it wobbled, her chin strap wasn't tight enough, dread was stirring in her stomach, regretful at how lax she had been in the weeks running up to this incident.

The ignition keys were missing, she was swearing to herself frantically as she searched for them. They were not there, but the call out tool bag was still under the passenger seat. It contained some fuses, tape, a yellow heavy-duty screwdriver, red ratchet screwdriver, an adjustable spanner, and a hammer. She had no idea what to do, this predicament wasn't part of training, unless you count two die hard movies as lessons learnt.

Bee pulled the heavy-duty screwdriver out and jammed it into the ignition switch. She was impressed with her own strength, no doubt fuelled by adrenalin as she managed to turn over the engine shouting, "Come on you shit, start!" It worked, it shocked her so much she almost looked around to share her triumph, but the gun shots and explosions hadn't stopped, and she knew any second, she could be killed. She reversed and hit something, she couldn't see what, then drove the tanker at the main gate of the compound where firing seemed to be drawn. She stopped short of ramming the gate and jumped out of the cab and ran back behind it as fast as she could, she kept running until she was behind the concrete shower blocks, where she took cover and waited to see what her next move would be. Three Marines crawled around the corner shortly after her and shot a rocket launcher at the tanker, it blew like a movie scene, taking out the gate and the insurgents behind it. There were a few short pops of gunfire to follow, like leftover straggling fireworks.

The Marine's radios signalled that the incoming fire had stopped. It was a short yet effective attack and there would be hell to pay. How had they managed to get close without notice and how did they penetrate camp? All questions to be answered in coming days but first, the casualties. Stretchers, first aid and get those in need back to the Medical Centre.

The Medical Centre had lost power so after Bee got there, she set to moving a large box shaped sixteen-kilowatt generator into place to provide temporary power. The humming of the generator started up with a cough and splutter and lights and power was restored. The screams subsided as morphine was administered to the injured, but the shouts between medical staff working seamlessly to save lives had only just begun.

Bee returned to her section for her next orders and to see if her team had any injuries. As soon as she got there, she was informed the communications were out and that the only comm's the camp had left was the aircraft tower to air control, and two satellite telephones that the Marines carried. One of which would be set up in HQ to call for medical evacuation procedures and support.

The head count for her section was down two. After giving orders for following tasks the Sergeant grabbed a radio and headed to the medical centre to find Staffy and Scotty, two mechanical engineers that were on duty during the attack and missing.

Chapter 49 –
White Noise

James was trying to stay positive, but he was frantic to hear if Bee was alive or dead. No direct communications with the base had meant they had to wait for the official reports to be filed, or the communications to be fixed. Bob tried his best to reassure James, but he was calm one minute and angry the next, pacing around like a tiger with a splinter in his paw he started chewing the skin on the side of his nails.

"James, mate, honestly, she will be fine, I am sure of it."

"How the hell do you know that? You don't, so don't say it."

"Okay, think about it. Bee is resourceful, she is also an engineer" – Bob pleased with James – "she will have been nowhere near the guardroom or the boundary. She would have been well inside the camp, safe and well from an attack."

"Bob, please stop, you're not helping. I just need to know the truth. It's killing me hanging around here and waiting."

In the squadron tea bar, the atmosphere was sombre, everyone had heard there had been an attack where Bee was deployed. They made their drink at break time and gave James and Bob space, choosing to take their mugs of tea outside, giving them the crew room to themselves.

The boss came in and sat on the green shinny seats. "James, can you sit please?"

"What is it, just tell me?" James begged for him to put him out of his misery. He was fearful he may have lost her. "There is no more news yet, I will tell you as soon as I hear anything."

"Then why are you here, shouldn't you be in the office, waiting to find out?"

"I'm here to speak with you and to tell you that, until further notice, you are grounded."

"I'm what? What the hell are you talking about, why? They may need support out there, we may need to go and if we are, I am not staying behind."

There was a panic and unrealistic tone to James voice which explained as soon as he spoke why he was grounded. The boss looked at him calmly waiting for the penny to drop for James, and that they were not punishing him. That they were looking out for him and the squadron. They were acknowledging the anguish he was bearing. Also, it meant they were accepting his feelings for Bee. James finally understood and he nodded quietly saying it was okay, resigned to the limbo he was stuck with.

He sat with his head in hands as the boss quietly got up to leave the room, gently patting James on the shoulder as he passed him. Bob sat next to James, their knees touching, each hunched over, and in the silence, James started to cry. No words were spoken, it was quiet except for the stifled sounds of a man's heart breaking with the fear of losing the best thing that had ever happened to him.

Hours passed and James and Bob stayed at the Squadron waiting for news, as did most of the aircraft engineers and the Ground Engineering crew, Paul with Charlie who had taken Bee's place while she was away.

Finally, Sam burst through the doors to the Tea Bar and announced with a scream of delight that Bee was okay. She stopped to watch the look on James face before telling him that the Boss has the details and wanted to see them in his office. Sam then ran out to tell the rest of the crew who cheered, and they all piled in to congratulate James as if he was now a new father, or as if he had saved her himself.

Bob patted James shoulder as they stood, James relief was clear as he looked up and let his head drop backwards with a sigh, he closed his eyes. *Thank you*, he prayed to his father. He had asked in his prayers earlier, that if his dad really was up there somewhere, for him to look after Bee and bring her back home safely.

"Come on mate, let's go and hear what the boss has to say." Bob ushered him forward.

The Boss was standing at his office door smiling, holding the door open for James and Bob and in his other hand was the transmission from headquarters with the news eagerly awaited.

Reports state It was an inside job. Three locally sourced canteen staff were blackmailed into passing information, their families held as security. One moving the tanker and placing it where the most damage could be achieved.

It was recognised that Bee's efforts had saved lives, yet she did not want any attention from the situation, people had died and been injured, it was no time to take any recognition. None the less, a note would be put on her file, and it would be mentioned on her end of detachment report. She was feeling guilty that she felt pleased and relieved her two direct teammates were found safe and well, as was Adam. She hoped Adam would be okay. He would be needed now more than ever.

Chapter 50 –
Unexpected Packages

It's a nice clear day today, no more sandstorms, no more attacks since last month. It seemed so cold last night which I find odd for the desert. The Sun seems like something powered by man, and it is on a strict timer. Instead of a sunset here we seem to have lights out, just like switching off a light switch. It's the fastest transition from day to night you could ever imagine. I don't think I will tire at the novelty of it, so I try to be outside each evening when it happens. I feel really down today and worried for some reason. I haven't heard from James. I expected a bluey today but nothing. No letter on Wednesday either. Maybe he has tired from the daily chit chat, it isn't like I have much news to tell him. I am just so used to him writing for every post drop, no matter what he has going on, he writes. Or maybe he has been out with Bob and found a nice civilian girl he is taken with, and I am about to be dumped? Let's face it, being with me will ruin his career, and maybe the distance between us has made him realise there are plenty more fish in the sea?

Nope, stop it, I know that's not true. Maybe there is a problem, and he is ill? Or there has been in an accident, I wouldn't know would I, as I am not family, no one would contact me? Or maybe it's something else? Argh, for God's sake, I am going demented having all these bad thoughts. I love him so much and I am pretty sure I can't feel all that on my own? That is it, I am going to get on with some work and concentrate. I should tell James when I get home that I love him. I haven't actually said it yet, and I should, I am sure he knows it though, I hope he does. I best make sure backup power is good, fuel topped up and a kit check is done just in case, it will keep my mind from torturing myself.

The hanger is a mess, I'll get stuck in, clear this dust off all the workbenches, put the mobile tool kits away too before I start. Besides tonight we have show night, we have a makeshift stage and lots of people gather around to hear who-ever wants to play, sing, make a joke and such. Both the UK and the USA take part. It's a military stage so you can't just wander on stage, you have to put your name down on the list the day before and you are allocated a slot. Nothing is without timing and precision; nothing feels free here. The last time I felt free was with James in Cornwall. Time stood still there, just us and nature, it was just perfect. I felt so happy afterwards, and I felt safe with James. So much laughing and time together since but, duty always called and the most time we have had is in between shifts and the odd weekend. Here I go again, it's all about James. How did I allow this shit to happen? Hell should freeze over before I let a guy in under my skin like this, it's pathetic. I should get out while I can, before it gets any worse. That's it, I'll dump him before it gets any worse. I can't do that by email, I'll call on Saturday and tell him it's not for me. Thanks James, but, no thanks, I'll have my freedom back. How dare he make me feel like this. I miss him more each day.

Just as I start to snap out of it and feel better the boss comes in. "Bee, you need to get out to the airfield to power up the generator on bay four, it's not holding power and a jet is due in, wait for it to come in and tuck in into bed. Oh, and take Scotty with you, he's driving me nuts, I need some peace." As the boss walks away, I gladly drop what I'm doing to go out for a drive with Scotty. He may drive you nuts, but he is funny, childish, and always happy. I need that right now.

As we drive over to the aircraft parking bays, we see there are more people than usual gathered there. Maybe the jet has a problem, this is not looking good, there are gaggles of aircraft technicians and vehicles. Scotty and I step out and wait by the van. We don't talk with the other technicians; Scotty will only put his foot in it and call them inbred or something or insult their families. He says he tries to make conversation and he's being friendly. I swear he has a death wish and enjoys really pissing them off, even if that means a few bruises or retaliation to the whole of our section. He claims it is all purely by accident, it's just his banter style. It isn't, and God only knows how or why he does it.

The jet is down and taxiing to the bay, it seems okay. No fire engine, no announcement over the radio signalling an emergency. It will take a few minutes to taxi over to bay four, so Scotty and I chat about home, he is missing his son Harry who is nine. He plans football tickets and playing in the park when he gets back. Scotty looks over my shoulder at the jet and raises his head to nod at the aircrew, who are walking over to us for some reason? I don't believe it, is it, am I losing it completely? Is it, is it James?

208

The world stops, I hear nothing, it's silence as I run towards him and throw myself at him. Tears are streaming down my face, I am so happy, I can't explain the excitement. It's like I have a sudden boost of energy and giddiness has taken over. When I finally stop kissing him, he says something to me, but I can't hear him, the guys are cheering and the jets are loud in the background, one taking off, one taxiing to be go up next.

"Why are you here? How? Why didn't you tell me?" So unromantic of me to ask but I'm in shock. As we jump into the back of the Land Rover, Scotty drives and is laughing. They all knew, they all bloody knew. James tells Scotty he needs to go to the Squadron office, and Scotty fake salutes like a boy scout to say he understands but hasn't actually said a word.

"Bee, I missed you so much and it was too good to miss, when the red flag showed in the control office that one of the jets was due back for a major service, I had to get out here to see you. It's driving me insane being apart, I worry about you out here. I only have one night, we go again tomorrow evening. Back to Cyprus first and then home to Scotland." I feel so sad instantly as it sinks in that we only have twenty-four hours before he goes again, and I'll have to wait another two and half months to see him.

We arrive at the Squadron; I have to let him go to a debrief.

"Bee, I'll find you after we de-brief." James kisses me in a longing wonderful warm kiss that makes me shiver, he always has that impact, I wonder when it will wear off?

"Oh, hold on, I'll be setting up the stage power and I'll be there until the show, there is a show by the mess, okay? I'll be over there."

Scotty chips in. "Bee, you lucky, lucky lady, I hope you get sorted with fly boy tonight, you've been a right grumpy cow. He better put a smile on your face." Scotty, always lowering the tone, didn't I say he ends up offending everyone at some point?

"Scotty don't be such a prat. Hey, did you know about all this?"

The Land Rover pulls into our section and Scotty looks so smug. "Mate, we all knew about this."

"Just unbelievable, you are supposed to be my mate. Thanks Scotty, you could have warned me, I look like a mess!"

With a real belly laugh Scotty simply tells me that the poor flyboy has rose tinted glasses on and I could look like a desert goat, and he'd be overjoyed. That come to think of it, I have a similar backside to a desert goat. The cheeky git and his quick-witted humour.

As we walk into the section the guys all throw similar remarks. Stu being the funniest, he thanked the lucky stars for this miracle and asked if my permanent PMT will now be gone, given he'd thoughtfully arranged for my bit of posh stuff to come out to play. Claiming falsely that he had some hand in it all. It's delivered well with his scouse accent, his comedy timing is twinned with scratching his crotch and him nodding in praise of himself, he had the guys in stitches.

*

Where is he, the stage is set, acts have started, no James? Bob is here and can read my thoughts.

"Bee, he'll be here in a minute, there was a lot of paperwork to do to change the jets over, lots of customs checks."

I just smile and nod. Bob seems distracted though, looking around he seems uncomfortable with our American counterparts who have been invited along to the evening. He doesn't take his eyes off them. I don't ask why; I'll quiz James about it later. Bob clearly doesn't trust them, or maybe he is gutted as some are way bigger and fitter than he is, I think there must be some steroids involved?

Wanting James is like a type of hunger, I feel it deep in my stomach, like I need to eat but, I know eating won't cure the cravings. The guys on stage have been good so far, a duo of guitars playing acoustic versions of rock classics. I didn't check the listings for the night, obviously not because I prefer a surprise, I just don't really care, it will be nice whatever it is.

That's him, I think it's him, I am so short in amongst all these guys, yet I can make out his walk and shape coming towards us, and I can't help but smile so much, he is just gorgeous. I jumped a little, how embarrassing. Hold on, why is he going on stage? Shit, does he sing too or is something wrong?

"Ladies, gentlemen and, well others" – James takes a pause and nods to Scotty which makes the guys laugh – "thank you in advance for your support. You see, I have foiled a plan and I want you all to know about it, and I want this on record. As many of you know, Bee." He is looking for me, god I am so embarrassed. "Come up here Bee?" Bob escorts me to the stage and there is cheering from the crowd. What the hell is going on? Bob just smiles warmly at me. Well, that's a first, this must be bad.

210

"You see gentlemen, this lady had a plan, and I have foiled that evil devious plan." He is confident, like a priest at a sermon. Cheers go up from the crowd, James is playing them and nodding as if he has caught a thief. "Hell yes, this little lady was so upset at coming out here on detachment it got me thinking" – James paused dramatically – "she is up to something!"

The crowd boos as if this is pantomime and I am the villain of the story. I am laughing too but, shaking my head, I'm lost to what he is going on about, just dreading what is coming next. "You see Bee is due to arrive home next year, on 29 February." James walks up and down the stage to build the tension. "Did you know fellas, that on this day, on a leap year, women can trap us by asking us to marry them?" The crowd boo's. "So sneaky these women are, just as much as we are clueless, they pounce. And they usually do this in public where we cannot possible get away or say no!"

The crowd boo and heckle more, supporting and transfixed on James and his address.

"Because to say no would make us a public enemy number one boys, a total looser right?" James is walking back and forth and then back to the middle where he stands next to me. Cheers go up in support of 'manpower'. He's a shit embarrassing me like this. "So, Bee, I worked it out, you are planning to ask me to marry you on 29 February, straight off the jet when it lands aren't you? What do you have to say for yourself?"

I laugh as he comes over to me with the mike and I shake my head, I hold my hands out to the side to protest my innocence and I tell him and the crowd that I wasn't going to ask him to marry me, I'm just pissed I won't have movies or a beer for two and a half months. The crowd laugh and cheer so hard I think I'm winning this battle. One American guy heckles. "Who are you kidding honey, he's so damn handsome I'd ask him to marry me!" James laughs at me and nods again, considering his new options, looking back and forth at the crowd.

"Okay, well, that's a bit awkward really." James looks at his buddy Bob who smiles at him and nods.

"Listen Bee, I didn't want to live in fear for the next few months worrying about what you have planned, so I have already picked up the ring to get ahead of the game." James goes into his pocket, pulls out a tiny black box from the Jewellers in Elgin. Oh my god I cannot breathe, and I will explode if I inhale any more. "So, Bee, I am so determined to foil your plan, I am going to ask you to marry me first" – he looks at the crowd nodding – "that'll teach her wont it guys?"

The crowd cheer, a few shout out, "Yeah, that'll teach her!" Another one adds, "Yeah mate, get across the line first, it works with my missus every time. Never let them win!"

There are laughs, cheers and banging tables but, they start to quiet as James looks back at me, he stares into my eyes, so intently I feel calmer, he is full of confidence, and he drops to one knee. I start sobbing as it really sinks in what is happening. I love him so much my chest hurts, and I am dumbstruck.

I think I said yes, I'm pretty sure I did, it's a blur, I am being swung around now anyhow and James is kissing me, I don't want this to end. He loves me, so much he did all this, it's crazy and it's perfect.

Loud dance music is now playing, *Rhythm is a Dancer,* aircraft flares have gone up as makeshift fireworks, air horns are sounded and people have gone wild, dancing on tables, chairs, big metal field boxes. The good old forces guys, suckers for a happy ending.

Although today isn't the happy ending, it is just the beginning and no matter what, whatever we do next, I'm in.

Chapter 51 –
Magical Moments

That night James sneaks into my tent, God knows why, everyone knows where he will naturally be. I think he is being sensitive as the Detachment Commander is a newly promoted Wing Commander who likes following all the rules, even the little ones that you wouldn't normally bother with in a desert. The show of public affection on the airfield and mixing with the ranks at the concert has made the boss very uncomfortable already, the whole officer dating junior rank thing and, he is already unhappy about a 'female' being on the detachment. Women do not belong. I'd put money on him being a public schoolboy who was held up in the countryside in an all-boys school, bullied, and that he has no sisters. Probably the only female in is life is probably his posh uptight, unaffectionate mother.

He isn't a well-liked man Wing Commander Dickson, nor was he a well fed one. He had to be the thinnest man in a uniform. He ran miles and miles every morning around and around the camp perimeter fence, he was nicknamed 'Forest Gump' as a result. We were convinced he joined the RAF on payment of a family dowry. An old-fashioned way of getting into the service for aristocratic families. The second Son born of a family is often sent to the forces and the father purchased a commission for him, the first born having followed in the family business as he is the heir. No one knew what to do should a third be born thereafter. The purchasing of a commission wasn't supposed to happen these days but, for some officers, you just couldn't believe they passed the gruelling physical and mental training that RAF Cranwell Officer training unit put you through. Lower ranks often discussed their suspicions that some were still buying their way through the back door.

James had brought some chocolate with him and my favourite crisps, and we had a picnic by tent light. He also brought some good quality tea bags, coffee and a huge box of sweets and biscuits for the boys at work, a small payment for their cooperation in his crazy plan. You don't get any treats on detachment unless you brought it with you and, a cup of tea or coffee just like you have at home, is a hug in a mug when you are missing your family. This huge hoard of goodies left little room for his flight bag to squeeze into the jet.

I was always amazed how light he travelled. I thought I was unusually light packing when travelling. I couldn't bear what other girls got excited about, a dozen pairs of bikinis, their dresses and shoes collections for their holiday. Even on detachment some thought bringing heaps of civilian clothes was a must and they became stressed about deciding what would fit in the bag and what wouldn't, which favourite gym t-shirt should they leave behind?

I am very much a wash it and wear it again kind of girl. I am not naturally organised, so it helps make life easier if I have less stuff to look after. One of the first things that impressed me about James was his lack of interest in material things. Other than big red and his music, there was nothing more he clung to that could be bought. We talked quietly, I was so pleased I could introduce James to Adam, I'd told James all about him back in the UK, he said it was great to put a face to him and meet in person, James really liked him.

We whispered until around three when tiredness took over and we fell asleep on the floor of the tent. James had told everyone back home on base what he was about to do. Bob was quite moody about it at first but came around and joined in. James told me that his boss had called him in for a meeting to discuss his plans, the RAF were not impressed, didn't he know how complicated this would be etc. We can't serve on the same unit once married for fear of junior ranks not respecting him and the Queens Commission that he holds. All of the discussions were reiterating the administrative burden we were placing on the RAF, and how inconsiderate it had been for James to decide to take this course of action. James laughed but, I found it harder to stomach, I feel uncomfortable with the complications and administration. James was every inch worth it all but, it made me feel anxious.

After just an hour and a bit I woke and looked at James, it was so wonderful seeing him, yet so uncomfortable on the floor. I decided to sneakily reach over and kiss him on the cheek as he slept. In an instant he woke and responded passionately. We moved quietly as if our lives depended on it, sliding off our clothes as we ached to get closer to each other. It was freezing cold, feeling James skin radiate beneath me, I clung to his body, the heat within me rose to match the heat of the moment. James kissed me and cradled my face to keep me quiet when we could feel the climax of our passions grow closer. The intensity of that moment was more than anything I had felt before. You may think it was the danger and inappropriateness of what we had done, it wasn't. It was the love that was given without fear for the first time, in full knowledge that now we would be together forever, and that no one could stop us from sharing every wonderful milestone together. It was the sealing of a pure promise of what was to come next in our lives together and our complete, unquestionable love and trust in one another.

Chapter 52 –
Farewells and Fairy Tales

Saying goodbye was tough, I waved him off as his jet taxied away and he blew me a kiss. Scotty was on hand with a childish remark which kept me from blubbing. It was so inappropriate to feel this way at work. I was reduced to an airheaded fairy tale princess, pining for her prince.

I decided upon a plan, I'd write to Mum and Dad to tell them the news and, to a few other friends and family. Once my armed ached from writing I would then pack this part of my world away in a little imaginary box and get on with my job. Only two and a half months left to go, and I'd be home. We won't have Christmas together but, that's okay, we'll have plenty of those. James has left me a present, and it's locked up in the section office. I am not to open it until Christmas morning.

The guys with kids feel Christmas most, missing the surprise on their Children's faces when Santa has been. Stu told me that he was dreading it, it was his second Christmas away from his wife and kids. The first time still haunts him. He called home on Christmas day hoping to join in with some part of the festivities, to fake his surprise as his son Scott received his construction set and Lego. Only to find they were all having a miserable Christmas back home. Scott had asked Santa for only one thing, for his dad to be home on Christmas morning. He didn't care for any toys, he just missed his dad so much and wanted him safe.

The disappointment of Santa letting him down sent Scott into a meltdown. He had such faith in Santa by the age of seven, that he had pent up excitement about seeing his dad and no need to carry the worry any longer. Three years on, it still hurts Stu to think of it, and he is dreading Christmas day again this year. Scott is older, he doesn't believe in Santa since then, that day put paid to that part of his childhood, but he has become angrier and more troublesome back home as the date draws near. Scott is angry, as he is reliving the memory this year too, as a heartbroken child in his mind's eye, it's a demon that has left its mark, and stolen a piece of his innocence.

We are sat in tea break in our small portacabin when Stu opens up and tells us this, he didn't look at any of us when he is talking, and when he finishes, he finally looks at us, as we haven't said a word to acknowledge him. Four of us are sat with tears streaming down out faces, unable to speak. Scotty gets up and tells us that the aircraft boys won't annoy themselves, and he heads for the door, patting Stu's shoulder twice as he passes him.

At that moment I feel the upmost respect for all the fathers who have the strength to carry on with their work in the forces this way, and even more so for the families left behind, I have such sadness for them. The wives are left to be single parents, miles from their parents and friends. Left to carry the children through one of the toughest parts of military life, separation from a father and worrying their dad won't be home safe.

James and I haven't talked about it, we haven't given it a thought, we have years yet to consider this but, I already know I am not that strong. I couldn't go away and leave my children behind. I could maybe be strong enough to be left behind, although I am not sure how, I just can't comprehend it. I just know I am not strong enough to leave without breaking.

Chapter 53 –
The Air Stands Still

Operations are heating up; flying is twenty-four seven, and when not flying we are in briefings and prepping a returned jet and crew so they can fly again. The ground troops are busy protecting the local community from the insurgents who try and intimidate them by random and frequent attacks, when they are not attacking the national police checkpoints that is.

They, and our troops on the ground are in need of full air support regularly. We go on more than ninety percent of the sorties, as the accuracy we can provide with the Tornado is over ninety-nine percent and the risk to the civilians is too great on most of the missions. So, with our eight jets, versus the other forty parked on the line from the USA and France, our engineering and pilots are used disproportionately but for the right reasons. We don't complain much, but we are worried about crew. Some of the groundcrew have a rant when there is silence, just before the jets come back. It's nerves I think hoping they all come back safely.

We are also taking out enemy strong holds and vehicles carrying weapons which is very reactive, not planned. We have jets with engines running, and pilots dressed and ready to jump in the seat and go when they are located, and the air horn sounds. The desert conditions are taking a toll on the equipment. The sand not only gets everywhere blocking up exhausts but, pretty much all moving parts at some point, it corrodes seals and gaskets. So, keeping the kit serviceable isn't quite a straightforward as it is back in the UK. Exhaustion for me comes in waves after long shifts. There is some down time, but it is sporadic not routine anymore. The team look after each other where we can, if we see stress building or tiredness affecting work then we step up and rally around to avoid a bust up. Sometimes, a flare up is the only thing that will clear the air, then the boys can be back to being best buddies afterwards as if there wasn't any fight at all. Only for the odd black eye or cut lip to show for it, you'd not notice anything happened afterwards.

Instincts play a huge part of working in this environment together, you sense a flare up is coming just as animals sense a storm coming. That and the wind ups. The humour plays such a huge part of coping in the British forces. If we are so stretched there is not enough time for fun, then the flare ups happen more often. James is the only thing keeping me going through the tiredness. Not dreaming of or planning the wedding or honeymoon. I've never been that type of girl. It's the thoughts I have of him and his smile, his smell, his laugh. He's sent me pictures of the flat, the bathroom will be done by the time I get back. He's learnt how to tile, it has a white sink and toilet suite and a silver and copper freestanding bath, with natural slate tiles. He's already decorated all the rooms from top to toe in white to compliment the warm polished wooden floors. We need a new kitchen, which he is planning to do in January. We discussed an oak worktop to match the floors and I said any units is fine with me. I am finally okay with having a surprise. There is a log burner for heat, but no central heating, I don't care though, I'm so excited. He refuses to buy furniture until we get back, we will only have the bed from his place and an old chair.

I can't wait to see James. I even love the annoyed look that he has when someone or something has angered him, through to the sight of him rousing from his slumber first thing in the morning with a smile. It all makes my heart race, my temperature rise, and my spine tingle just thinking of him. When I let myself, these flashbacks remind me that I am human, not a machine, and that there are good times coming again soon, just eight weeks to go. Then I will be in the one place on earth where I am completely human. Somewhere completely safe, and it's James. In James's arms I have peace.

It is so easy to become robotic and ruthless in this place. You have few emotions; you need to leave real life at the door most of the time and focus on why we are here. Don't get me wrong, I miss James on the bad days so much I'd do almost anything for this world to stop and for me to back in his arms, just lying there quietly with him. I call James sometimes on the forces network, we are privileged to have the Satellite comms. Oddly I don't call him when we have a fatality, those are the days that feeling human could potentially break me. I must stay machine like on those days and support everyone else, I have that healing nature, they see me as their big sister. When the shit hits the fan, I find the right thing to say to comfort or to spur someone on to keep going naturally. I don't know how I do it, I just read people, empathise, I guess. I see it as a part of my duty just as much as getting the kit working so the jets can fly. It's tiring though, it drains me. I need a break. I feel sick when I am tired and I'm feeling sick most days now. The heat doesn't help. It's forty-four degrees in the day and the below freezing at night.

It's six at night and I'm in the daily briefing tent, stood near the back when the PTI, Charlie comes into the tent and calmly walks to the front and pulls the boss to one side. Charlie is a funny chap, only about 5' 8'' which is short for a PTI. He played county cricket for Essex though and is super fit. So, that's why he was accepted. Most PTIs are obsessive on health and fitness to the point of being arrogant and egotistical. Not Charlie, he has the humour of an engineer and a complete obsession with ladies who are seriously unfit and morbidly obese. He calls them his cherub goddesses. His fiancé was over eighteen stone but, they broke up when she got fit for the wedding. It devastated him as she announced she loved feeling so healthy that she'd keep it up. Charlie had to admit he didn't find her attractive anymore which, at twenty-six years of age, and as a red-blooded male, passion was very important to him. So, he called off the wedding. He said he couldn't even buy her a take-away anymore after a night out, that she wasn't fun anymore. She now obsessed with what she shouldn't eat so much she just wasn't the carefree girl he fell in love with. Other than this he is a stereotyp-ical PTI, tanned, styled hair and meticulously kept. He wears factor fifty sun cream and reapplies constantly as he doesn't want wrinkles or cancer when he is older. We think the orange tan he has is fake, although we haven't quite managed to raid his kitbag for evidence. Anyway, Charlie spends too much time worrying about his beauty routine and how he will look when he is older when he should be worrying about getting home alive.

It's strange, the briefing is called to halt since Charlie called the boss to one side. He has a piece of paper in his hand and is talking fast, he's shifting his weight from one foot to the other, over and over and changes from having his hands on his hips to having one of his hands rubbing the back of his head. What-ever this is it looks serious but, I don't understand as Charlie isn't communica-tions staff, so why he was sent with the intel I don't understand, it's quite odd. He hangs out in the HQ tent as being the only PTI there is nowhere else to send him.

They are looking into the tented briefing room now, still talking but scanning the crowd. The boss sees me, then Charlie does too, and they stop scanning. I feel a sensation like a huge punch under my ribs. I know this is bad news and that it's for me. The Boss takes a deep breath and with his chest enlarging, he rolls his shoulders back and he shouts over, "Bee, please come." He gestures me with his arm, calling me to him like a policeman directing traffic. My knees are trembling, and I feel my breathing is quickening. I haven't moved yet even though the crowd has opened to let me through, everyone is now silent, or have I stopped hearing? I start to walk towards them and as I do, they just both stare at me transfixed. Charlie has wet eyes, they are glazed. His hands are on his waist, and he is still shifting left to right on his feet as I trip and catch my hip on a chair back. "Shit, that hurts." I feel so sick I am not sure I can do this, it's my parents, my dad, yes, his heart, or an accident, Mum? Maybe it's Mum. It must be my parents. Christ only knows, but I feel like turning and running in the opposite direction as far as I can and never coming back to hear this news. The Padre, lovely Adam has made his way to the front, shit, shit, shit, this is bad.

Somehow, I don't run, the armed forces 'do as I am told' training is pushing me to where I am summoned.

"Bee, I am really sorry…there was a training exercise over the Cairngorms, the jet had a bird strike, there was nothing that could be done, the jet went down in the mountains. James didn't eject, we think he was trying to avoid the A9 which was gridlocked with holiday traffic. I am so very sorry Bee, Flt Lt Jamieson, James, was killed on impact, as was his Nav."

The world stops turning, I felt it halt with a huge jolt as the Boss asks, "Bee, do you understand? Bee?"

The pain, it is indescribable. It has soared from my chest to every bone in my body like I have been kicked by a horse, then electrocuted until each bone throbs as if they are about to explode from the inside out. I can't breathe, but somehow, I manage to scream with every ounce of my pain pouring out…no words, just screaming.

My legs begin to give way and Adam catches me, his arms are a steady stronghold wrapped around the top of mine, as I can no longer carry myself. He gently eases me to the ground. I can't hear anything now, it's quiet. The most painful quiet, like I have been sucked into a vacuum, and I can't stop sobbing. My mind flashes through my memories, the proposal on stage, the look he had when he saw me at outside the shop in Elgin, flying over Cornwall, our first kiss in the Land Rover, and our night in the tent. So many memories are now so painful as they flash back through my mind, and I just want to die too. Breathing in hurts so much, I really think breathing at all is too much for me to bear.

Please let me die too and I will be with James. I don't want to know who I am without him. Please, please, no, please don't take James, not my James, my home, my safety, my life.

Chapter 54 – Forever

Bee returned to camp greeted by Paul and Sid who take her straight to the flat where Bob is waiting. She hasn't spoken other than to say thanks as they open doors and carry her bags. Nodding where possible to avoid speaking. She simply doesn't have the energy to interact. Bob opens the door as she arrives. His eyes are red. This is the second bereavement for him in three weeks. First his father, a man who he spent his childhood terrified of, but loved regardless, now James, a man he loved and cared for, and without question was willing to risk his life for.

The irony was, he wasn't there with him. If he wasn't at the funeral, maybe he could have done something, and James would be here now. Although, initial reports say not.

"Bee, I am so very sorry."

He looks at Bee, she doesn't raise her head to look at him. He takes this as a sign she is angry with him, as angry as he is with himself. "My dad died Bee, I was at the funeral, I am so deeply sorry. I should have been with James."

Bee is shaken and looks up, startled by Bob's fragile news, tears begin to leak from her eyes and drop onto her cheek, thawing her face from the coldness she has been unable to shake since it happened.

"Bob, it is not your fault. I am so sorry your dad has died too." She breaks down and covers her face with her hands as she sobs. Bob wraps her in his arms and they both cry, her tears more vocal than his, they both feel the painful loss of James intensely.

In an attempt to lighten her spirits, Bob tells Bee he is keen to show her around. She has only seen the estate agents sales brief and so much has changed. Especially, the bathroom and the main bedroom which James completed first. Then to examine in more detail the lounge, with a log burner and the second bedroom which was currently full of boxes. The new kitchen units had arrived, and James hadn't yet fit them, Bob was going to help him with it before Bee returned, Paul had asked the section to check the electrics, which they had duly sent someone to take a look. They were impressed with James's drive and commitment to Bee.

Bee smiled and was in awe of the bathroom. The natural stone floors and wall tiles and the freestanding bath were elegant and tranquil. The chandelier above the bath was possibly a step too far, too glamorous for the small room but, Bee had joked about having one and James pushed the electricians to fit it until they gave in, amid their warnings of it not meeting regulations.

The high ceilings meant once the bath was installed below there was no way of knowing how they'd change one of the lightbulbs but, James thought it would make her laugh, so he decided he'd figure out that detail at some point in the future.

Moving onto the main bedroom, the familiarity of James's Bed, the duvet covers and his every day belongings scattered around the room caught her by surprise. She knew he had moved in, but she wasn't ready to see his things. She grabbed a t-shirt from the laundry basket, sat on the bottom of the bed and held it close, smelling James's scent one more time she kept her eyes closed. She was struck frozen by the pain of loss and all she could do was lie onto the bed in the foetal position, grasping the material as tightly as she could to her chest. Bob placed a blanket on top of her and retreated, leaving her to her thoughts.

Bee's parents arrived the next morning. Bee's Warrant Officer had been in touch to notify her parents of what had a happened straight away and to make arrangements for them to come up to Scotland and be with her. He had kindly arranged for the family's house near station to be made available to them. It was a three bedroomed bland building set aside for broken families to spend time together. Somewhere for the separated and divorced airmen to stay with their kids on school holidays, those in search of their lost and treasured normality.

Bee was oblivious to her parents travelling and these arrangements. She didn't hear most of what had been said to her since she was told James has died. She couldn't bring herself to eat, she only slept and sat still, unless ushered along by someone else. She drank little that was put in front of her and Bob was becoming increasingly concerned about her but, at the same time he felt the pain she was in and understood.

As Bee's parents Sue and Peter arrived at the flat, Bob was relieved to see them. He had stayed in the lounge that night, slept intermittently in an old brown leather chair. Bob had to go and get ready for round two, meeting James's mother, stepfather, and sister at the airport. They were flying in from Canada, via London, they were to stay in the Officers mess. Bob hadn't been there with James on that day, but he was determined to be there for him now. He made silent promises to James to look after Bee and James's family forever. Whatever they needed, he would do his very best to deliver.

Bee could hear noise of people talking, it didn't register that it was her parent's voices. Once the talking stopped there was a short silence followed by a small tap at the bedroom door and the noise of an old door latch lifting. "Bee, it's me, Mum." Bee didn't move an inch, she felt a stabbing pain in her chest and chose silence as a way to force the physical pain to pass over. "Love I am so sorry, we got here as quickly as we could." Hearing her mum's soft caring tones meant the pain in Bee's chest hadn't subsided, it spread to her throat strangling her airways and she couldn't hold on any longer. She sat up quickly and flung herself at her mum and the pain screamed out of her in a primal way that was unbearable for Bob and her dad to listen to. Bob had a tear fall on his cheek and nodded at Bee's father, pointed at the door as he took his bag and left. Bee's dad didn't break the silence he simply nodded back to acknowledge Bob and as he did, he rubbed his chin to sooth himself from the feelings of helplessness that had overcome him.

After the sobs started to subside Bee's mum quietly whispered in her ear, "We are here as long as you need us." Bee lifted her head from her mother's chest and looked at her, unable to speak. "Bee love, I'm afraid there is a lot to do, so how about we start with getting you cleaned up and fed so you have some strength to get through the day?" Bee's eyes opened a little wider as she heard her mum suggest to her that she'd make it through the day. Bee felt she couldn't make it any further than that very moment. Bee's mum read her thoughts. "I know Bee, I know. You will make it through today, and you are not alone." Bee broke and sobbed and as her mum held her tightly again, she prepared herself, she tried to take deep breaths as she knew that her mum would soon rub her arms and insist that she make a start and get cleaned up.

As Bee was in the bathroom her parents stood in the small kitchen, Mum Sue looked out of the window as she talked to Peter. "I don't know what to do, I have considered this situation, what do I say to her?"

"There isn't much we can say is there?" Peter replied.

"What do we do then, I can't bear it. She shouldn't have to go through this, she looks awful." There was as silence for a while, water cascading in the shower across the hall sounded like heavy rain. "It's not fair Peter, he seemed so perfect for her." She turned to him for support, she felt angry. "This is my little girl! What do I say to my little…" her anger turned to sorrow in an instant when she heard herself say the words as they tumbled from her mouth 'little girl'. Those words meant so much to her and if her little girl's hurt, she is too. Peter held Sue while she had an almost silent cry. She was desperate for Bee not to see she had been crying, so she pulled all her strength to make it stop and straighten herself out, asking Peter if her eyes looked alright.

Soon after Bee emerged and joined them in the kitchen. Bee's dad put the kettle on, and her mum pulled out a chair on the tiny table that sat alongside the wall opposite to the kitchen worktops. The kitchen was old and in desperate need of refurbishment, with bright orange paint on the outlines of the kitchen units, faded white paintwork on the doors, and royal blue walls. It was a headache of a space.

"Bee, you look very pale love." Bee looked at her and shrugged her shoulders, she really didn't care how she looked. "I will make you some toast." With this thought, Bee stood quickly and ran to the bathroom to vomit, overcome with emotion. Bee's dad Peter slowly shook his head as he looked at his wife and passed her a cup of tea and told her to sit and rest a while. He didn't say much, they both needed his silent support and patience right now. He then turned to make the toast, he made sure his wife ate some first before making some for Bee and lastly himself.

Bee's parents had started speaking slowly as they checked their words before they allowed them to air. They had come close to joking about the kitchen and how it needed someone to overhaul it. They stalled a few times, almost asking if Bee if she was feeling better after her shower and such, she was anything but okay. So many of their go to phrases would cause offence or pain right now, it was a minefield.

That night they would let Bee talk if she found her voice, make sure she ate something wholesome and they hoped to make a list of what she wanted to do, and what they needed to arrange. Bob had told them that he would bring James's family over the next day, so it was important to Sue and Peter that they knew what Bee wanted before then, just in case it got confused or so busy that her wishes weren't heard.

Bee's parents would convince her to come with them to the family's house so they could stay together. They could come back to the flat every day if she wished but, they all needed to be in one place and there was no way they could all stay there in the flat. One lonesome brown chair and a bed in the biggest bedroom was not enough for a sleepover.

Chapter 55 –
Moving at Speed

At ten in the morning, they were at the Families house when the bell rang. Bob was at the door with James's family, and they wanted to talk to Bee. James's mum is as cold as she remembered. Her eyes were red from crying, yet she seemed empty. She sat upright on the edge of the sofa, her husband and daughter sat alongside her. She held a tissue in a ball in both her hands resting them on her skirt.

"We would like to have the funeral here at Lossiemouth, with a full guard of honour, instead of a burial we would like to take his ashes home with us to Canada."

Bee said nothing, she sat across from her and just listened.

"The Chaplain said he can hold the ceremony next week, providing his body is released from the investigation. On Thursday."

Bee nodded slowly, a tear escaped from her eye and rolled down her cheek, but she didn't move.

"We have picked the songs for the service, one is the same as was at his father's funeral, *Let it be,* by The Beetles." On hearing this Bee bolts up from the sofa and heads for the back door. She gets there just in time to open the door and be sick in the back garden. Bee's dad makes swift excuses for her and follows to hold her up. "It's all been too much for her, she isn't able to talk yet." – her mum adds – "I've not seen her like this before, I'm afraid I don't think anything you are saying is sinking in."

James's mum nods but looks angry. Monica asks quietly, "Is there anything I can do?" Bee's mum's eyes glisten, how sweet she thinks Monica is. "I think James would want me to look after Bee if I can," James's mum is quick to close her down.

"How do you know what James would want? He isn't here is he and I know your brother better than you do." With this Monica starts to cry, her mother remains steadfast in place as her husband steps in. "Don't do this Margaret, there is enough hurt here, and you need to remember you are not the only one hurting."

The atmosphere turns darker, and James's mum is about to explode when Sue, Bee's mum, speaks directly. "This is not the time nor the place, now drink your tea and let's start again." She caught them off guard, they are not used to a stranger taking charge, and she continues. "Monica, that is a lovely thought, and I will think on it, I am sure there will be something you can do to help and, of course we want to help you too if we can, you have lost your brother and it must hurt terribly." With this Monica smiles through her tears, thankful that someone has noticed and validated her feelings exist. "As for you 'Margaret', I won't beat around the bush, I cannot comprehend how you are feeling but, I wouldn't be surprised if you are the most angry person on earth right now. You have a strong man sat next to you and you can give him both barrels when you get home, for now though, you need to look after Monica and make the plans for James's ceremony." James's mum is shocked at her forthright attitude but succumbs to the helpless situation. She cannot look at Monica, she already regrets what she has said to her, saying sorry doesn't come easy to her. She reaches to her left and takes Monica's hand and takes it to her knee to hold it gently. This is enough for Monica, she leans in closer, feeling the warmth meant by these awkward affectionate actions.

Bee returns to the room with her dad, sits back down on the edge of her seat and says an almost inaudible choked 'sorry' to the floor, intended to be an apology to the whole room it is received without question. She keeps looking at the floor as she agrees to the plans for the service, adding nothing in. The only professional funeral flowers are to be from close family and Bee. Those flowers would travel on the day with James. Guests could bring flowers, but nice bunches and bouquets. Not funeral flowers, and they are to swap them with someone else who attended so they could then take them home.

His mum explained that when James was grieving for his father, he asked why the flowers people bought were made so gloomily into wreaths and then thrown away. Only eleven years old, he said with the wisdom of a 90-year-old that it would surely make sense to give a bunch of flowers to someone who was at the funeral to cheer them up, that that's what he thought should happen. The conversation made his mother smile all those years ago, just when she thought smiling again would be impossible. James was a logical but caring young man and he meant well. James cared about people and obviously didn't like anyone being as sad as he was when he lost his father. She had remembered the conversation all these years later and everyone thought it was a lovely and fitting tribute, a way James could have some say about what happened on the day. So, these instructions were to be listed on the funeral notification.

The Station Padre explained that James was very popular, although he didn't go into detail about operation Cinderella and how Bee and James's romance had captured the minds of the station staff, he simply informed James's mother that they expected a sizable turn out at the funeral.

It was arranged that the service would be at St Aiden's church at eleven, and then close family were to return to the Officers Mess, as the station held a hanger reception, with food, tributes, and a place to gather for station staff. All service personnel who wished to attend would be asked to wear number one dress uniform. The visit ended after arrangements were made, it had taken many hours even though it went smoothly. Plates of sandwiches were made by Bee's dad and placed in front of the group and tea refreshed often. It remained respectful and quiet throughout the discussions but regardless the arrangements took their toll, everyone was exhausted.

As soon as James's family and Bob left, Bee's dad ran her a hot bath and told her to go have a soak and a nap, that he'd wake her when it was time for dinner. Bee followed orders and slowly rose and headed to the stairs when her dad stopped her in her tracks by placing his hand on her shoulder. "I'm proud of how you are dealing with this Bee." Bee nodded and tried to smile a little. She wanted to say, 'thank you', 'I can't do this without you, and I can't thank you enough', but the worlds wouldn't come out. A small, resigned smile is all she could manage.

Once Bee was safely in the land of nod, her father sat Sue down to talk. A rare occasion, having only instigated half a dozen grown up discussions in their twenty-five years of marriage.

"Sue, I think things are going to be more complicated than you can imagine."

"What do you mean Peter, how could this get any more dire? What is it?"

"Well…"

"Spit it out then," Sue barked.

"I think Bee might be pregnant."

"Oh, don't be ridiculous. She can't be that unlucky. Isn't losing James enough."

"Is it unlucky, a child I mean. If the worst thing to happen is a little baby. I can think of worse things, Sue."

"Look, I'd know if she was pregnant Peter, it's absurd. She's just stressed and bereft."

The pair bickered for a while until Sue agreed to approach the subject, tactfully when she woke.

*

It was seven in the morning when Bee woke, she felt dizzy and nauseous. Her parents couldn't wake her for dinner the night before, she was too tired so after trying in vain they left her a drink on her bedside table and tucked her in for the night.

"Morning Bee, come and sit here honey, your dad will get you a cup of tea, won't you, Peter?" Bee sat next to her mum as asked and her dad without reply went to fetch tea.

"Bee, please don't be annoyed at me but—"

"But what, what is it?" Bee asked, finally finding her voice.

"Do you think you could be pregnant, Bee love?" As tactful as a brick, Peter held back his criticism in a bid to make this as painless as possible for Bee.

"What, no, of course not. Why are you saying this, why now?"

"You've been sick a few times that's all Bee. Look, I sent your father out last night to get a test, to put your mind at rest."

"My mind at rest. Really, yours you mean. I hadn't given it a second thought." Bee looked at her father for back up. "Dad, for crying out loud, tell Mum, she's wrong."

"Bee darling, if you take the test, I'm sure that will make your mum, stop worrying."

As Bee put her head in her hands her mum added, "I'm not worrying Peter. You are the one worrying."

"Okay, stop it. I'll take the test and this madness will be over." Bee's mum stood and held out a packet in a paper bag. As Bee took the packet, she stated with full conviction, "It will be negative and then I'll wish it wasn't. Thanks a bunch, just what I needed." She then stood and stormed out of the room like a nonchalant teen, headed for the bathroom upstairs to take the test. Her mum started to follow her when her father called her back. "Let her do this on her own Sue, Bee needs space. She'll be back down in a minute or two."

The door opened and Bee quietly walked in holding the test and sobbing. Her mum couldn't wait. "Are you pregnant, love? Is that why you're crying?" Bee sobbed louder and nodded. She couldn't move any further, she felt lost and abandoned and the pain of James not being there was as raw as when she first heard he died.

As her mum rushed over to her to grab her in her arms, she was flustered. "See Peter, I told you she was. I knew something was wrong, I could sense it." Behind Sue, Peter rolled his eyes. He was beyond caring about who knew what, he was hurting. He knew in an instant that his daughter now has so many bittersweet years ahead of her, and it would be impossible for her to have a day in the future when she wouldn't miss James. Until then, he had selfishly hoped in a year to two she could move on and only think of James every now and then. Keeping her freedom to live the rest of her life without the sadness getting in the way.

He turned and walked back to the kitchen, placed his hands on the sink, he looked out of the window. *How much more could his daughter take?* He thought. *When would she have some peace? Would she be on her own now forever. How could they help with the baby? Would she leave the RAF and come home?* So many questions flooded through his mind until one thought stopped him dead in his tracks. He was pleased and excited at the thought of a grandchild, and he realised he had no right to feel sad, or pain at this news. He hadn't lost his daughter; he didn't lose a child, Bee hasn't died. How dare he be so wrapped up with his worries for Bee. His worries were nothing compared to the thought of losing her. The challenges they would face are for the living, and therefore can be overcome.

Chapter 56 –
Goodbye for Now

Bee slept for more than four hours straight once she finally went to bed. She was worried that this meant she was odd. Bee had heard of others losing a loved one and not sleeping a wink the night before the funeral. The day before was so busy with friends and family arriving, each dropping in to visit her and offer their condolences. Afterwards her head hurt so much that she couldn't settle, pacing back and forth, hovering by the kettle or, talking to her parents about the funeral and of course her pregnancy.

Her dad was shocked when Bee insisted and pleaded to him that she couldn't go through with having a baby. The thought of trying to be a mother right now, even for James, was too much to bear. She wanted to stop the world spinning and get off. Bee found it difficult to breath each day, even this basic instinct drained her willpower. She hadn't seen much of James's family, Monica popped by just to escape her mother as much as check on Bee. She was thankful for this but felt that at any minute James's mum would call Bee to summon her or come around.

"Bee love, your father has finished in the bathroom, it's time you got ready now too."

"Okay," she muttered, took a deep breath, exhaling slowly before she headed to her room to get ready.

"I'll get you some ginger biscuits and plain water. It will help stop you from throwing up on the vicar."

"Padre, Mum. They are called Padre's or Chaplains here."

Her clothes were laid out, she had decided not to wear her uniform. A simple black dress felt more appropriate. They had to be at the Officers mess on camp by ten, a car would pick them up at nine forty. They would meet James's family there and James would arrive at the mess at ten twenty. Bee was told the route, but she couldn't remember anything more than where she needed to be. After this first step, she knew that she would be ushered to each place by others. She knew of the two songs to be played.

Right then, in this moment, it felt like the most surreal out of body experience. She felt disconnected from all around her now it was time. She went through the motions of getting ready and there was no sickness, it was as if her body knew to go easy on her today. Ready and waiting in silence for the car to arrive, Bee sat with her mother while her father stood at the window so he could see the car pull up.

"The car is here now, it's time." Finely tuned to perfection the car slowed to a stop at the house.

Bee's parents left first standing outside the front door so they could flank her on each side and walk her to the car. As Bee left, she looked up and stopped dead in her tracks. The house is surrounded on the street by forces family homes. At the front door of each one, men, women and children stood outside their homes silently and respectfully watching from afar. Some with flat lipped smiles and a nod, some with tears. Bee was shocked to the core. This gesture was recognition that it was all real, that she really had lost James, that he wasn't coming back, that she wouldn't wake up and this was not a bad dream. She fought with all she had to stop a tear leaking from her eye. Not now she thought, not yet.

At the mess, Bee was greeted by Monica and Bob with gentle warmth. James's mother was as frosty as usual. *Of all days, couldn't she at least be civil?* Bee thought. Bee's father quietly spoke in her ear, "She has lost her son Bee, grief is a terrible thing, let it go." She felt instantly disarmed by her father's words.

As Bee and Monica exchanged pointless pleasantries to fill the awkward void, behind them James was carried into place in front of the Officers Mess by a long black gleaming hearse. As three men got out of the car, the mourning friends and family hushed. Bee felt a bolt in her stomach as if she had been shot. She didn't want to turn around. She didn't want to see the box James lay in. No one had seen James body, it was a closed casket and Bee had decided it was good that she didn't have a choice, that she didn't have to face seeing his empty cold body.

"Bee, come on now love, you need to walk to the car." Her mother spoke gently and placed a guiding arm behind her.

"I can't. I can't do it." Bee was frozen. She couldn't turn around and was starting to panic.

Her breathing started to speed up when Bob came over to her. "You can do this Bee. Just take a slow deep breath and I will walk you to the car in three, okay?" Bob's assuring confident command brought her RAF obedience to the fore, and she nodded agreement. On three she turned and saw James's coffin right in front of her. She almost tripped and fell, Bob caught her arm and walked her slowly to her car, with his head held high. She could do this she thought, she had to do this, for James.

Part of Bee wanted to run to the hearse and get close to James and talk to him, it was illogical but an instant reaction to knowing he was just a few feet away. Not considering that he wasn't really there in that box anymore. The box simply held his redundant and broken body.

Bee sat in the middle of the car with a parent sat on each side of her. As they drove away, she saw that every road was lined with uniform, each spaced ten feet apart. Like a wave they each saluted James as he passed by, Bee thought it was beautiful and her mouth dropped open as she watched it entranced by the elegance of it. As she passed out of the main gate, she noticed the station flag was at half-mast. This made her well up again, a lovely sign of respect to James, and she knew it could only have been ordered by Jeremy Biggleswade, the Commanding Officer.

In Lossiemouth village the route was lined with locals from the village. Shop keepers, homeowners and businesses had come out to stand like statues to pay their respects to a man most had never met. They had heard of him through the news on tv and from chatter in their everyday lives. James the hero, who took his damaged jet away from the holiday makers and paid the price with his life. His actions were admired, and many were grateful to him.

The journey to the church seemed to take a long time, probably as a man in a top hat and pace stick walked in front of the procession for the entire route. Bee was lifted by everyone's kindness and thought to herself, *I can look at the stained-glass windows of the church and I don't have to hear what is being said. I can get through it that way, I can do this.*

In the church Bee's plan was foiled when she heard her name read out. "James also leaves behind his fiancé Beatrice. Recently they were engaged and hoping to start a life together as man and wife."

She was there and heard it all, every moment of the service from then on. Unable to block out the intense pain, unable to stop the tears, rendered unable to speak once more. At eleven forty the ceremony had come to an end as James's old boss stood to speak. He asked everyone to gather outside in silence for a final RAF farewell, which was obeyed.

At eleven fifty the rumbling of jet engines broke the peace, and everyone started to look up. Only the staff from his squadron knew about this farewell, that Bob had instigated. Bob had gained his Boss and the Station Commander's blessings with ease, and far beyond.

Nine red jets flew across the skyline in arrow formation headed out to sea, a final salute to James. They turned around and upon their return a couple of the jets broke from the arrow to corkscrew around the others, coloured smoke followed behind them in red, white, and blue. This was James favourite childhood memory and why he had ended up an RAF pilot.

It was now clear to Bee that he trusted Bob enough to tell him that he was in awe of them as a child. That he had seen them with his father all those years earlier and that the corkscrew was his favourite manoeuvre.

Bee was smiling but crying and a small laugh broke through her sobs as she wondered how on earth, they had pulled this off. James was given the upmost respect, it was as if they all knew he was someone special, not just her someone special, and it made her feel immensely proud.

Afterwards, many came to offer their condolences. Bee smiled as she saw the rugby team. Paddy was first in line with Taff alongside, leading the team line. "I'm so sorry Bee, you lost a good man there." Taff chipped in. "We lost a promising teammate too by the way. We had convinced him to try a game and he stunned us all, he was going to be our fly half, a natural he is. Was I mean. Sorry…"

The team all passed by shaking her hand and barely looking at Bee, looking at the floor, a sentimental bunch, they each felt the sadness that surrounded them.

After returning to the Officers Mess for the private wake, Bee's college friends gathered around her all in their dress uniform making small talk and every so often saying what a beautiful service it had been. So did a few of the guys from her section. Paul, and his wife, both puffy eyed, holding hands, they said little. Yet it meant a lot to Bee that they stood there beside her. Bee's parents took a rest and sat and watched her from across the room. Callum leant in and spoke softly. He placed a hand on the small of Bee's back. "Bee, I have been thinking. I can come up at least once a month to see you. It is going to be tough time and I want you to know I will be here for you." Her other college friends echoed the same, vowed that they'd all visit. Bee knew they meant it and was touched at their support.

At the station hanger reception, the squadron hanger was full. The mess had set up a barbeque to feed everyone. Pop up tables were covered with crisp white linen that carried salad, paper plates and a makeshift bar, staffed with mess volunteers. Paddy and Taff made speeches and afterwards, two minutes silence followed and a toast. "To Flight Lieutenant James Jamieson." There were three cheers and all in attendance were ordered to drink the bar dry as a sign of respect for James.

Back at the officers' mess, James's stepfather Eric asked Bee's dad if they could bring Bee over, as James's mother would like a quiet word with her. Peter knew this sounded a bit odd and as if they needed to be present, so dutifully both Peter and Sue quietly approached Bee to bring her over to the Jamieson family table. James's mother stood and as Bee arrived, her husband stood up next to her as she spoke.

"Beatrice, I will be leaving for London tomorrow. We head back to Canada a few days afterwards."

"I understand, I am sorry you are leaving so soon." Bee didn't know what else to say, surely this wasn't the time for goodbye. "Shall I come over to see you in the morning?" She added.

"I don't think you do understand. We won't be seeing each other again. So, I will need to have the keys for James's flat. I want to tidy it up in the morning and then pass the keys to an agent so it can be sold."

"What?" Bee needed it explaining. She hadn't thought for a second about what would happen next, she could barely get through each day as it is. Yet somehow, she had expected to go to the flat on her own to curl up in James's bed when the funeral was over. She thought she find solace in the quiet, surrounded by his things, in what was going to be their home. It wasn't about money it was her only place to be close to him and she had assumed it would be okay. He had moved her out of the block while she was away with help from Gillian, and her boxes and all her belongings were there. It was her home now, their home.

"It is simple Beatrice, you weren't married, you have no entitlement to James's estate, I am his next of kin. Not you." Peter looked at his wife as she was about to say something in retaliation, his gaze silenced her. Instead, she put her arm around Bee to let her speak for herself.

"I erm, I can't move out that quickly. I don't know how…" she was not sure what to say and her eyes filled with tears, she begged inside herself that one wouldn't fall.

"You have until nine tomorrow morning. You can collect your stuff before then. After that, I don't want to have any contact with you I'm afraid, we have no connection." – There was silence, so she continued to fill the void – "I don't owe you anything."

Beatrice's mum was livid. "Hold on a minute, how dare you speak to Beatrice like that? Today of all days." James's mother look horrified that someone had spoken back to her.

"I explained and it is quite simple, I am leaving tomorrow, so it all needs sorting today."

"Is your heart made of stone? Why today, to cause harm, to be cruel? This could be sorted out at any time, it's just stuff. It's not important."

"If it isn't important, it isn't a problem being out by the morning is it." James's mum had no care for anyone else's feelings. Bee's mum wasn't letting her off the hook.

"You are a nasty and bitter woman. I bet James is looking down and is ashamed of you!"

With this Bee started to cry and as the room grew quiet, she caved. "Stop it, please just stop. I'll leave and you'll have your keys by morning, just stop." Bob was there and heard the exchange, he could also see the venom in James's mother's eyes. He knew she was bitter and wanted to lash out but needed to step up for Bee as James would have wanted.

"I'm afraid it won't be that simple. James would have had to re-write his will when he bought the flat. I know because he also had to write his letters for his admin file."

Monica spoke up. "What letters?"

His mother spoke next. "What will, why would he need a will at his age?"

Bob took a deep breath. "Because your son and I have flown in many dangerous places, and we have done some very dangerous things together and had planned to continue to do so." He took another deep breath as they hung on his every word. "If something happened to us when flying, we have letters held on file for our family."

"Well, where is my letter?" James's mum demanded.

Bob was tiring of James's mum but wanted to stay respectful. "They will be sent onto you with the final RAF report. In a few days I suspect. There is also one for Bee as James considered her his family and future."

Bee wanted to curl up and sob, she was anxious to leave and managed to shout. "You can have it all I don't care what is written in any will. It won't bring him back and the only thing I want is James."

Bee turned to leave, everyone was quiet and watching the emotion fuelled exchange. She felt humiliated enough, but her mother grabbed her arm. She was still angry and thinking ahead of that day, keen to protect her daughter. "No you don't, don't do this. You might need it. No rash decisions Bee."

James's mum scorned. "She doesn't need anything, she's young, she didn't die! She can make her own way. Who knows, they may have split up before the wedding. James will have seen sense at some point." James's mum seemed full of hatred at this point and there was no stopping her lashing out.

"What are you trying to say about my daughter?"

"That they are not suited, are they? My James was an Officer."

"James loved Beatrice and told me so himself. He had plans for a long future ahead, and a rank doesn't make someone a better person or different, you sound ridiculous, have you heard yourself."

"What do you mean, he told you himself, Mum?" Bee was keen to hear anything new about James.

"He came to see us love, to ask if he could marry you. Didn't he tell you?"

"No, he came to Devon? Wow." Bee's eyes widened.

"Yes, yes he did. Your father gave him the third degree and made him sit and write about how he saw his life with you, before he gave his blessing. He sat at the table for over an hour writing a list of things he had planned for you to make you happy."

"What, how could you Dad?" Bee was instantly embarrassed and cringed at the thought of it. She knew immediately how she would apologise to James when he told her about it, and how James would laugh when telling her about it. She loved the creases in James's eyes when he laughed and his enthusiasm when he told a funny story. She was lost for a moment, it felt almost as if she was thinking of a real memory.

Bee's dad interrupted her thoughts. "It was a bit of fun Bee, I was always going to say yes. I liked him the minute I met him."

"Bee love, your father took him to the pub afterwards. When they got back, they stayed up until gone two in the morning laughing. Your dad was chuffed to bits that James was joining the family, he introduced him to everyone in the town that he saw. They really hit it off."

Bee thought to herself that it was obvious they would, why wouldn't they like each other. They were both great men, both calm, kind and witty. Everyone liked them.

James's mum broke the reminiscent talk with defiance. "This won't happen, regardless of what WAS going to happen, it didn't, did it. There is no connection now, I want it all closed and, for it all to be over."

"Well, it won't be that simple I'm afraid and you will regret speaking to Beatrice this way."

"Mum, stop it." Bee pleaded for her mum to stop now and look towards her dad for help.

"No Bee, she will know soon enough and this way she gets to sleep on it, stay and make amends."

Bee's mum hadn't taken on board that Bee may not have the baby, she assumed Bee would change her mind and taken it for granted that it was a foregone conclusion.

"Amends for what, for speaking the truth. Why would I want to do that?" James's mum was smug and even her husband found her actions distasteful, shaking his head and looking upwards.

"Bee is pregnant with your grandchild, that's why!" Gasps in unison from family and friends nearby were soon followed by mumbles spreading across the mess, and one lady a good twenty-feet away theatrically burst into tears at the news.

Bee looked over at Bob and started to cry. She had been having stomach pains all day and was starting to worry she may not have a choice to make about the baby at all. She couldn't bear any more drama or attention. Bob snapped into action, took control, and escorted Bee and her parents out of the mess.

Bee's mum, full of adrenalin started to worry and needed answers.

"Bob, will Bee have to leave the RAF now, because she's pregnant?" – Looking at Bee – "Bee love, you can come and live at home, we'll help you with the baby."

Bee's father was tired of the talk it had been a long day. He simply interjected to support Bee.

"That's Bee's choice Sue, she may want to stay in their place, it's beautiful up here, she may want her friends and her memories."

As Bob held open the door for Bee, he reassured them all,

"Today is not the day to fight or to figure out what to do. You have all the time in the world for that starting tomorrow, and I'll be there to help you Bee, whatever happens and whatever you decide. Just rest today, the future can wait until tomorrow."

As a soothing silence was restored Bee saw clearly why James was so fond of Bob.

"Thanks Bob, thank you."

When Angels Fly...